I0721265

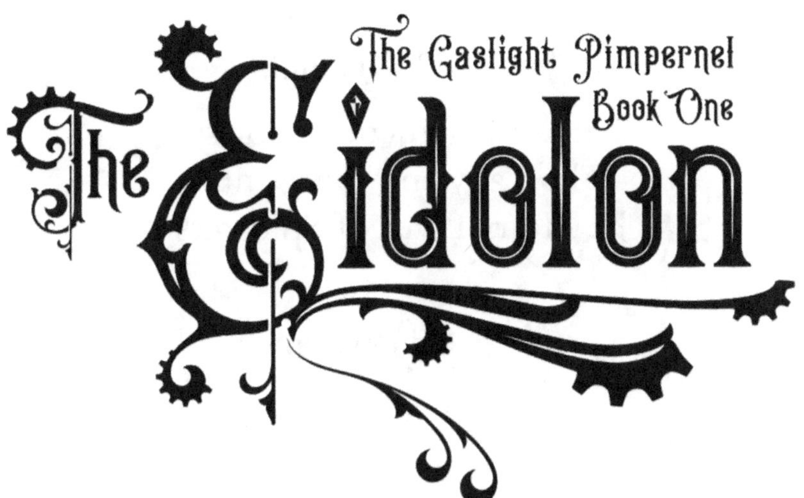

The Gaslight Pimpernel
Book One
The Eidolon

Also from Phase Publishing

Rebecca Connolly

An Arrangement of Sorts
The Lady and the Gent
The Merry Lives of Spinsters

Grace Donovan

Saint's Ride

Emily Daniels

Devlin's Daughter
Lucia's Lament
A Song for a Soldier

Laura Beers

Saving Shadow
A Peculiar Courtship
To Love a Spy

Ferrell Hornsby

If We're Breathing, We're Serving

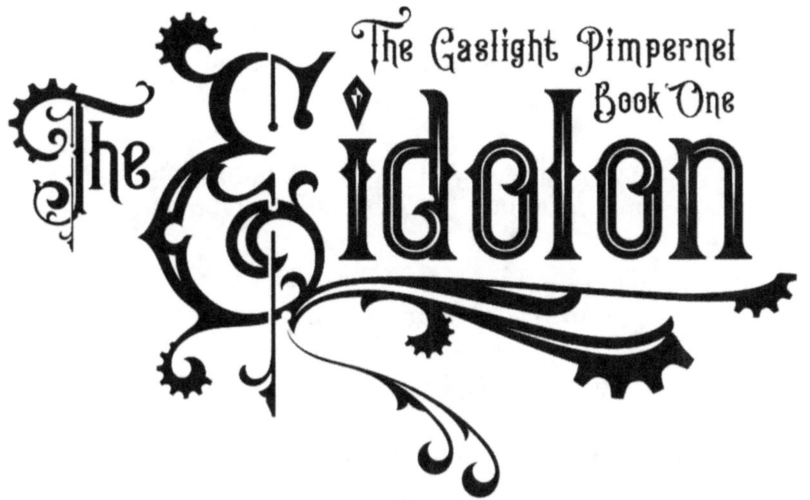

The Eidolon

By

Tiffany Dominguez

Phase Publishing, LLC
Seattle

Text copyright © 2020 by Tiffany Dominguez
Cover art copyright © 2020 by Tiffany Dominguez

Cover art by May Dawney Designs
https://covers.maydawney.com

http://www.phasepublishing.com

Phase Publishing, LLC first hardcover edition
May 2020

ISBN 978-1-952103-11-7
Library of Congress Control Number 2020906731
Cataloging-in-Publication Data on file.

Dedication

To Karlene, Sheila, Kristen, and Chris. Thank you for a decade of creating and designing stories together.

To GEWA, for inspiring the final touches. To Julie, for always encouraging me.

To my beta readers—thank you for making me feel like I had a chance.

And to all my favorite authors who have so brightened my life.

Chapter One

Lady Veronica raised her Tesla-ray and shot the guard in the chest. His mouth gaped open and a wheezing sound escaped his lips. He sank to the ground, stunned, falling with a sickening thud. His whistle dropped with a small clatter on the cobblestones.

She stepped back into the shadows of the alleyway before addressing the children. Their faces were streaked with grease, their thin cotton shirts hung limply on scarecrow frames. Veronica wanted to kneel in front of them, take their hands, and tell them they were safe. That no one could hurt them now. But she couldn't. Not yet.

"I'm the Eidolon. Have you heard of me?" Veronica spoke in the rough, deep voice she'd spent many hours perfecting. The children would see and hear what they always did—a fine gentleman. One they could believe in.

The younger children gasped. The older ones, with empty, dark eyes, simply stared. They all looked brittle, like bags of bones, not soft as children of their age should be. Veronica could only hope, as she always did, that they had strength enough left to leave.

"The gent wot saves kids? The Angel?" a small boy asked quietly.

"Yes. If you want to escape this place, you must go with my manservant. He doesn't speak, but he is strong and fast and will get you to a place of safety. Do you understand?"

Twenty heads turned toward Clank, her automaton, and then back to Veronica. Clank moved and appeared as an average-sized man, hidden inside a mask, top hat, and simple attire like her. Underneath, he was stronger, faster, and more intelligent than any human she'd ever known.

"Yes, sir," they answered quickly, voices hesitant, as though that response came often and automatically.

Yet even the youngest among them, a boy of not more than four, stood straight and at attention. A girl saluted Veronica and then dropped her chin to her chest, likely fearful of showing any spark of personality. They starved it out of them in this place.

Veronica smiled. The courage of this motley group steeled her for what lay ahead. The fallen guard had alerted the Enforcers, a foe she'd avoided facing these many months, and one she wasn't certain she could conquer. These children, with their brave faith in the Angel of the Grave, inspired her. She would keep them safe, no matter what happened to her.

"Go! And do not look back," Veronica ordered. She nodded at Clank.

Clank bowed, his long, leather jacket billowing behind him. He swept up the four youngest, placing one on each shoulder and making them wrap their arms around his strong neck, then cradling one in each arm, and ran. The others followed, their eyes lit with a desperate hope as if waking from a dream.

One boy, a thin, blond specter, stopped and called back, "Thank you, sir!" before joining the others.

Veronica spared only a moment to ensure they'd all disappeared before turning to face the Enforcers. The Grave's overlord, Grillett, would have them here any moment. They were chosen from among the fencing elite and armed with sharpened steel blades that could cut through metal, rarely leaving anyone alive. She knew of them from the terrified confessions of the children she'd saved.

She'd slipped their grasp before now, but tonight was different. Too many children, too much noise. Grillett had created bigger groups, set more guards. All to counter her.

Veronica wiped off her goggles, enabling her to see more clearly through the mist and hiding the flare of rage in her narrowed, blue eyes. She need only delay the cursed Enforcers, giving the children and Clank enough time to reach the steam-powered carriage waiting outside the slums.

She heard the flutter of fabric above her and rolled to the side just in time. An Enforcer landed directly in front of her; a tall, sharp-featured man dressed in a red cape, his sword already in his hand.

Veronica blocked the strike she anticipated. The Enforcer obliged, moving far quicker than any foe she'd ever encountered. She moved just as she'd practiced hundreds of times, fast and controlled. When she saw the opportunity, she ducked, stepped to the side, and knelt. She drew her Tesla-ray and squeezed the trigger. The Enforcer's sword clattered on the cobblestones and he fell forward, face frozen in pain.

She stood and whirled around but was too late. A second Enforcer's blade sliced her upper left arm. She leapt back, almost out of range, minimizing the damage to a shallow cut instead of losing the entire limb. *Cursed sharp blades.*

"So, you're the Eidolon. The deity of the gutter trash." The new Enforcer sneered. He tossed his blade from hand to hand, circling her. "You're a little smaller than I imagined."

He was faster than she'd ever seen. Yet he was only a man, and the worst possible kind. One who stole, beat, and imprisoned children and felt stronger for doing it.

With a sneer that made his face even uglier, he said, "No one's coming to save you, *Angel.* To end up like this, after you rescued all those street rats. They won't thank you for it. They'll turn on you. We try and give them a purpose, but they are worthless in every way."

This one is a brave bricker with a God complex. I don't need anyone to save me. I never have. And I can save them, too. Veronica's thoughts raged, but she never voiced them. To anyone. Not to her father, the duke. Not to Clank. Not to her brother, Alec. Definitely not to this Enforcer, even though his words painted pictures in her mind of what she knew Enforcers did; secreted bodies in cart loads out of the Grave. Silenced whimpers with a thud.

He lifted his sword and paused. Cocked his head. "No lecture on how unrighteous I am? No final prayers? Would've expected more. Maybe they already did turn on you and got you scared of what you done. You risked it all to save stupid… worthless… rats." He swung his sword.

Veronica raised the leather guard on her wrist to block his strike. The blade sliced clean through, cutting into her scarred skin.

She didn't scream at the pain. That was the one gift the duke had given her; she could block it out. Regular beatings developed that skill.

At the same time, Veronica shot the Enforcer with her Tesla-ray, enveloping him in a beam of circular light. He scrambled backward and fell, yet she continued to fire. Her anger rose again as bright as the beam, and her thoughts raged on.

Murderer. Devil.

This man spoke to her like every other man in her life, as though females served no intelligent purpose. This man told her what she could not do. This man cut her, threatened her. Made her bleed.

This man, like Grillett, stood guard on the other side of the door, keeping the weak and helpless locked inside. Her thoughts roiled and agitation spread into her chest and through her arm, then her fingers, squeezing the trigger tighter.

How many moments passed, she didn't know. The smell of burning flesh stung her nose. She blinked and lowered the Tesla-ray. Rancid smoke rose from the Enforcer's charred body, scorched too long by her gun. His shirt was singed nearly to pieces, a gaping hole revealing red, puckered skin, still steaming. Most of his face was unrecognizable now. He didn't look human anymore but rather like something out of nightmare.

Her arm fell to her side and she sank to her knees. Dr. Hoch, her only mentor, had warned her about this; the stun setting could turn deadly if she fired too long. All her anger seeped down into the cobblestones, now stained with her blood.

What had she done?

She crawled over and checked for a pulse. Nothing. The heavy clouds above opened, drizzling cold rain that drenched her in seconds and doused the Enforcer's skin.

No. She'd lost control and burnt a man to a crisp. She'd killed before, a guard here and there when it was necessary, always quick and clean. But she'd never tortured a man.

Heavy footsteps splashed nearby, the boots of more of Grillett's guard. Veronica picked up the Enforcer's sodden cloak, now cleansed mostly of the charred smell and blood by the rain, and wrapped it around her shoulders. She left the Enforcer and stumbled through the empty streets.

It was now past curfew in the slums. She headed toward the rendezvous point. Clank would be waiting there to take her back to the Clarke townhome. The steam carriage only took minutes to make the trip to the workhouse, Bridges, hidden under the auspice of a laundry.

Her arms ached with the fire of a hundred suns, and she could feel her forehead heating in spite of the chill. Veronica tore off a piece of silk from her shirt and wrapped it tightly around the largest cut on her lower right arm, but the fabric did little to staunch the flow. She leaned heavily against the wall as she continued on. Only one more block.

Veronica pushed the pain further down, narrowing her focus to the drops of water as they fell, pinging on the stone. She wrapped the cloak tighter around her shoulders, but it couldn't staunch the chill.

Cold. It was always so cold. In her childhood home in the country. In the fancy townhome in the city. In her memories. In her scarred skin. Warmth was an illusion.

She heard the sound of metal hitting stone a few moments before Clank appeared, eyes whirling beneath the goggles.

"Take me home, Clank. Through the back door, please. And get Matilda."

He swept her up into his cool, metal arms and sprinted for the carriage.

Chapter Two

Clank placed Veronica carefully onto the soft seat bench of her steam-powered carriage and wrapped her in a soft, dark blanket. As he stepped onto the driver's standing platform in the front, he pulled the lever forward with one fast motion, shooting them out of the side street and into the main thoroughfare.

Clank didn't light the gas lamps on the front of the carriage. The glow of the streetlamps was enough for his sharp, rounded eyes that consisted of nothing more than cogs and whatever Dr. Hoch animated him with.

"They're safe?" Veronica asked.

They always had been, in his care. Though nothing had gone as usual tonight. Her horrible thoughts churned, clacking inside her head as loudly as the carriage wheels on the stone streets. She pressed her hands to her ears. So much trapped inside of her.

Clank turned his head, the whirring of his metal eyes slowing, as though hypnotizing and reassuring her. He nodded.

She felt the din ease and lowered her hands, wrapping her arms around her middle. The carriage hissed and spattered along, after a while joining in the chorus of grinding gears from a few other vehicles. When they passed into the merchant section and into the fashionable part of town, Clank lit the front lamps by turning a knob on the control board.

To others, they would look like a driver and his gentleman coming home from a nightcap at White's. Most of society dined or danced at this hour, including the duke, so they thankfully attracted little notice. The twin lamps on the front of the vehicle and the gas lamps on the street spouted yellow flame, the only illumination in this murky, black night.

When they reached the townhouse, Clank pulled into the empty barn and shut down the carriage. Moving swiftly, he snatched Veronica up again and ran through the shadows into the house and up to her room on the second floor. She gripped his shoulder through his leather coat, trying to find purchase, though she needn't have. Clank never dropped her.

He set her down on her feet and pulled the bell to summon Matilda, her companion.

"Thank you, Clank," Veronica managed to say.

She could only keep the pain at bay for so long. It always felt sharp and invasive when she was on the wrong end of a rapier. Somehow, tonight, it seemed to have penetrated the ever-present emotional shield she carried on her person as well. She stumbled, feeling weak and spent.

Clank bowed and then returned to his usual place in a hidden compartment behind the armoire. He'd been programmed to conceal himself the instant they returned to the townhouse. Before he closed the door, his eyes whirred even faster, as though he wasn't pleased to be put to rest. Veronica didn't trust her father's servants, especially the ancient butler, Critchton, who was as mean as Matilda was kind.

Veronica had long ago tossed the Enforcer's cloak onto a rubbish heap during the ride home. She used her left arm, the one with the shallow cut from the first swipe of the dead Enforcer, to draw her knife and cut her shirt off. When she got to her right arm, she steeled herself, drawing on her regret and anger, and tore off the sleeve and wrap together. The pain inside and out engulfed her for a few bright moments, but she knew she wouldn't faint. The duke had proven that in his quest to raise a child that would contribute to society.

Veronica staggered into the washroom, shrugged off her underclothes and britches and sank into the waiting bath with a groan, almost too tired to sit up above the water. She had no idea how Matilda kept the water warm when Veronica never returned at a consistent time.

Matilda flew into the room, closing the door silently behind her. When she saw Veronica, her already pale complexion turned ghostly. "Oh, my lady! What have you done this time?" Strawberry-blonde curls fell forward on her face as she leaned over to examine Veronica's arm.

"I'm sorry, Matilda, I know how much you love doing this, but I'm going to need some stitches. I'm afraid I ran into some rather sharply armed company tonight."

Veronica hated that it fell to her only human friend to piece her back together, but she had no one else to turn to. The Eidolon's work had to be done.

Matilda shook her head, stood up, and got to work. She tossed Veronica's bloodstained clothes into the false bottom of a drawer in her dresser and placed the ray gun and goggles in a locked suitcase beside Clank in the armoire. Then Matilda picked up a cloth and began gently washing and disinfecting Veronica's cuts.

In spite of Matilda's obvious horror, her hands worked expertly over the injuries. Veronica, for her own part, shoved aside the pain. She'd saved twenty children tonight. She closed her eyes, savoring the hope she'd seen in their faces.

"There now," Matilda said after a few minutes. "You may have wrapped this gash tightly enough to begin with, but when you tore it off…" She shook her head. "Don't know that it'll stop bleeding 'till we get it stitched up."

Matilda gently wrapped the cut and then held out a towel for Veronica. In spite of the warmth from the tub and from the fireplace burning in the next room, Veronica could not stop shaking.

"Enforcers, was it?" Matilda asked as she helped Veronica into a shift of soft, fine material.

"The very same. Please do try to minimize the scarring, if you can. The duke knows exactly how many are his." Her back told the story of most of her scars, though smaller, almost imperceptible ones marked her skin in the area her gloves covered.

Veronica sat in the chair by the fireplace and gripped the arms to still her shaking. When the needle pierced the flesh on her upper arm, she embraced the stinging feeling. It distracted her. Steadied her.

"Did you get them? The children?" Matilda worked quickly, stitching a neat, straight line.

"Yes. Yes, I did," Veronica said.

Matilda glanced up and smiled softly. Matilda's compassion for the children at Bridges, where she'd initially been hired as a teacher, amazed Veronica. Enough that Veronica had taken a chance with her. However, that same compassion now directed at Veronica made her uncomfortable, as she was unused to such care. It felt frivolous, in spite of the severity of her injuries.

"All finished, my lady." Matilda's wiry arms helped Veronica into bed, fussing with the covers as if Veronica were a little child. "Did something else happen tonight? You don't seem yourself."

Veronica stilled Matilda's movements by capturing her cold hands in her own. "I'm fine. Don't concern yourself. Go, get some rest. I know it must weary you to attend me at all hours." She squeezed her companion's hands reassuringly and then waved her out the door.

Matilda sniffed. "I know you better than that. But you can tell me after you've rested. I've left a tea with that herbal tisane that will ease your pain. In the meantime, I'll make sure you're not disturbed." She turned down the lamps.

Veronica shifted, the pain of movement holding back tears at her companion's kindness. "Thank you," she said stiffly.

When Matilda left, Veronica drank the entire cup of tea. The tisane smoothed the sharp edges of her aches. She slid into her covers and pressed her face into her pillow, perhaps thinking that if she couldn't see her injuries, she would not feel them—both the burn from her cuts and the regret from what had just happened.

She'd never deluded herself into thinking that no one would ever get hurt. But in the past year since she'd become the Eidolon, a name the residents of the Grave had bestowed upon her, she'd been well in control of every situation. Everything was timed precisely, every strike, every grab.

Tonight, she'd lost control.

Perhaps she'd been a fool, thinking she could defy the duke and create something more of her life than he intended for her.

She laughed once. The sound felt cold as it left her throat. Yes, her dear papá, the Duke of Richmond, expected nothing of her, save that she be the perfect lady of high society. Save that she never reveal that the duke hated her, despised her, wished he'd never been burdened with such flawed progeny.

They had rescued her, those orphans. Suzie, Claire, those that she saved. Children were so generous with their love, even after being broken. They warmed her in this townhouse that more accurately entombed than housed it's residents.

There was no one but her to save the children at the factories. No one else had the means, nor such tools as Dr. Hoch provided her.

No, it was too late to care about the consequences of her work. She had vowed to save as many children as she could, and if that meant embracing the guilt of torturing and killing an Enforcer, she had no choice.

If she couldn't live with the violent side effects of her destiny, she was truly useless, as the duke always said.

And that was something Veronica vowed she would never be.

"My lady! The duke requests your presence in the library. We must hurry!" Matilda stripped back the covers on the bed and opened the drapes. Sunlight streamed into the room in a blinding rush. "He doesn't know you're not up yet."

Veronica could never plead an excuse, despite of her exhaustion. She had to keep just enough goodwill with the duke so that he'd continue funding Bridges. He had no idea where the children came from, likely thought them war orphans, but the venture gained him favor with the queen.

Veronica used her less injured arm to push herself up to a sitting position. Matilda lifted each bandage, examined the wounds, and wrapped them with a clean cloth. "They're closing nicely, but it will be many weeks before this big one heals. It'll scar for certain."

Matilda helped Veronica stand. Today every part of Veronica hurt, ached, and burned, even with the aid of the tisane.

"Come. After you've spoken with His Grace, we can pay a visit to Bridges and meet the new children! Here, drink some more of the tea."

Veronica waved away most of the petticoats and settled on a pale pink muslin dress with puffed sleeves. Layered with rosettes, it was fluffy and girly and perfect for her affected society persona. She pinned a decorative watch on her chest and winced as she put on long, pink leather gloves to hide the cuts on her arms. She looked utterly ridiculous and rather like a frosted pink cake.

If she wore it out, this ensemble was sure to make *Ladies of High Society*. Veronica occasionally appeared in the *Defunct Debutants* section, causing the duke endless embarrassment. It hadn't taken much to convince the duke that she failed at yet one more valued accomplishment, looking the part of a fashionable lady.

Veronica pulled out the chain she always wore around her neck and fingered the butterfly made of small gears and cogs. It was the only thing she wore that she considered truly a part of herself.

"Did the duke tell you exactly why he wanted this audience?"

Matilda shook her head. "It's likely the same thing he tells you every time. Maybe if you weren't *quite* so bad at mixing, just at Almack's…"

"I have to be terrible at mixing. If I show even a little promise, those matrons will pounce. Besides, I wouldn't know what to say even if I were to drop the persona." Veronica dabbed rose water on her neck.

"I know how hard it is for you. I know what it's like to not belong anywhere."

Matilda gathered the used bandages and tucked them in her apron. She always looked smaller in the light of day than she did by lamp light, stitching up Veronica and caring for her.

"We do belong somewhere," Veronica said. The only place she ever wanted to be. The only place that mattered in her world. Bridges.

Matilda nodded, the light that came from the children brightening her expression. "His Grace might relent if you at least try to find a suitor," she said. "They cannot all smell as revolting as you say."

"But they do. It is mostly their breath. Oral hygiene is nonexistent and underappreciated."

Matilda laughed and tossed her hands into the air. "You cannot go on like this forever, you know. He has expectations for you."

Veronica nodded. "I know we can't. Someday, the duke will find someone to take me. Hopefully an earl on his deathbed, for there is no man who would fund Bridges or let his wife dress as a man."

Matilda sighed. "I hope that someday you'll find a man who will understand." She shooed Veronica out the door. "I'll have some breakfast waiting for you in the dining room when you're finished."

With both arms still aching, Veronica took her time descending the grand staircase and making her way to the duke's library. She'd had this discussion so many times that she could surely give the lecture herself and save her esteemed papá the wasted breath. But Veronica would listen. She always did. She had learned that lesson years ago.

It reflects poorly on me, a man so favored of Her Majesty, for my daughter to appear in society so dull and frumpy. Yet in spite of your looks, you have a sizeable dowry and a title; any man would gladly offer for you.

For the duke, Veronica's marriage would be one of his boldest moves in the political chess game he played. The candidates he had chosen, and whom Veronica subsequently scared off, held titles no less than his own.

All of them, without exception, had no more spine than a jellyfish. Quite a few were enslaved to the gaming tables, some to gurney racing, and others to their own vanity. Their lives held no meaning beyond their own pleasure. The duke would easily control them and their not insignificant resources.

For Veronica, though, trading one male dictator in her life for another held little appeal. It was her love of her work as the Eidolon that kept her conniving her way out of each proposal. As long as she remained the hapless spinster daughter of the duke, she knew the rules and how the Eidolon fit into that game. She couldn't afford to bring her alternate identity to another household, another man who might expose her or cast her out.

"I wouldn't go in there, Peanut. The bear is suspiciously calm this morning," Veronica's older brother, Alec, said. He approached her and flicked the lace on her sleeve.

She swatted him away. "You know I hate that nickname. Why couldn't you think of something flattering like—"

"Chicken legs? Buttercup?"

"Perhaps you've heard of Circe..."

He grinned and swept a bow. "You wouldn't respect me if I did that, *Peanut.*" He replaced his top hat and goggles and grasped both her shoulders. "Now, I mean it. Be careful with dear old papá. In his current state, he's likely to punish you should you give him one wrong look." Alec sounded less playful than usual. Perhaps even a bit worried about her.

Veronica tried to shrug him off but stiffened when the movement sent a flash of pain down her arm. She ducked and twisted away.

"I promise not to bait him, *dear brother.* Not that it's any concern of yours."

He had lost the right to care about her when he'd deserted her, leaving her alone with the duke. He had gone to Eton, then on to Cambridge. Alec never returned home, not once. Never wrote. He vanished from her life, like the late snow in spring that is here one day and gone the next.

Until last year, when the duke ordered him to either return home or go into service. Alec chose the former, swaggering back into her life a stranger, full of charm and confidence. Nothing like his brittle, clumsy younger sister. They managed a stiff, polite kind of peace. But he didn't ask for forgiveness, nor did she offer it. They both knew, without the spoken words, that such a thing was impossible.

Alec seemed to hesitate. But then he grabbed his walking stick and flourished it as he bowed to her.

Critchton entered the room, shuffling like an animated skeleton. Alec moved past him and ambled through the front door on a cheerful breeze, most likely headed to the track. His tastes ran much simpler than hers. The scent of burning oil and the harmony of a strong gurney engine, and he was lost for hours in a simple enjoyment Veronica could never understand. Rather than dealing with the duke's expectations, he avoided them altogether. Veronica could no more avoid them than she could the memory of the charred Enforcer.

She turned toward the tall, ornately carved wooden doors of the library and knocked sharply once.

"Enter," the duke said in a mild voice.

Veronica instantly recognized that tone. She was its ungrateful recipient daily.

She swung open the door and curtsied to the duke. He stood behind a large, expensive, oriental desk, its legs carved with the narrow airships of the Far East. With his hands clasped behind his back, his broad chest looked all the more imposing, rather like a brick wall. His brown velvet town coat, matching vest, and cravat were scarcely wrinkled, though Veronica knew he had been up for hours. A walking stick that hid a blade rested by him on the corner of the desk.

For the past year or so, since Her Majesty placed him in command of her air fleet, he had slept little, preferring to pore over airship plans, tactical journals, and maps.

"Sit," he ordered.

She spread out her skirts and alighted in the only other chair in the room, directly across from him.

Her father's bushy eyebrows furrowed. "You've been out three Seasons now."

Here it comes. She had long ago stopped caring about the duke's opinion of her, so his speeches meant little, though she could not at any cost let him know that.

"You've failed in every single instance to ensnare the few men worthy of a Clarke. Your utter lack of charm is incomprehensible."

Yes, it wasn't hard to convince them they wouldn't want to be married to a girl so dull and awkward, she would embarrass them at every turn.

The duke sighed then. He did so rarely, preferring not to show such weakness. She sat up straighter and clasped her arms in her lap. Would it be a cane this time? Or hours of posture practice? Even while the thought of punishment made her bones feel brittle, the children, her life's work, shored her for what he might say.

"So, instead, I've arranged it myself. The marriage contracts have already been signed. You will be presented to him at the ball tomorrow evening. Your fiancé, Prince Durad Jurinic of Sombor."

Chapter Three

Veronica couldn't move. Couldn't breathe.

Marry. A stranger. A foreign stranger. A man she had never heard of. What if he were worse than all of the others put together. He might be, with the way the duke looked so pleased.

She wanted to retrieve her Tesla-ray and stun that horrible expression off his face. But she wanted so many things she had never had. Impossible things.

She dropped her gaze to the floor.

"Her Majesty needs an alliance with Sombor, and the prince's unmarried state provides the perfect opportunity. Sombor is a country newly independent of the Ottoman Empire and has rich natural resources." He picked up his walking stick and rapped it on the desk. "You will not chase this one away, or you will lose everything. Matilda. Bridges. Any freedom that you possess."

She didn't respond, afraid of what she might say. Afraid that even one word might betray her. If she sounded pleased, he would be suspicious. If she betrayed her anger, he would enjoy it.

The duke lowered his cane. "I take it by your silence you do not like this plan. Veronica, I've gone to every length to provide for you and teach you, yet you are a complete failure, even in showing gratitude."

She considered for a moment. "I'm sorry, sir. It's just that this announcement surprised me. I will do as you say. Can you tell me about him, please?"

He began writing a letter and did not look up as he replied impatiently. "The prince is former landed gentry in Sombor, and the man who fought his way to the throne. He was crowned last year. You are to treat him with the respect due a soldier of his caliber."

She thought of all the foreign officers she had met at court. The duke was forcing her to marry one like them; privileged, entitled, narcissistic. And obviously underhanded and violent, if he had just staged a coup d'état.

"Tomorrow eve. Almack's. The queen and I will be there. Have that ridiculous gearman Hale take you, and don't be late."

The duke was going to the ball? She had never heard of such a thing. He did not care to deal with the public and found balls in particular to be a hideous waste of time.

The duke began flipping through the journal again, his shuttered face declaring the conversation finished. She rose from her chair and left the room.

Once she shut the library doors, Veronica lifted her skirts and ran. She didn't stop until she had reached her room and locked herself in. She wrapped a blanket around her entire body and shivered.

She knew this day might come. Veronica couldn't, after all, scare off every single man her father tossed her way. But she hadn't expected marriage to a complete stranger, a foreigner. She should know better by now to expect the very worst when called in to speak to the duke. He was always several moves ahead of her, always plotting, always strategizing. He never lost ground, least of all to his own daughter.

What could she do now? The contracts were signed and Bridges was at stake. Even though the little girl inside of her had never found such a place, the adult Veronica knew what she had to do.

She dropped the blanket, too restless to sit. She clasped her hands behind her back and paced erratically. The duke couldn't mean to ship her off to Sombor with this violent prince right away. They would most likely be tied up posting banns and planning the wedding for several months.

She would stall as long as she could. There had to be a way to save Bridges. That was the most pressing dilemma to figure out. Get it out from under the duke's control. She needed funds.

She'd thought of a million ways to do get the money that wouldn't work. Offering a skill of her own for hire. Yet the skills she had, she could not acknowledge in polite society, nor could the daughter of a duke work for coin. She considered penning novels under an assumed name, which required time she did not have.

Think, Veronica.

Nothing more came to mind. Her chest burned with each breath. Maybe if she could stall this wedding, she could come up with something. Veronica had spent a lifetime enacting a farce, playing the dutiful daughter. She could do it again as a fiancée.

She would find the means to save the only good thing she had ever done. Even if she had to beg, borrow, or steal from those too blind to see the price of their way of life.

Chapter Four

"Emil, why in heaven's name are we speeding toward London, and therefore my impending *demise*? Can't we take a few moments to enjoy the… open air?" Prince Durad spread his arms in a wide gesture from his stance on the deck, encompassing the enormous storm cloud bearing down on the lightweight frigate. They were high above the open plains of Sombor in Emil's own vessel, the *Hırsız*.

Emil smiled beneath the scarf always wrapped around the lower part of his face. It was endearing to see that even after so long, Durad still hadn't overcome his fear of flying. Though Durad hadn't ever confided to Emil the reason for his fear, Emil suspected it had something to do with their time in the factories. Now, however, Emil thought the recurrence of this "fear" might have more to do with his friend's upcoming nuptials.

"If you want to spend the night being tossed about like the Vizier's name in a house of ill repute, then of course, Your Highness, I will do precisely as you wish. Stall, take the low skies." Emil tossed a small coin up into the air, one of no value any longer in Sombor, and caught it behind his back. "But don't forget, the sooner you bag the English biddy, the sooner we get paid."

"Bag the biddy? *Get paid?* I'm the one who has to…"

"Careful, Highness, you would not want to speak badly of the woman you choose to love, honor and cherish."

"I did no such thing." Durad stalked toward Emil. "And you are not getting a single coin from my—"

"Dowry?" Emil said. "Now, I could never accept such a generous offer, even when I am obviously providing you with such an invaluable service. Not to mention the country I stole for you."

He stepped up to the helm of the ship, waving away one of his officers.

"St… stole!" Durad sputtered.

"More speed!" Emil said into the com-piece, his voice carrying through his scarf and the winds that now wrapped the frigate on all sides as though they meant to surround her at once and fling her to the earth.

The crew was calmly securing the loose items on deck and tying up the smaller sails. They were used to their mad captain's orders. Few would sail into such a gale. Of course, that was one of the first tests all of them faced. Emil couldn't have weak-minded misses in his employ. He quite liked his crew at the moment. They were all ragtag, rough looking, and insane.

Emil turned to Durad and shouted. "It is time for the pretty fiancé to take himself down below. Get to my quarters and latch the door. Move!" He couldn't be risking his friend's royal neck, now could he? Emil had complete confidence in his ability, and that of his crew, to navigate the riskiest of weather, but it would still be better if Durad was below deck.

Durad reached out and wrapped one of the safety lines around his waist, securing it with an expert hand. In spite of the color bleaching out of his face, he grinned. "If it's all the same to you, Emil, I'd like to have one last adventure before I'm wed. Carry on."

Emil let go of the helm with one hand and yanked on the prince's line. This impractical soul, one always game for adventure, was the friend he'd missed. A year had passed since Emil left Durad, left Sombor. A year since the prince had broken his promise to Emil to fan embers of change through the industrial world.

If he wasn't glocky mad, Emil hardly recognized Durad. What happened to the feckless youth who had charged the Ottoman's line with a handful of men? He became captain, then general as he challenged the old, frightened regime. He led an insignificant country to win its independence from an empire barreling its way through Europe like a juggernaut.

But once the crown set securely atop his head, it pulled him, dragged at him like an anchor. Durad hesitated, a half-witted glock, worried that he couldn't be what his people needed. He'd abandoned the cause that had fired Emil and Durad from their youth. He'd betrayed Emil, their shared past, and all they stood for.

Now, Durad paled and sweated at the idea of an arranged marriage. He, who once inspired thousands. How rippin' rich.

Watching Durad, shivering as rain pelted his coat, smile wide, Emil nearly sighed. His friend surely needed him, more than ever. He needed Emil to remind him where they'd come from, what they'd overcome, and what they could do to help the kids that carried scars identical to theirs.

Emil secured his own line and nodded at Durad. "Right. Just stay out of my way, princess. I cannot be responsible for losing king and country to a little storm."

Durad lowered his goggles. "I would be shocked if you didn't need my help before the dawn. You forget, *captain*, that I used to have my own command."

"And you hated every moment of it," Emil couldn't stop from pointing out.

The prince tilted his head. "Yes, but we still won."

Emil matched Durad's grin. "We did."

The rain overtook them then, drenching the crew above decks, including Durad and Emil, with curtains of water so dense they could hardly see. Emil consulted his compass and pushed the altitude lever all the way forward. He lifted the com-piece by the wheel and shouted, "Up!"

The officers and crew grabbed the rails of the ship just as she tilted back, fighting her way up through the solid shower of water threatening to drown her. Emil wiped his goggles and held on, keeping her steady. He had always loved this part of being a captain, when it was just him and his ship. Where the struggle between man and nature was real, honest; not hidden behind veiled phrases and selfish motivations. He would get them out of this storm and into the cool, grey skies above London. It might even be challenging.

For a few moments, the feel of the icy water on his cheek and the wind diving in and out of his clothes would bring him to life. Emil would allow it to take him to a place where flesh and bone existed and the future was no farther than the horizon.

"Have any wagers been made?" Emil asked.

Claude Paget, Durad's new valet straight from the heart of Paris, stiffened even further and ignored Emil's question. He did this often.

Emil popped some kompot into his mouth and chewed loudly, causing Claude to press his hands over his ears. Emil leaned forward and said, "Do not hold out on me, Paget," he pronounced the name *pa-jet* instead of *pa-jay*. "You and the staff, you're running some type of betting pool on the prince's upcoming nuptials and I want in."

Claude paused in the middle of folding His Highness's royal hosiery and shrieked. "I am *not* a common gambler, you pirate. Now, get out! It is enough that I am pressed into service for this barbarian. But *you*, I do not have to endure!" He pointed at the door with the royal shoehorn.

Emil laughed. "These are my quarters, Paget."

He threw his hands up in surrender and left anyway, whistling. Paget was proving to be an endless source of entertainment. The last few days on the ship, following their escape from the storm, would have been dull without the Frenchman around.

Pierre Rosseau, first mate of the *Hırsız*, swung down from the ropes and approached Emil with a crisp salute. The faded white shirt underneath his leather vest alternately billowed and clung to arms corded from years of labor aboard the ship.

He had been Emil's first hire, a man with whom he'd shared a cell deep in a Russian prison years ago; the man who had killed several guards upon escape, saving Emil's life. The entire plan, of course, had been Emil's, but it would've been futile without a second man.

There had been little reason to part since then. Rosseau refused to do so, and Emil had never felt inclined to force him. Now, Emil couldn't do without the large, reserved Frenchman, who inspired obedience within the unusual crew.

Rosseau turned his brown, weathered face west and nodded. "We're coming up on the hotel, *capitan*."

"The landing is open?" Emil took out his scope and looked in the direction of the Imperial Hotel. The gilded structure soared higher than nearly any other building in London, over twenty stories tall. The newly laid asphalt landing strip on the northwest side of the roof looked clear, while several dozen ships were lined up and docked along south side. Two gearmen waited by the strip to assist with the landing.

Emil collapsed the scope. "They still do not know the passenger we carry?" With Sombor's rich natural gas deposits, all of EurAsia coveted the fuel. Many foreign emissaries would be waiting to court Durad's favor.

Or kill him before allowing the English to ally with Sombor.

"No, sir. But the men are prepared." Rosseau nodded in the direction of the rest of the crew. None had been with Emil less than a full year. Dressed in the flowing white robes common to Sombor, they appeared no more than peasant folk. Their sunburnt faces minimized the differences among them, their long sleeves hiding their scars. They stood at attention for their captain, guns and swords hidden but always ready.

"Where is Durad?" Emil asked.

"In your quarters, sir." Rosseau placed his palm on the hilt of his sword.

"Toss ropes!" a rigger shouted from the helm.

The crew rushed to the sides and shoved off the waiting lines. Two of them leapt over the rail of the frigate along with their rope.

Emil placed both hands on the rail and watched his crew land the ship on a pillow of air, without so much as a jolt. He leaned forward, steadying himself as the ship rolled into her reserved dock.

A door slammed as Prince Durad flew out of Emil's quarters, his turban askew. "We've already landed? *Aman Tanrım*, Emil, your men move like ghosts."

"And yours did not, Your Highness. Which is why I sent them packing. You are very welcome, though you failed to thank me for it. Come, let us freshen you up and get you ready to meet your intended. Cannot be late!" Emil slapped the prince on the shoulder. He was looking forward to meeting this mental English lady. With a horrible reputation like hers, she might actually be interesting.

Best to keep a close eye on Durad, though. Emil didn't trust anyone else with Durad's safety. They had both attended Cambridge, so they knew how dangerous the English gentry could be. At every turn, those rotten nobles could twist an innocent remark into whatever they liked. No longer a simple country lad, Durad would be under siege from all sides.

Durad swatted his hand away. "Blast it, why did I agree to have you along again?"

"Rosseau, find that fussy countryman of yours and bring him along to the prince's rooms. We have a ball to attend!" Emil clapped his hands together twice. "Chop, chop!"

Durad's face turned red and he opened his mouth to say something. But when he saw Emil waltzing around the deck, he let loose his breath and laughed long and loud.

"Oh, let's get on with it, shall we?" He turned with an added flourish and a little kick of his heel and headed toward the ramp.

Emil smiled. It might work after all. He could remind Durad what they had suffered together, won together, and then he'd understand anew what they needed to do. How they could change everything.

After so many years without enough food, without a bed, without warmth, Durad now huddled inside his newfound comforts. Frightened and small. That's why Emil had returned, to scrub the grease from his friend's oiled hair and scented skin. To uncover what he believed still remained; a heart braver than any he'd known.

Chapter Five

Ten years ago...

"You know it'll only make matters worse to hide from him, Peanut." Alec's voice carried through the gardens, disturbing the stillness Veronica never ceased to crave.

In the middle of January, among all the long-dormant rose bushes, she found a breath of peace. The sound of the brittle branches snapping off in the wind, the cold kiss of snow as it flurried... It was the only place on the Richmond estate she could remain for hours. She found serenity, somehow, in the winter silence.

Yet ultimately, it mattered little where she went or why, the duke always found her.

The crunch of snow under Alec's boots. An impatient sigh fogging the air. "Come out. Endure what you must for now. I'll stay with you. Always."

The soft admonition didn't ease her anxiety for what was to come. She had not lived a day without fear. If she gave in to it, she would lose what little remained that was wholly her. Wholly Veronica. Her light, albeit a small, flickering one, would be extinguished.

"He's not in such a mood today. Good news arrived from the front. Please, Peanut, you know the longer you wait..." Alec trailed off, looking this way and that for a sign of her.

She watched him without moving. Family life had sculpted both of them, Alec perhaps more so than her. Though only thirteen, his cheeks had lost the roundness of their youth, now sharp and edged. His build bordered on gaunt, his shoulders and knees poking out at an angle. He wore a coat with padding, one the duke gave him to hide the weakness of his build.

He was tall, just as she was, but neither of them felt it. They both drowned inside their own skins, like Alec in the coat he wore now.

Today, Veronica felt a heavy tiredness, like a scratchy woolen blanket, descend upon her. She couldn't face the duke. Not this time. She huddled, shivering, wishing that for once, Alec would tell the duke she'd gone away or left or anything to grant her a day's respite from his tortures.

"If I return without you, he'll just send Critchton. Please, Peanut, it's cold as the devil's nose out here. You must be frozen." He pulled his coat tighter around his frame, shivering violently. After a moment, he sat on the bench, eyes cast down, and waited.

Something about the defeat in his posture made her stand up, walk over and take a seat beside him. Alec wasn't strong enough to stand against the duke, though she never ceased wishing he were. Alec didn't have to come out here now. He had already paid his toll for the day. Yet here he sat, shaking with cold. For her.

Besides, she hated the creaky Critchton.

It's going to be fine. She wondered if thinking the words might help her believe them.

Alec wrapped his coat around both of them. The warmth penetrating her skin was painful.

"Someday, we will escape," he said.

She didn't want him to say it, even if part of her was glad he still had hope. "Do you think Mamá will ever come back?" she asked for the millionth time.

Alec sighed. He didn't respond for several moments. He never answered that particular question. He always remained silent. This time, he said, "I'm sorry, Peanut, but no. I don't think she will."

She ducked her head into his chest. Finally hearing the words was actually a relief, to know Alec thought the same thing she thought.

"Why did she leave us? Did we do something wrong?"

Alec rubbed her arms up and down, trying to keep her from freezing altogether, she supposed. "I think it was the duke. He wasn't very kind to her."

"Like how he treats us?"

"A little differently. Strict, but in a grown-up way. Like telling her how she needed to look and act all the time, to be a good wife."

"A perfect one. Just like he wants us to be perfect children." She fingered the butterfly necklace she'd found under her mother's dresser after her mother left.

"I suppose."

"Why, Alec? We haven't met many kids yet, but none of them seem perfect. They sneak off and do things they aren't supposed to do. They shout at one another, at their governesses."

He shrugged. "Don't know for certain. My guess is Grandmother and Grandfather taught the duke to be like this. I overheard Critchton speaking with Higgins. You know how those two talk, all stiff and high and mighty about their respected master. How proud they are to be in his service." Alec pulled her in a little tighter. "Peanut, we're both of us older than we ought to be so I'll tell you what I learned. But you can't ever let on to anyone that you know. Swear it?"

Veronica nodded against his chest. She held everything inside, this would just be lumped in with the rest.

"Critchton said the duke grew up in a prison, but that it made him an even stronger, better duke. Grandmother and Grandfather asked to be stationed there. Something about wanting to help reform prisoners. Make them useful to society."

"No, he didn't. Really?"

A prison? Somehow, that brought to mind dirty, unkempt places with terrible sinners. Not the orderly country home they now lived in. Nothing sounded more unlike the duke. Veronica forgot the cold, forgot why she came out here in the first place.

Alec nodded. "That's what Critchton said. The duke was raised among murderers and thieves. But he doesn't want anyone to know. Ashamed of it, I think."

The duke, growing up in such a place. Among the lowest in society. But no. She didn't feel sorry for the duke, not even close. Images of rats and rotten hay and unwashed people flooded her mind. The duke with his fine manners and high reputation. Among them. It didn't add up at all.

The only thing that did was the duke acting like a criminal. He should be locked up for what he'd done to her and to Alec.

When Alec shuddered again, Veronica let him take her back into the house.

Chapter Six

"Which prince are you to marry? Have you met him? Is he handsome?" Matilda looked hopeful. She and Veronica waited on the front steps for the gearman Hale to pick them up.

Veronica stared. "What are you going on about? This could be the end, Matilda. I'm going to try to delay, but what if I can't?"

Matilda glanced at the place on Veronica's arm where the glove covered her gash. "Maybe there's a way to keep the children and make you happy. I think there's a law stating princes must be handsome. And cultured and charming. He's most likely a better choice than you would find at Almack's. I'll wager he at least cares something for politics and his people." The carriage puttered up in front of them with their Hale at the wheel.

"He must, if he's marrying you," she muttered.

"Matilda!"

She huffed. "Well, it's true. If he didn't care about his people, he would never have agreed to marry someone he's never met. With the reputation of a nitwit, no less."

Veronica eyed her companion suspiciously. "Of course. To Bridges, Hale," Veronica ordered as she settled inside the Clarke family carriage with Matilda beside her. She needed this visit to her precious children if she were to face the ball tonight as a meek, bridal offering.

"Yes, my lady."

The burly driver leapt up in front and pulled the lever. Instead of the duke's navy-blue livery, Hale wore sturdy, brown leather breeches, a matching leather jacket imprinted with the Richmond family crest, large goggles, and thick gloves. His tall boots were covered in grease with the rest of his clothing in similar disarray.

Big and absent-minded, he looked like a cross between a boxer and a scientist.

He was young to hold such an important position in the Richmond household—barely older than Veronica—but only the New Era set seemed to be capable of driving the sleek, new steam carriages. Though he wouldn't admit it, she could see how the lever and dials baffled her father. Just as on an airship, he was more comfortable barking orders.

"Can't we pull the curtains, my lady?" asked Matilda.

Veronica smiled. Her companion detested the harrowing ride from the townhome to Bridges, even while Veronica thrilled at Hale's driving. He should be gurney-racing, with how quick he could respond to sudden obstacles, and how smoothly he guided the steam carriage through the narrow streets.

Perhaps she could take Hale and Matilda with her to her new home. She refused to think otherwise, she couldn't live without either of them. Veronica lifted her hand to the rope binding the curtains and loosed them. Matilda buried her head between her knees.

As their carriage passed through the wide, clean streets of the fashionable section of London, Veronica peered through the curtain, recognizing a few of the families and their gearmen also on the road. Hale tipped his top hat to some, calling out a greeting.

Veronica pulled back the curtain a fraction and waved gaily, not shrinking away from the sneering glances of the rich and titled. She knew they whispered about her. The duke's position with the queen, his title, and his estate made her family an endless source of fascination during the Season. She cringed as she remembered they would have even more to gossip about when they heard of the engagement.

Her engagement. Merely another phrase contrived by society to create excitement about submitting to its rules and its whims.

Veronica peered through the curtain again. They were getting close now. The Richmond house banner rising from the engine on the front of the carriage waved from one side to another as Hale entered the merchant district and swerved away from an apple cart and a flower peddler. One of the thin trails of steam on either side of the carriage caught one man directly in the face. He sputtered and cursed at Hale, who, of course, paid no attention. His focus was solely on the road.

"When do you meet him, my lady? The prince?" Matilda asked.

"I'm to be presented to him at the ball tomorrow eve," Veronica replied.

The thought exasperated her. Presented. Like goods for sale. The entire affair was ridiculous. Why add all the pomp when it was simply a transaction? Why did society have to pretend to romance?

Matilda lifted her head from her knees. "Tomorrow? So soon? You must at least try with this one. I don't know if you can get out of it as easily as the others."

Trying meant Veronica had hope that something she did would change the outcome. She intended to stall for time, not to try to win a savage prince's favor. Matilda, thankfully, had not lost all hope for romance, as Veronica had.

An imposing brick building materialized out of a cloud of steam a half block away from them with the sign, "Send-out Laundry Workhouse: Bridges." Sandwiched in between a book shop and a ladies' trinket store selling goggles, pendants, looking glasses and the like, the ten-story workhouse dwarfed the adjoining buildings like an encyclopedia between novels.

It was a place of miracles, where they raised boys and girls from the hollow graves they had stepped in, restoring the pink glow to their cheeks, and life to their lost souls. Though it certainly didn't look like it at first glance.

Hale eased them to a stop by the bookshop. They never used the front entrance to Bridges. It would look odd for a lady of her stature to visit such a place, even if society praised the duke's financial contributions. Save the gutter rats from a distance, not up close, was their motto.

Veronica accepted Hale's proffered hand to help her down from the carriage. "Now there will be no more talk of princes or engagements. We're here to be with the children."

Matilda's eyes flicked to Hale as he helped her down the step to the pavement. "Of course, Lady Veronica," she said.

Veronica raised a brow. Matilda's manner was always remarkably stiff in public, and even more so in front of her gearman.

"We'll be done at four o'clock, Hale. Please return for us then," Veronica ordered.

He bowed, his leather jacket creaking and stretching over his large frame. "Yes, my lady."

Veronica and her companion waited until the street was empty and then slipped behind the bookshop. She heard a rustle of fabric, possibly the soft pad of a footstep. Veronica glanced back down the street and then upward but saw no sign of anyone. She remained still, watching.

"Something wrong, my lady?" Matilda asked in a hushed voice.

With the advent of tin trash collectors, even the alleys in the market district were impeccably clean. If she did indeed have a pursuer, they had nowhere to hide.

She couldn't conceive of a reason for anyone to follow her. She dressed conservatively enough, a footpad wouldn't mark her as a great score. The duke had many enemies, though none had yet shown an interest in her. No one cared about the comings and goings of an admittedly vacuous, frivolous lady. Men and women both snubbed her as thoroughly as penniless gentry looking to marry money.

It would do no good to worry her companion. "I'm sorry. I'm nervous, that's all. It's just this marriage business," Veronica said, resuming their progress toward Bridges.

Matilda squeezed her arm gently. "It might not turn out as badly as you think."

Veronica didn't want to scare Matilda, but her ears listened for the smallest sound. The step she'd heard had been too heavy for an animal, or even for a woman. If anyone worked out how and why she was connected to Bridges, her reputation would not be the only one at risk.

I'm going to have to start bringing my Tesla-ray when we go out. Heaven only knew there was room inside her monstrous dresses.

Matilda rang the bell on the servant's entrance. They heard the answering squeals of the boys and girls.

Mistress Phillips flung open the door, her face flushed, and her apron covered in paint. She curtsied. "Bless my soul! Good day, my lady!"

"Good day to you, Mistress," Veronica said as she stepped in behind Matilda, shutting the door quickly behind them and flipping the lock.

"We've just been teaching the girls how to paint a proper portrait. The boys are in the science room. Who would you like to see first?"

Veronica smiled and then asked in a low voice, "Did they all make it through the night?"

Mistress Phillips nodded. "Yes, my lady. Every single one of this lot did."

Veronica's heart lightened. They had lost about a dozen children in the past, when the transition to freedom had been too much of a shock for them. Too institutionalized, too used to living as nothing more than slaves, they couldn't bear the tender mercies of Mistress Phillips and her staff. Their minds shut down, unable to cope with the light after an existence of darkness.

A stringy-haired girl of the night before peered out from behind Mistress Phillips' apron, revealing nothing but a set of large, blue eyes.

Veronica squatted down until her gaze met that of the little girl's. "Hello, little miss. My name is…" She gasped and her hand flew to her open mouth. "Why, I don't remember my name!"

The girl looked at her solemnly.

"Perhaps you can help me! Can I borrow yours?"

The girl seemed to consider Veronica's request very seriously and then said, "Agnes."

Veronica laughed delightedly. "What a fine name that is! Agnes, since we share the same name, might you show me up to the arts room? I'd like to see these brilliant portraits." She smiled and held out a hand.

Agnes dropped Mistress Phillips's apron and placed her small, delicate hand in Veronica's. Now that she could see her little charge, Veronica noticed Agnes's hair and face had been scrubbed and her clothes replaced with a blue workhouse smock and collared shirt. Veronica guessed her age around seven years, though she appeared much younger with her hollow cheeks, but also much older with that serious look in her eyes. Her fingers gripped Veronica's as she led her up the stairs.

"What a little doll she is, my lady," Matilda whispered.

As they climbed the winding staircase, the newly mopped floors sparkled, and the fresh flowers in every corner brightened the dull place. Mistress Phillips and her husband lived on the first floor along with the cook and a single guard. The main floor also contained the kitchen, dining area, and laundry. A large, hidden cellar underneath the kitchen served as an emergency hiding spot for the children. The second, third, and fourth floors housed the school and recreation rooms, while the rest had only bedrooms and washrooms. With the new additions from the previous evening, the orphanage now had over two hundred children. They had run out of space. Heaven only knew where Mistress Phillips placed the refugees last night.

Since Veronica refused to turn any away or send any of her children into precarious or unknown situations, she now faced a rather large problem. She needed more space. That is, she needed to build another workhouse. Quite obviously, she had no funding to do so without asking the duke.

She also did not know how much longer she could keep hiding the number of children like this. London prided itself on not having children on the streets. Society thought Bridges provided an orphanage-type service, housing and educating those left alone from EurAsian wars. It would be unusual for Bridges to pick up twenty children in one night, as scarcely twenty were to be found on all the streets of London all together.

Laundry carriages, the supposed business of the workhouse to keep orphans out of trouble, arrived daily with deliveries. It left with bundles of clothing. The children did perform actual light work here, such as folding and sorting. The building even had a front office to greet customers. But if anyone were to inspect the place, they wouldn't expect masses of starved, bruised children. She needed more space, more resources, more places to hide the children.

Veronica hadn't decided upon her final plan for the older ones. Perhaps some type of apprenticeship programs with reputable craftsman and businessmen and women. A few could stay on at Bridges, help instruct the younger ones. She needed to start approaching the locals she trusted and making inquiries. It was simply another problem she hadn't yet solved.

Agnes led Veronica into the large art room, her steps shy and tentative. Girls of all ages sat in pairs around the room, one drawing while the other sat for her portrait. Some couldn't remain still or refrain from making silly faces at the "artist" opposite them. Many were stifling giggles and snorts.

"They've been hard at work all morning on math and science. I thought I'd give them a bit of a break, my lady," said Mistress Phillips with a curtsey.

"I am not displeased at all."

While Veronica pushed for her charges to learn all they could, she also instructed Mistress Phillips to allow them to play. To learn who they were, now that they could scrub off the filth of the Grave.

When they spotted her, the students squealed, "Lady Flowers!"

A tide of girls dropped their brushes and hurtled toward her. She knelt and flung open her arms. Twenty sets of hands grasped at her skirt and tiny mouths kissed her cheek. They rained questions upon her and she answered them each in turn.

Since Veronica hesitated to use her real name in front of the children, one of them solved the dilemma for her by commenting that she smelled like flowers. So, Lady Flowers she became.

"My little ladies, I hear we have some new arrivals. Can someone introduce me?" Veronica asked.

Suzie, one of the older girls who had been rescued on Veronica's first mission, stepped forward. She curtsied properly and pointed out five girls at the back of the group. "That's Beth, Erica, Leila, Marcia, and Madeline, my lady. Oh, and the one behind you, that's Agnes."

"Lady Flowers' name is Agnes too! Agnes Flowers!" Agnes said and then hid behind Veronica again.

"Really?" Betty said.

"Lucky! Can I change my name to Agnes?" Joan asked.

"Aww!" many of them said together.

The girls all chimed in with their opinions of Veronica's new name.

Veronica laughed and motioned the new girls forward. They came in a pack, each step heartbreakingly hesitant. She plopped down on the floor and, one by one, they followed her lead. They sat just far enough away that she couldn't reach them.

"Has Mistress Phillips told you our three rules here?" Veronica asked them softly enough that they had to lean forward to hear. She felt a slight tug when Agnes sat down behind her on one of her skirts.

The newcomers nodded as a group.

"Can you tell me what they are?"

"Please, miss. Don't be afraid is one," one of the girls Veronica had identified as Leila, a brunette of eight or nine, said in a small voice.

Veronica smiled and nodded. "I know it will take time for you to trust us here. You've had an awful time of it. No one blames you for being cautious. Suzie, come here, dear."

Suzie nudged in beside Veronica.

"Suzie has been with us since the beginning. Were you frightened when you came here?" Veronica asked.

Suzie nodded vigorously, her short, dark hair brushing her cheek. "I was in Grillett's factories for eight years. I thought this place might be mental or just plain crazy dunlops. No one could get past those coppers wot kept us in the Grave."

The new girls shivered, and one curled up into a ball.

"But the Eidolon scooped me up and dropped me 'ere a year ago in this 'eaven. I never been back. It took a while to get used to regular meals and the like." She looked directly at Leila and then the others. "But the nightmares stopped, and this became… 'ome."

The wild edge about the new girls' faces softened a bit while listening to Suzie, and one or two looked at Veronica with frantic hopefulness in their eyes. None of them ventured a question, but she could tell they'd heard Suzie and wanted to believe her. Veronica didn't expect much progress the first day, or even the first week. But children were resilient, and just like the others, they would eventually start speaking and interacting.

"And the other rules?" Veronica asked.

"Stay inside," Beth squeaked.

"Very good! These walls will protect you. They may even be … magic!" she whispered.

A few of the girls who had been at Bridges for a while giggled.

"The last one is to make friends," Suzie said. "We're family now, we are." She hugged Madeline to her side. The girl's eyes went as wide as saucers.

Agnes scooted closer. Veronica motioned for Mistress Phillips to hand her a book, the one she read to all her new orphans. "Now that you know the rules, I'd like to read you a story.

"This is the tale of the twelve-year-old orphaned girl, Melilot. When her parents died, she was all alone without food or family."

The newcomers all watched her warily. Suzie bounced and asked, "Then you have to tell the one about the hero pirate, *Kartal!*"

Veronica shook her head. "We save that one for later on, after the new girls and boys are settled. After all, he's very fierce!"

Suzie giggled.

Kartal. The common soldier who had saved the Somborian fleet from the Turkish invasion. The children loved hearing how a man who came from nothing saved his friends and countrymen. The Eidolon's cause could use such a fighter. Even if he was only a man.

Veronica opened the book and began reading, lowering her voice to a soothing cadence. She told of Melilot, a young girl about Agnes' age. Melilot was afraid when her parents died, and she was left all alone. The first people that she encountered after leaving home were three ugly, frog-like creatures who bade her enter their cottage. Taught to be brave and polite, Melilot did so.

She told them of her plight, how she had neither food nor the physical strength to dig her parents' graves. The creatures consoled her, followed her to the gravesites of her parents, and buried them for her.

As soon as the burial was complete, bread and milk appeared on the graves. Melilot gave the creatures the food and drink. She ate only when they had finished. That night, she invited them to sleep in her parents' bed.

When yards of beautiful cloth magically appeared, she sewed them each a magnificent dress. When the creatures put on the clothes, they transformed into fairies. They revealed how they had been cursed, but Melilot, through her generosity and selflessness, had freed them. Then they each bestowed a magical kiss upon her, granting her magnificent clothing, transforming her cottage into a beautiful mansion, and giving her all the food she could possibly eat.

"Melilot went outside the cottage and knelt on the ground. 'But all is changed about me. Why do the walls flower and why is my dress covered with glittering stones?' " Veronica read.

Some of her new charges had nodded off, their heads resting on the shoulders of the older girls next to them. The story was not yet finished. She said to those still awake, "So you see, my dears, that when night is darkest, when you have gone without even the barest of necessities, you can yet be brave and kind. If you do, you may not have a dress covered with glittering stones, but you can still shine just as brightly."

Veronica thought of the dark days ahead of her. Orphans like Suzie, both girls and boys, proved themselves as brave as Melilot, who was kind in spite of her loss, choosing to face their fears and charge into the future.

Perhaps she needed to borrow some of their courage.

She wouldn't deny these heroic children a future simply because the thought of giving up her own, the idea of losing her freedom, made her throat swell until she could hardly breathe. She placed a kiss on Agnes's head and pulled Claire, the girl who'd been there the longest, tightly to her side.

Claire leaned her head against Veronica's shoulder, her hair smelling of the apple-scented soap Mistress Phillips favored keeping on hand. No matter the darkness she was called to face, Veronica vowed these children would never live in the dark again.

Chapter Seven

Emil squeezed oil onto the hinges of the window before sliding it open and tossing out a rope. The prince finally slept, encouraged to do so by a bit of tea spiked with some sleeping herbs Emil had collected overseas. Rosseau, Emil's first mate and the crewman who'd been with Emil the longest, had been left in charge, not that much supervision would be needed.

No one would even know they'd arrived at the Imperial Hotel. A prince on an obscure ship with a ragtag crew, checked in under a German name? They were beneath everyone's notice. No one liked the Germans these days. They held onto their steam-tech with tight fists, like a child with a coveted toy.

Rosseau saluted Emil as he slid out the window and pushed off the wall of the hotel with his heels, his gloves slowing his descent down the rope until his soft-soled boots touched the dirt amidst the pruned bushes on the south side of the hotel. He tugged once on the rope, and Rosseau pulled it back up into their room on the tenth floor.

Instead of his traditional robes, Emil wore breeches, a long town coat and a top hat. With his scarf still securely covering his nose and mouth, he lowered the brim of his hat and headed toward Grosvenor Square.

The streets smelled thickly of oil. The darkness at this hour of the night obscured all but the circle of light surrounding the lampposts set in odd intervals. All was improbably still, as though London were suspended, caught between worlds. Emil heard nothing above the sound of his own breath.

The black paint surrounding his eyes and the dark threads of his clothing seemed unnecessary now, when so few walked the streets, and those that did averted their eyes from the shadows.

Emil continued to weave his way through the darkness, savoring the quiet. Savoring the time to think.

Years ago, long before he won his throne, Durad had fought side by side with Emil. The sparring ground they chose was dark and reeked of the unwashed and forgotten, forgotten by all but Emil and Durad. They smuggled the boys and girls out of the factories, a few here and there. Most of them made it back to Durad's plantation home, where they grew in size until an unlikely army formed, unflinchingly loyal and insensibly brave.

The memories—the faces of each child—never left Emil.

Perhaps Emil should drag his prince through the slums of Varna, Bucharest, or the Algiers. *Change doesn't stop with Sombor, Durad! We planned on changing the world, not just how we dressed.* Ah, but Emil would find a way to make him remember. He would dangle Durad from the yardarm of his airship until he admitted he'd gone soft, that he'd lost sight of what was important. Admitted that this alliance could give Sombor the stability it needed. Admitted that with that stability, change could spread across continents, razing kings like wildfire, leaving new shoots to flourish amidst burnt embers. That they could be that change to save the families broken apart by war and by factory enslavement.

Change.

You promised me, Durad. No more factories. No more children like us.

While Sombor had embraced Durad's hard-won regency, they had grown restless. They knew the truth; peace faded and vanished as quickly as the rising steam, dissipating in the stronger air. With threats on all sides, their people wanted more of Durad. More of what he promised when he seized the throne; action and passion.

Emil stepped around a corner and leaned against the side of a five-story mansion in Grosvenor Square, opposite the Duke of Richmond's townhome, and settled in. It was time to see what had a prince and military hero whining like a nursery-age child. If Lady Veronica Clarke were addle-pated, vain, cunning, double-crossing, or loose with her morals, he would find out. He'd take care of this ridiculous situation, knock some sense into Durad, and return to his crew, to the work that could not wait long. Not even for a prince.

Several hours later, a steam carriage chugged up to the front door of the townhome, steered by a rather large and impressive gearman. He brought the long, sleek six-wheeled contraption to a smooth stop and hopped down to open the door with more enthusiasm than grace. A tall man in evening dress exited the carriage with the assistance of a walking stick. He took the stairs slowly, as though unhurried, but Emil spotted the slight limp. Guessing from the gentleman's apparent age, it might've been from the last continental wars.

Shouldn't his daughter be with him? As an unmarried woman, she would hardly be out in society alone, even with a companion.

The boxy gearman shut the door. *Blast Durad, needing my comfort earlier like an un-weaned pup and delaying me.* The daughter must've returned home already. She would not remain home in the evenings, a woman with her standing.

Still, the situation made Emil curious. What social or business gathering brought the Duke of Richmond home in the early hours of the morning? He was not young, nor, from what Emil guessed of such a well-reputed man, prone to gaming houses or women of the night.

Before the front doors shut, the duke turned, and for one moment, Emil saw his face.

Something clicked in the recesses of Emil's brain. That face, he recognized it with sudden certainty. There was no mistake. He knew this man, not as a duke, not as a member of civilized society. But as a shadowed profile, a sweeping fist masked by an iron gauntlet.

With an instant plunge, his past memories stabbed him in the chest, opening a wound he thought long healed. A small face appeared in his mind. *Suzanna, my little* canım. *Sister.* Image after image flashed in no particular order, jumbled together with snatches of dialogue. *No! You cannot take her! Stop! STOP!* Fingers, slipping through his. A face, red with terror. A small voice, nearly drowned by an engine, pleading with him. Tears burning his eyes. *My* canım, *I will find you!*

And then it was over, and he was clutching his chest and kneeling on the freezing stone. The memory vanished even as he grasped for it.

The doors closed behind the duke, the night just as it had been.

Emil stood and scrubbed the stones with the soft heel of his boot. He pressed his hands to his chest over his heart. Nothing seemed amiss, yet a pressure still remained, sharp and heavy. Suzanna, he still missed her, still ached for her.

He rubbed his eyes and tried to focus on the height of the rooftops, the likelihood of discovery from his current position, the possible angle of attack, his mind reaching, calculating, sensing, diverting his thoughts until his heart iced over again.

Emil lifted his eyes, staring at the heavy iron door the duke had shut a few moments ago. He had thought those memories long faded, like the sound of his mother's voice or the shape of his father's face. Emil ran his fingers along the scars beneath his scarf and wondered at fate, at how he could be here, now, about to meet a shadow from the past.

He'd been given an opportunity. And though Sombor's future, and Durad's, fluttered in the wind like a sail from a broken mast, he would not hesitate to chop it down to reach the duke. The man who had taken his sister from him.

"Absolutely not."

Emil tossed the velum invitation onto the desk. The prince had awoken late and was now in an annoyingly cheerful mood.

Durad snatched it up and held it aloft, waving it like a ship's sail in the wind. "This is my last chance to have a bit of fun before I meet my loony bride. I'll be wearing a disguise, Emil, what's the problem?" He grinned as he used to, his eyes shining, the corners of his mouth only slightly lifted. That look had led Emil into far too many battles.

"But a masque, Durad?"

"Just think of the beautiful women who will don a mask, wanting to escape their lives for one evening in the arms of a glamorous stranger. Even you would not look out of place there, my odd friend, with that feminine frippery on your face." Durad flicked Emil's scarf.

"We had an agreement about my eccentricity, *Your Highness.*

This *thing* is as much your fault as it is mine. If you had not traveled all over Sombor spreading wild rumors, I would not need this disguise."

Durad laughed. "It wasn't *entirely* rumor. Besides, what are the chances a few stories about a Somborian war hero have reached fashionable London? Your scars will fit right in with the other veterans. The women will hardly notice. Or if they do, they'll want a personal account, if you know what I mean."

Emil ripped off his scarf, baring the crisscrossing raised scars on the lower half of his face. "I will not show these in public, no matter how far we travel from Sombor." He turned, leaning his palms on the desk, breathing heavily. His scars burned, as they sometimes did, a phantom pain from an injury long healed.

As he rubbed his scars absently, he noticed the full, black facial mask sitting there, having arrived with the invitation. Durad reached over his shoulder, grabbed it, and held it up to Emil's face.

"Look in the mirror, my friend," the prince said.

Emil snapped his head up. "Why did you have to choose now to relive old times—" He paused, his eyes connecting with his reflection. The mask did indeed cover his scars.

"I'll send Monsieur Paget out to find us two costumes that will make us look *devilishly* handsome and mysterious. It'll be just like old times." Durad popped open a bottle of cider and poured two glasses, handing one to Emil.

While Durad toasted his ingenuity and the upcoming evening, Emil continued to stare at his masked face. He could be anyone. He could be invisible for an evening, without slipping through alleyways or climbing ropes. What kind of information could he gather in a setting where the gentry's tongues were loosened by wine, their dispositions sweetened by anonymity? Information about the gentry?

As he listened with half an ear to his old friend, his thoughts turned to the duke. Not one day had gone by in the eight years since that rippin' man had taken Suzanna without Emil contemplating the prospect of finding him. Now that Emil had, the discovery was not welcome. The duke was near invulnerable, plated with an armor of money and influence.

Still. Without the lenses of fearful youth, Emil saw the duke for what he was. A man of flesh and blood. With a name.

And a daughter. Who was about to marry Durad.

His friend might never forgive him for what he was about to do, nor might Emil ever forgive himself for such a betrayal. He'd barely obtained the prince's forgiveness for leaving him this past year. Now, he planned on killing Durad's future father-in-law.

Yet he lifted his glass to Durad and drank.

Chapter Eight

Eight years ago…

Emil's shoulders tensed and his hands shook as he assembled the rotors on the drive wheel. The parts were so small. The damp nervousness of his fingers made it difficult to complete his shift quota, especially when Master Craig was on duty.

The whip cracked an inch above his shoulder, and Emil nearly dropped the last wheel he needed to finish for the day. The cattail left a thin line of blood where it grazed the skin. He didn't feel anything though, the skin on his shoulders was too scarred and his focus too narrow. Emil knew what would happen if he failed.

Next to him, Durad whispered, "All right?"

Emil barely nodded. They weren't allowed to speak. Durad shouldn't be taking the risk, but his friend had never been good at following rules. Emil had been here for years and knew how to survive. He'd seen dozens of boys like Durad come and inevitably go, too broken to fix. He didn't know what exactly happened to them, but he knew those who ran the factories and how they treated the boys. Commodities. Efficiency. Production. Quota. They weren't human beings, only cogs in a machine.

Emil glanced over. Durad was short three wheels. When he noticed Emil's look, Durad slumped. Every shift, his frantic work inevitably fell short. It seemed to Emil as though Durad's fingers were simply not designed for such work.

Emil cursed silently. This wasn't his problem. If he helped… there was a reason he'd lasted this long. He'd built a shell, day after day, around the soft part of his heart. The part that would help boys like Durad, that would show weakness in front of the guards.

Why should he break his shell for this boy? What made Durad special?

Rippin' rotors, but he liked the boy. Saw courage in his bones, light in his eyes. Something different from what usually came and went. Durad blinked brightly in this heavy darkness.

Emil shut his eyes briefly. He'd been here so long.

Too long.

Voices broke free of his hardened shell. One after another.

You're nothing more than a slave. Worthless. Scum. Gutter trash. Get it right! Again. Again. Again! No one will miss you. No one cares. NO ONE.

The memories layered, building up inside his mind. The piercing sound of the whip, the screams as it tore through flesh. The shame as he looked away. Agony as he felt it upon his own back.

Anger burst through and ran like a current through his entire body. Thoughts multiplied, one upon another until a plan formed in his mind.

Now. Today. Before they broke Durad, he had to act.

When the shift bell rang thirty minutes later, Durad was still short two wheels. His eyes dimmed, but he turned, feet together, shoulders straight, like all the other boys at their station. For the first time in hours, silence fell, heavy and dense, like a moonless night in a dark forest.

Master Craig rose from his chair, stretching up to his full height, at least a foot above the tallest boy, and slapped the handle of the whip into his palm. The crack of leather on skin caused several boys to jump and then hastily resume their stance.

Emil waited for Master Craig's one-word assessment of the boys' work, which would determine the type of punishment doled out. Two wheels short, Durad would get last draw for sure.

Master Craig surveyed the room and barked, "Lazy."

The sharp inhale of breath marred the silence. That indictment was one of the worst.

He strode down the row, noting the number of wheels in each boy's station. The boys faced forward, every moment drenched with tension while they waited for the final tally. All stations were neat and orderly, with the exception of Durad's. Emil wiped his damp palms on his trousers. He pushed three of his wheels silently over to Durad's pile. Durad's eyes widened and his mouth lifted slightly in what might have been a smile.

The sound of heavy footfalls, dense and crisp, arrived before Master Craig did. Face darkened with soot and streaked with oil, he leaned forward to count Durad's wheels. He snorted while his hand shot out to grip Durad's chin. "Impressive, boy. You made quota for the first time. But your station is a mess. And you know how much I care about workplace safety. You will be last."

Durad's eyes met Emil's, resigned. He lifted one shoulder in a half shrug and nodded his head, showing he didn't blame Emil for trying.

Last draw. Emil hadn't planned for that. A line of sweat dripped from his temples. He wanted to tell Durad to hang on, to survive. Just one more time.

Master Craig's fetid breath turned toward Emil and hitched for a moment when he surveyed Emil's station. His large fist immediately lashed out, catching Emil's ear. Master Craig turned back and tossed an order over his shoulder.

"Cuff this one."

A guard, one Emil didn't recognize, shot up out of his chair, ran to Emil and snapped a set of cuffs on his wrists. The sound echoed in the cavernous factory room, and several boys flinched.

"Take him to the furnace," Master Craig ordered, waving them away.

The guard, his face shiny with sweat, nodded and pushed Emil down the hall. As they left the room, Emil heard Master Craig order the boys to the hitching post. Before the door closed behind them, Emil heard the sickening crack of a whip on bare flesh.

Emil stumbled down the hall, imagining Durad tied to the post, and the scorch marks of the cattail as it bit into his poor friend's back. Master Craig, though not a fan of personal hygiene, cleaned his whip regularly, reserving the vinegar dip for the last boy.

Emil hardly noticed where he was until the guard shoved him through a door and a wave of unbearable heat hit his face. He didn't know why he was here, nor had he heard of this brand of punishment before. But he knew better than to ask questions.

The guard snapped the cuffs onto the side of the furnace. Emil's hands brushed the metal door and he jumped, yanking back. He turned to the guard.

"What is this?" Emil asked, while a horrible idea rose violently in his mind.

"It's your fault, kid. You know Master Craig doesn't mess around," the guard said.

Though his words seemed sympathetic, his tone was smug. He turned and left the room, the lock clicking into place behind him.

This wasn't a punishment. It was an execution.

Emil frantically yanked at his hands again and again, trying to get them away from the heat. In minutes, his clothes were drenched with sweat and he could hardly see. He managed to position his hands so his skin wouldn't burn, but the effort of maintaining the pose made him tremble.

No one could survive this heat or the torture of being burned over and over. Emil inhaled a breath of warm, sooty air and forced himself to think. After a few moments, he glanced down at his cuffs and yanked again. A plan formed in his mind, and with new resolve, he thrust his hands toward the fire.

Chapter Nine

"You simply must go, my dear. I will not hear another word on the matter." Veronica's brother, Alec, swung his walking stick up to poke her in the chest, emphasizing each word with another jab. "Despite what our estimable papá thinks, you are too," jab, "much," jab, "of a stuffed," jab, "shirt."

She whipped her arm up and grabbed the stick. "I'm a proper society lady, remember? I'm supposed to be boring."

Alec rolled his eyes. "You've succeeded very well at that."

"Yes, well, the duke does not exactly think I'm a jewel of the *ton*," she muttered.

If Alec thought her boring, wait until he heard she was engaged to a prince. No one had less fun or less freedom than royals. Or so she could imagine. If she thought her life restrictive now, what would it be like to never have one moment of freedom? To be constantly analyzed by a people she didn't know or couldn't understand?

"*Hello.* Peanut, pay attention, darling. If you don't go, I'll be forced to drink until I'm well in my cups at some club and disgrace our family name."

"How is that different from what you do every other night?"

Alec laughed, but it lacked mirth. "Ah, but this time, I'll set up shop at the gaming tables."

Veronica let go of his walking stick, making her brother stumble back a few steps. "You wouldn't. You know how much you lost last time. You've little enough left for your future."

Alec simply raised one brow.

"No," she scoffed.

But he continued to stare at her. Underneath the mask of

humor and devil-may-care attitude her brother always wore, she recognized the Clarke stubbornness. He *would* do it. He'd never cared much for himself. The duke's indifference toward Alec since his return had nurtured a kind of desperation in him.

If Veronica wouldn't listen to him, or care what happened to him, who would?

Quick as lightning, she snatched his walking stick and held it up to his neck like a sword.

"All right. I'll come to your silly masque, but I'm only staying until midnight. And Matilda is coming, too."

The corners of Alec's mouth turned up into a polite smile. "Are you sure you want her tagging along? She's about as lively as you are."

Veronica removed the stick and handed it back to him. "You don't know what you're getting yourself into, brother dear."

"I'd rather marry a dozen princes than go to this absurd event," Veronica said to Matilda as Hale handed her up into the carriage.

Dressed in a flowing black gown edged in white that may have been considered morbid by some, she had finished off the costume with a silver metal corset, tied together with white ribbon. Worn, as was the style, over the dress. A butterfly bracelet snaked up each upper arm, matching the chain she always wore at her throat. Matilda had piled her hair on top of her head in carefully arranged curls, securing them with a single, wide, decorative silver band, with Alec directing the entire affair.

"Nonetheless, you look magnificent, my lady." Hale bowed before shutting the carriage door.

Already in the carriage, Matilda added, "Of course she does. Really, Hale, no need to go on stating the obvious."

The gearman eyed her and said, "Then I guess I won't say anything about your costume, miss. Or how much it reveals about you." He winked at her and hopped up front.

Matilda folded her arms across her chest, covering a modest white gown that looked more suitable for a debutante at Almack's.

"I should not need to remind him, my lady, how improper it is for a gearman to share his opinions with his betters. I'll have a chat with Critchton."

Veronica laughed. "Matilda, our old butler stopped trying to change Hale long ago."

The door to the carriage swung open again and Alec alighted in what looked like an outfit of Hale's; a leather jacket with several flapped pockets, tight leather breeches, a flowing white shirt, and a cap and goggles. Though Alec usually appeared elegantly slim in his tailored clothing, the leather he now wore clung to a more muscled physique than Veronica had guessed. *He certainly plans on having a smashing time.*

Alec glanced at Matilda's gaping expression and unbuttoned the top buttons on his shirt. "There, is that better?"

Veronica's companion sputtered for a moment.

"Honestly, Alec, stop torturing poor Matilda. That whole costume really is quite shocking."

He waived aside her comment. "I forget you've never been to one of these before. Though you look," he held up both her hands and glanced at her corset, "nothing like you usually do. I've done excellent work here."

A sound escaped Matilda. It sounded halfway between a laugh and a snort. At least she'd managed to stop gawking.

Veronica tugged her hands away, swatting at Alec. "You promised to behave."

He leaned back and grinned. "Why, *that* was never part of the agreement, dear sister."

Dozens of crystal chandeliers glittered in the dim light of the gas lamps. Metal flashed, studded with diamonds, sparks of light and color in the near darkness, as couples waltzed across the floor, scandalously close together. Not one person disdained a mask, with the exception of those that had already left the gathering with a partner they may or may not have recognized.

Veronica tried to inch further away from the heavyset man in an unoriginal black cape and matching suit who was currently leading her in nothing resembling a waltz. His fingers pressed into her back, unyielding. She glanced at another couple nearby, the man and woman seamless and perfect in their movement. He pressed the side of a long, lean torso to her soft one and she seemed to melt into him with each step.

Heavens, why didn't they just leave the party in favor of the gardens?

All the smoke and mystery, the seductive music, the license to be free… It seemed to her as though these people couldn't handle even the minimal responsibilities of a privileged life. They had organized an evening when those obligations, those *burdens,* vanished into liaisons with people they might cut tomorrow evening at Almack's, perhaps not knowing or remembering who they'd danced with.

Or maybe they did know, maybe they did seek out a person in particular; a second son with no prospects but a pretty face, a bored, younger woman married to a wealthy, older man, a rough member of the serving class even.

She reached up to adjust her mask, the movement one of habit, and she nearly stopped moving altogether. She'd found a way to deal with her burdens through a disguise. Not just a few times a year, but several times a month. Instead of romance, she heated her blood in a different way, wielding her Tesla-ray and her rapier. For the first time, she'd found something she had in common with members of the *ton.* Albeit the morally questionable.

Veronica resumed the bumbling dance with her partner, her mind spinning along with the music. She was, of course, different from these pleasure seekers. She saved innocent children, for heaven's sake. Suzie. Agnes.

Thinking of her orphaned charges lightened her heart for a moment and helped pass the remaining steps of the dance. As soon as the song ended, she stepped back and turned, searching for the quickest route to the exit.

But a man stood in her way. She stopped only because she recognized him as the same one she'd been watching, the one who'd been waltzing in a shocking manner with the woman in white. Up close, he was even taller, larger. His clothes fit a bit too snugly, showing off a figure best suited to a soldier. It looked as though his tailor had measured his costume a few inches too small, though instead of revealing any flaws, it simply made him look a bit indecent. Rather like Alec this evening.

After the long moment she spent gawking, instead of asking her properly for a dance, the man swept her up in his arms and into the next waltz. She nearly froze, stiffening in obvious rejection.

"I mean to leave, sir. You will unhand me. Without making a scene, if you please." She tugged, but he didn't relent. What was it with sticky-handed men tonight?

"I saw you smile," he said in a clipped voice that revealed a foreign lilt.

"Pardon?" He surprised her into ceasing her struggle for a moment.

He turned his face so his eyes met hers. Sharp and black, they made her stumble, but his hands held her firm. A mask covered the rest of his face, making her relieved he couldn't use whatever other power he possessed over her. He moved without appearing to exert any thought, pulling her along with him, making it all feel so natural.

"I..." she tried to reply, and then realized he hadn't asked a question.

"What were you thinking of, just then? When you smiled?" he asked. Oddly, his words didn't sound muffled in the least. "It looked for a moment as though you were not... here." He inclined his head toward the other dancers, some stumbling more than waltzing. Her last partner among them.

What was I thinking of? It took her a moment. *Ah. Suzie.* The reminder brought her out of the fog and back to her senses. She straightened.

"Nothing you would understand."

"Perhaps I would surprise you."

I very much doubt it. But then, her earlier thoughts returned about the similarities between the mask she wore as the Eidolon and the mask she wore tonight, and she snapped at him.

"If I give you one minute to convince me *not* to leave, will that suffice?"

He leaned in close, his forehead nearly brushing hers. When he spoke, his voice was soft and dark. "Is your life so perfect that you do not need an evening off every once in a while?"

Her reply came out sharp, swift, "An evening off from *what?*"

"The obligations of your position, of course." He sounded amused.

"The obligations…" Veronica sputtered as she missed a step. Something shook loose inside her.

Yes, she took nights off, but not for gratifications like this. What she did mattered, changed lives. The irritating smoothness of this attempted seduction, and his comparison to her own need to be free loosened her tongue. She wore a mask, there was no need to filter her words. Her opinions burst out, a strong, steady stream of steam flowing from a hot engine.

"Why does everyone speak of the *burdens* of title and yet do nothing with it but waste their evenings at Almack's or silly masques? Waste their days flying above London, too intoxicated to appreciate the irony of their position. They've done nothing of real worth.

"When have one of these people here visited the factory district? The place they call the Grave? The orphaned children from the latest Continental Wars work twelve hours at a time, just for the opportunity to be starved and beaten by unregulated guards."

Her partner missed a step in the waltz, forcing her to stumble into him. She tried to wiggle free, but he kept her even closer, flowing into the next step.

Veronica could feel him from her toes to the tips of her fingers. It made her words stream even faster, harder.

"Why do they refuse to see? How can the feel of a silk dress compare to the embrace of a lonely child? How can they waste money at the track, betting on gurney races when so many thousands have never left a table with their stomach filled?

"It sickens me." She finally stopped, still breathing hard. She tried to tear herself away yet again, but her partner held her fast. *One kick and I could make you release me. One second more…*

"So passionate, madam," he said in a voice no longer soft and seductive, but as hard and cold as the metal bracelets snaking up her wrists.

"Is that not what you were seeking tonight? Someone *passionate?* Do I not fit your ideal?" She laughed, a hard sound. "My apologies, sir, but I'm not the girl that's swept into a dark corner. Nor one to be considered seriously. I spout foolish nonsense."

"A man listens little enough to what a woman says. And your figure is pleasing." His eyes swept her body.

She tensed. "Now, as I may have said, I have somewhere to be."

He allowed her off the dance floor, but then he did what no partner of hers had ever done; he pulled her away from the others and toward one of those dark corners she'd just mentioned. Shock, once again, made her compliant. And morbid curiosity. Such words were usually enough to earn her the cut direct, in spite of her station.

Veronica tossed a glance at Matilda—her attention engaged with yet another earnest suitor—before Veronica found herself on a balcony. The outdoor lamps had been turned off completely, and when he shut the doors to the ballroom, she could barely make out his figure.

"Why are we out here? Haven't I said enough to scare you off? Can I leave now?" she asked.

She watched him carefully, scanning for an opening, in case she had to defend herself. This man must be one of those that enjoyed a chase. The thrill of being denied fueled some kind of sick excitement in such men. Yet the putrid, furtive smell that usually hung about them didn't afflict this one. He was all confidence, his movements deliberate, calculated.

He laughed quietly. "You do not seem nervous. Are you not frightened of what I might do? A proper woman should at least feign to be." His voice was once again soft, the words honeyed and draped in his accent. In spite of his taunts, he stood as far across the balcony from her as possible.

She leaned on the railing and looked out into the black night. *Two, maybe three moves, and he would be flying into the garden below.*

"I can take care of myself."

"I would like to see that."

She shrugged, and then realized he probably couldn't see her. They stood in silence for several moments and, surprisingly, she felt herself relax. Without the stench of cologne, the murmur of gaudy conversation, or the beady eyes of the males in the room upon her, she breathed in the fresh air. Her teeth unclenched; her shoulders dropped. It felt wonderful to say what she really thought. Even if her partner appeared not to care one whit for her opinions.

"Why did you come tonight?" the man abruptly asked.

She had no reason to not tell the truth. "I was blackmailed."

He laughed again. "Of course."

What did he mean by that? Did she seem like the type of person susceptible to blackmail? Since the moment he'd so rudely grabbed her, she hadn't once shown any type of meekness or submission. He must then be laughing at her. It *was* a rather unconventional reason.

"My family," she said.

"Ah," he said, without appearing to understand her comment at all.

She turned in the direction where she thought he stood. "My turn, oh mysterious one. Why did *you* come to this delightful party? And please don't tell me it was to bring a girl out here, because you would not have chosen me."

It was a moment before he replied. "I, too, came here for family." She heard the black cape he wore flutter as he moved to stand next to her by the railing.

She couldn't imagine this man had been blackmailed to come, as she had. The way he moved, stood and spoke, she had no doubt he ever did anything he didn't want to do. For some reason, his confidence didn't dissuade her from his company, it had the opposite effect. She found herself wanting to verbally spar, to hear him challenge her. Perhaps because he did what few men ever did… he listened.

Of course, the whole idea of her having a civil conversation out on a dark balcony, with a foreign stranger with beautiful eyes and a strong figure, was utterly ridiculous. What would happen next? Would she sprout wings and fly off into the night?

Still, she stayed. She allowed the rising steam from the buildings' pipes to both warm and then chill her, wondering what the man was thinking.

"I'm sure you wanted to come?" she asked.

"No," he replied. She thought she heard him shake his head, but it was hard to tell. "Though I think…" his voice trailed off and she felt a hand brush her neck.

"What?" Her skin felt hot where he'd touched her. What was he doing? Was that a caress?

"I think it is nice to speak with a woman like this."

"Out in the darkness?" she asked.

She smiled, amused by the idea that a man would touch her, the ridiculous spinster. Then she remembered that tonight, she didn't play that role. This man heard her spout nonsense and still, he drew closer. A society man would never find a silly woman like her to be attractive. Desirable. There must be something off about him.

Then again, there was more than a little something off about her.

"Actually," he paused and when he spoke again, it sounded like he'd lifted his mask, "yes." His hand trailed down her bare arm until his fingers laced with hers. She didn't dare look at him. Nor move.

"Does that mean you don't mind hearing a woman prattle on about orphans?" she asked with a laugh that trembled only slightly.

He didn't answer for a moment and then asked, "Everything you said as we danced… does it really matter so much to you?" His words traveled into the night, as if he now stared off into the distance.

She could hardly prevaricate now, not after her impressive rant. "It is all that matters to me."

Another pause. She waited. Glanced down at their hands, still laced together, his palm warm and rough in hers. She hoped his next words would not crush the growing respect she had for him.

He spoke, his voice sounding closer. "I grew up in one of them. A factory."

"You did?" The strumming beat of the party faded even further into the background. The night seemed to close in on them, as though the world faded to this moment, to him and his confession.

"Yes."

The hand in hers tried to pull away, but she held fast. "You survived. How?"

"Another depended on me." The words came out raw, as

though it hurt him to speak.

"You both escaped?" There was no leaving the factories, except as burnt ashes in the wind. Or in the Eidolon's carriage.

He didn't answer but moved her fingers to his wrists. She felt raised bumps circling them, scars. From shackles most likely.

"I melted them off, and…" he trailed off. After a moment he continued. "We left on a dirigible, one we had just completed."

She gently felt the scars. They encircled both wrists, ugly and thick. *Mercy.* A few of Veronica's orphans, the older boys, bore the calling card of the cat'o'nine, but their skin was young, new. Once they were in her care, the scars faded little by little, as the child himself healed. Each time Clank cracked his whip on a guard, Veronica felt no regret.

Until last night. When she'd allowed anger to overpower her control.

She folded both of the man's hands inside hers. They were large, calloused. Though he might be fully-grown and more than capable, perhaps he needed a bit of Lady Flowers's magic. The man didn't pull away. After a moment, he shifted and sighed, as though her touch relieved him.

"You're a miracle," she said.

He flipped his hands out and grabbed hers, placing them on his heart.

It drummed, strong and quick. She kept her eyes straight forward, unwilling to break the spell. This man couldn't have admitted this to just anyone. The *ton* would not hear it, but her rant, the darkness, this anonymity, it must've made him want to confess. Veronica may be the only person in that prodigious ballroom who comprehended his words. She considered what it meant to be a survivor of the factories, and comfortable enough to move among the *ton*. Perhaps she wasn't as alone as she thought.

"Shall I tell you a story in return?" she asked finally.

"I have already told you I like the words from your enchanting mouth," he said, his tone lighter. He moved their hands down by his side, fingers now entwined.

She smiled and related the same tale she'd told Agnes and the new arrivals, of Melilot and the creatures. He listened without moving, without making a sound, as though this were a natural state for him. His calm kept her speaking, the story flowing as effortlessly as it did when she gathered Suzie and the new arrivals by her, their eyes large with wonder, and taught them about hope. It felt natural to tell him, a factory orphan, the same fairytale. The story that lit her dark corners as a child, that now served the same purpose for the orphans she rescued.

When it ended, she asked, "Does your tale have such an ending?"

"It did tonight."

He used their hands to suddenly pull her close. Her calm evaporated. She felt her eyes go wide and her pulse flare wildly out of control. What did he intend to do? Kiss her? She was now closer to this man than she'd ever been to any male.

She nearly reacted by taking their joined hands and twisting it around his back, but something stopped her. Good heavens, but she really liked how this felt. A strong man, a factory survivor no less, smelling lovely and touching her with confidence and longing.

His free hand reached up and landed on her mask. He left it there for a moment, as though giving her time to decide.

Decide what? Did he want her to slide up her own mask? She still couldn't make out the features of his face. What would be the harm? She wanted to. Wanted to see what would happen. Wanted him to kiss her. Wanted this more than anything.

But what if someone discovered them? A scandal like this might not only ruin her engagement but also give the duke the excuse he needed to pull the funding from Bridges. No, there was too much at stake…

His hands cupped her face. It felt a little painful, like the shock of a dip in a cool pond on a hot day, but then it livened her senses, as though she were waking up for the first time.

Heavens. She felt her feet freeze to the cold floor. Her eyes searched the darkness for the features of his face. The sound of his breath hung heavy in the air between them. She should slide up her mask. Right now.

He swore and then pulled away, placing his hands on her shoulders, to steady whom, she couldn't tell.

"I have never," he whispered. His voice trembled slightly.

Never what? Kissed a girl? Surely, he had. They stood there, not moving. She contemplated stepping forward, into him again, tearing off her mask.

But his hands dropped, and he turned away.

Veronica felt her cheeks flush. She'd missed her chance. She unnecessarily straightened her mask, taking several moments to adjust it, telling herself she was lucky she hadn't given in. Doubt swirled and settled in her mind. She might've given him insight on how to sweettalk her when she'd ranted, then he'd spun a tale that made her knees weak. That was the manner of rakes, was it not?

But then, he would've seized his moment, done what he'd planned.

It had all felt so real, sounded so real.

Veronica might have escaped ruin, but the idea didn't make her as relieved as she thought. Her heart ached. Then her body began quivering. She had to get out of there. Away from this man that made her want too much.

Without a word, Veronica turned and swept aside the curtains, placing her hand on the doorknob. She heard fabric flutter behind her, and when she opened the doors, the light revealed the balcony to be empty. He was gone.

She rushed to the railing, but even with the dim light from the ballroom, she couldn't see over the edge. Veronica sank back against the wall and pressed her hand to her forehead. Maybe it hadn't happened at all. Maybe she'd imagined the whole thing. Yes, that seemed more reasonable than the confession she'd just heard, and her nearly kissing a man she didn't know on a dark balcony at a masque.

She had to find Alec. Surely whatever had just happened satisfied what her brother had in mind for her this evening.

Veronica stepped back inside the ballroom. A wave of sickly-smelling heat doused her as she moved through the crowd, searching for Matilda. She was easy to spot, her white dress shone like a diamond amongst coal.

She was attempting to gain shelter by the chaperones, but men continued to approach her, bowing first and then offering a palm for a dance. Matilda's stiff posture never waivered as she declined each prospective partner with a shake of her head. Her eyes searched the room, most likely for Veronica. When they settled on her, Matilda shoved her latest suitor aside and marched toward her charge.

"Where have you been?" she asked with a tight smile. "I've not seen you these past twenty minutes."

Veronica shrugged, her heart tender enough to ache. "Oh, you know me. I was out on a dark balcony with a stranger, sullying my reputation."

Matilda relaxed. "I'm sorry, my lady. I'm being ridiculous, aren't I?" She placed her hand on Veronica's shoulder and laughed. "As though you would take part in all this. If it weren't for that foppish brother of yours… just look at him. Why does he enjoy this so much?"

Veronica glanced in the direction Matilda was looking. Alec sat in a velvet-cushioned armchair with one woman on his knee and several more by his side. All were clearly younger, sporting flashes of metal around their upper arms, shortened skirts, and drop-waisted belts. The one on his lap leaned in, placed a hand on his exposed chest, and breathed something in his ear. He laughed and pulled her in for a hearty kiss.

Veronica stared for several moments at the way the girl's cheeks flushed and her eyes fluttered closed. Is that what it would have felt like? To kiss the stranger? His masked face flashed in her mind, and her skin tingled with the remembered sensation of his hands on her face.

She narrowed her eyes and shut out the image. She had to tell herself that, in the end, the stranger was no different than any other man in this room. He was simply more skilled at persuasion than any she'd met.

Had things been different, had she been a normal debutante from a normal, titled family… but then, how could they be? Veronica never would've chosen otherwise. Her course as the Eidolon was set. Still, her world had tilted, pushed off its axis by a man with a crisp accent, scarred wrists, and a thrilling touch.

Suddenly, the ballroom air felt musty and dirty. Veronica had attended one too many balls, cotillions, and musical events. She'd watched the same events unfold, with the same ending. Except tonight. Her eyes sought out the foreign stranger, wishing she could catch one more glimpse, but he'd vanished. She had to leave before she spent the night looking for him, or even worse, found him again.

Veronica swept up her skirts and waded through the slow-moving dancers until she reached Alec. She snatched the timepiece hanging from his neck and held it up to his face.

"I believe I've satisfied your requirement, brother dear."

Alec glanced at the watch and arched a brow. "Ten minutes yet remain." He inclined his head at the crowd of females gathered around him. "I plan on using that time to its utmost."

She used the chain from the piece to yank him closer to her. "I'm leaving, brother, with or without you." She let it drop and turned to move away, but he stood, shoving the girl off his lap and grabbed Veronica's arm. He pulled her aside and spoke in a low voice.

"Peanut, what happened?" He lifted his mask, revealing the concern in his eyes.

She shrugged him off. "How can you do this, Alec? How can you join them?"

Veronica glanced at the ballroom, at the dancers and the observers, duplicity reflected in the shiny surfaces of their trifles. Guilt nagged at her for her accusation, but she ignored it. On the other hand, she wanted to know if Alec felt as she did on the balcony, when the foreign stranger took her in his arms.

Alec snapped his mask back on and turned away. "Why not? I have few enough diversions in my life."

"Alec!"

Diversions. The same word he often used to describe the racing track. This could be simply a temporary thrill for him, the thrill of winning. His prize was to feel something, anything, good for a while. But only for a while.

Which was why she herself was leaving. She was not immune to the same lure.

Veronica lowered her voice. "Don't let your anger at the duke turn you into *this*."

Alec smirked. "What a quaint idea. Now, if you will excuse me, I have an appointment with a young lady." He took the arm of the girl he'd kissed openly and strolled toward the same alcove Veronica had occupied minutes ago.

Matilda approached. "I am quite ready to leave. I find the company here tiresome. Shall we, my lady?"

Veronica allowed herself to be led out to where Hale stood waiting by the Richmond carriage. She tossed off her mask and threw it aside as they descended the steps of the dance hall. When Hale saw the action, he hopped down from the driver's box and opened the carriage door.

"You'd best keep that mouth of yours shut, Hale. My lady is in no mood for your smart remarks," Matilda said.

Hale bowed and lifted Veronica into the carriage. "Why your ladyship, when have I ever been so bold as to express an opinion on any subject of importance?" Veronica felt one corner of her mouth turn up. "Therefore, I will not say how glad I am to see you leave this place," he said.

"Well," Matilda sniffed, "then I will not stop you."

Chapter Ten

Emil watched the woman, the one he'd battled and nearly kissed earlier, Milady Trouble, leave the ballroom. Her gait was steady and fast, her full skirts unable to hinder her as she marched through the front door. He'd waited outside the entrance in the shadows, hoping to catch a glimpse of her, maybe even learn her name.

A smaller woman followed Milady Trouble through the front door. He presumed the girl to be a companion, dressed in a white so bright as to be nearly blinding. As they passed, he noticed gentlemen averting their eyes in a rather guilty fashion, as though the reminder of innocence made them uncomfortable. Emil smiled, liking the statement she made.

Milady Trouble rushed down the stairs, the silver in her corset catching the flickering light. She paused for a moment, released her heavy skirts, and removed her mask. He caught a glimpse of a bright blue set of eyes and a pursed mouth that thinned and hardened as she tossed the mask heedlessly in his direction. She hadn't appeared to see him, and when the mask fell at his feet, some impulse made him pick it up.

He wanted to applaud the gesture, dismissive as it was of the entire event. Though he'd not admitted it to her, he felt the same way about this farce, this "ball", where the *ton* removed all pretense in a room of candlelight and shadow. He'd goaded her, for her answers were the only interesting part of the evening.

Out on the balcony, Milady Trouble's words had stirred something in him. He couldn't believe he'd confessed such a thing to her, but when Emil spoke the words, they felt right.

And then she'd touched him with fingers that were warm and,

oddly, a bit rough. He couldn't move, frozen by her tenderness. The story, her voice, neither too high nor low but somewhere pleasing in between, scratched at his barriers. He thought, he *felt*, that she might know something of his life. He'd wanted to kiss her with all his darkness, absorbing her passion and kindness.

For the first time since he could remember, a woman intrigued him with not only her figure, but with her rough, honest words. Plenty of women in Sombor had wanted the hero, but none had been interested in the factory orphan.

Why hadn't he kissed her? Something kept him from taking what she might have given. He could imagine what it would feel like, the way it would make his heart pound and his skin burn… but no. The decision was quick, *leave, now*. Before she turned into a greater complication. Before he got distracted. She'd given him an opening with her sweet hesitation. Maybe like him, she'd found it hard to believe that neither of them was as alone as they thought.

He watched now as she took the hand of a familiar burly gearman and stepped into a carriage, never once looking back at the white columns of the dance hall. Sound still pulsed from the pillars and the smoke of a hundred candles still wafted through open windows, but her face did not appear in the window of the carriage after the door shut. She made no pretense of her eagerness to leave the venue.

Emil continued to stare at the boxer-type gearman as he shifted the carriage forward. With a small puff, the fancy machine shot into the darkness but not before Emil recognized the purple crest on the door.

His eyes narrowed and he cursed under his breath.

Hayır, olamaz. Her? She was Richmond's daughter? The nitwit promised to Durad?

This innocent girl, who danced the proper length apart, who froze when he touched her, who knew his secret, *she* shared the same blood as the duke? He glanced at her mask, still warm from her skin. He nearly crushed it in his palm. He turned and headed toward the hotel, his stride quick enough to nearly make him a little winded.

Why would she bring up the unfashionable subject of the factories, of all things, with *him*? With anyone? He was certain she could not know who he was.

Before he danced with Richmond's daughter, he'd heard nothing more than praise for Grillett's new air cruiser, or discussion of the latest steam-tech. He'd even heard complaints of husbands spending too much time at the gurney races. Some wanted their figures admired in leather corsets or skirts, or the shape of their arms in metal bands that writhed from wrist to shoulder. It made little sense that Richmond's daughter had been fixed on the orphans and the blind eyes of the *ton*.

Surely, she did not oppose her father's past business activities. It provided her that ridiculous carriage and the other comforts of a lady in her position. Why would she be any different?

He stuffed the mask into his cloak pocket and slipped deeper into the shadows. Nothing about this woman added up. He would need to keep a close eye on her. Nitwit, indeed. She was no more fit for the white coats of Earlswood Asylum than he was.

She did fit into that charming dress quite well. With such a figure, and with her wealth and position, men should've been lining up, hats in hand, fairly drooling. She'd thoroughly pulled the wool over everyone's eyes, to have them miss such a jewel.

The feel of her oddly rough hand, so gentle, and the moment they'd almost kissed wouldn't leave his mind. The memory assaulted his senses. His heart thudded and he could hardly think straight.

The mere thought of this woman drove him mad. Mad with longing, hungry for more answers, questioning when he might see her next.

Several minutes later, he found himself back at the hotel. For the duration of the two-mile walk, he realized he'd thought of nothing but her.

He straightened his shoulders and cleared his thoughts from the distracting woman. Thank the skies he hadn't kissed the woman, or the straits he might be in now. He had only one objective, the only one that had ever mattered to him. The duke. Richmond. The man who'd snatched his bright, innocent sister. The man he'd hunted. Hated. The idea that fueled him in the darkest corners, where nothing else could. Fueled him to a relentless pace, across borders, into the impossible factories, the ones everyone deemed impregnable. All in search of what now lay within his reach. Revenge on Richmond.

The duke's daughter, intriguing as she may be, would serve not only to distract him from his life's goal, but could lead him into a dangerous place. One where he might hesitate. As he well knew, hesitation was a cost he couldn't pay. His sister deserved more than a fickle brother who could be swayed by a little bit of kindness and a striking figure.

He would steer his ship starboard, clear out of the lady's path. It was the best chance he had of success.

As Emil crossed the lobby, he spotted a masked, caped man stumbling toward the lift with that French valet, Paget's, help. The man hummed the *Kartal* song the Somborians had started singing shortly after the famous battle. The one that saved Sombor but made Emil too famous for his liking.

Emil strode up to the prince and slung Durad's other arm across his shoulder. Durad turned toward Emil and laughed. His breath made Emil shudder.

"Paget, get yourself to bed. Rosseau and I will take care of this."

Emil signaled Rosseau, who waited across the lobby. Paget bowed, dusted off his hands and scampered off, muttering something in French as Rosseau took his place.

Emil laughed. "Did you enjoy yourself, Your Highness." It was not a question.

"I'd forgotten how lovely English women are. I danced with so many skirts."

It struck him suddenly that Durad might have met his intended. The thought disturbed him for some reason. "How about the lovely creature in the silver corset?"

Durad's head tilted to the side as they entered the lift. "Silver corset… there *was* one with no corset, she was so soft." He sighed and then sagged. Rosseau heaved him back up.

Something like relief shuddered through Emil. Ridiculous.

"Thank you, captain, for taking me out on this fine evening," Durad said to Emil in a jesting voice. "I know this is not, it's not…"

"You are so very wrong, my prince. I adore a good party." Emil swung his cape in an attempted half-flourish.

Durad laughed until he doubled over. "If only you had such aspirations at the ball. I saw you dancing, but not one of them caught your interest. Did they?" He shook his head. "In all my years, I have seen few boast such conquests as you have had. Even before you donned your scarf and you… the war her…"

Emil feigned examination of his figure in the lift mirror. "Alas, no woman can match such perfection. See how sharp my profile? How fine the cut of my cape?" He removed his mask. "These puckered scars on my face serve only to highlight the perfect height of my cheekbones, like so." He turned in profile. The view startled him for a moment, as if he'd forgotten, just for this night, that his face told his morbid story.

Even Rosseau chuckled at his antics, as he said, "*Capitan*, it is not safe."

Emil saluted his first mate and replaced his mask, hating his relief at its protection.

The prince turned to him, his eyes eager and open. "I am sorry you did not find a good prospect tonight, my friend. You seem quite… lonely since you've returned."

Emil laughed. "And you, my prince, will be lonely no longer after tomorrow. Go sleep off that wine, you will need to look your finest for the new princess."

Durad snorted.

Though Emil hadn't thought to confess to Emil he'd found Suzanna's kidnapper, seeing him now solidified that decision. He was too weak in this state, too annoyingly fragile. A silent plan, known to few, always made a better one, in any case. Emil would find a way to anonymously take from the duke what he had stolen from him; the duke's life's purpose, whatever that may be. Money. Power. Position. Hopefully without ruining the English-Somborian alliance.

Emil looked up and glimpsed Durad's heavy-lidded, bloodshot eyes in the mirror of the lift before his head fell to his chest. The prince would be fine. His new princess would not suspect who'd destroyed her father. Once married, neither of them would want for wealth or power.

As with all things that mattered, Emil would do this alone. This was too important to trust anyone with, not even Rosseau.

"Sir, I will take him to his quarters," Rosseau said as the lift opened.

Emil shrugged off Durad's arm and smiled beneath his mask. "Are you ordering me to bed?"

"You have not slept in several nights."

Rosseau pulled a key out of his pocket and shuffled toward the prince's room, the stiffness of his back clearly stating his opinion on the matter.

Emil shook his head and opened the door to his suite. He headed over to the window and pushed it up as he tilted his head back to breathe in the night air, tinged with English roses and a steamy mist.

Tomorrow, he'd accompany Durad to meet his friend's new bride. The duke was certain to be there. Emil would stand only feet from him. He thanked the gods, or Suzanna, or whoever watched over him, for giving him this chance to make it right. To wrest payment for the lives of so many, including his sister's.

The involvement of Richmond's daughter and Durad changed nothing.

Chapter Eleven

Veronica nodded at Clank. His eyes whirred, and he returned the gesture, understanding without specific instruction that he was to wait. The clock had just chimed two o'clock in the morning. The shrill of the factory whistle followed, somehow sounding louder in the early morning stillness.

These streets, reeking of sewage and hot steam, smelled better to her than that duplicitous ballroom. She rolled her shoulders back and stretched, felt a stitch pop in her wounded right arm, and grimaced. This was where she was supposed to be. This gave purpose to her life. The masque had been a clever illusion and she had nearly been fooled. The thought made her reach for her Tesla-ray. She simply refused to believe she had nearly been taken in by a handsome figure and strong hands. Veronica was not that woman and she never would be.

The guards posted outside Factory Thirty-Three tossed aside their coffee and opened the doors. A line of pale-faced children marched through, eyes never lifting from the ground in front of them. Veronica counted—one, two, three … up to twelve. A smaller shift than normal. And the children were younger than she'd seen before. Some appeared no more than six years of age. With their hair cropped short, and the same shapeless, gray rags, she could not even tell their gender. One, a thin prospect at any age, stumbled and fell to the ground. The others were too dazed to help their comrade. They simply stopped and waited, slumped in place.

Veronica pointed to the smoker Clank held in his hand. He pumped the small bellows and aimed it at the lamp directly above the factory doors. The device spewed a generous amount of thick, dark smoke directly into the lamp's beam.

One of the guards, having noticed the fallen child, removed a sleek club from his belt and headed toward the line, but the smoke quickly obscured the scene, leaving the guards swearing and the children whimpering.

Veronica secured her goggles and rushed into the opening. She squatted in front of the group of children and spoke quietly. These children were too young to understand who she was, and she had no time to explain.

She simply said, "I have orders to take you to your next home. You will follow this man," she pointed to Clank, "and do so as quickly as possible, or there will be consequences. Do you understand?"

They all nodded, sleepy eyes growing large with fear. She hated to terrify them so, but after her last encounter with the Enforcers, she feared discovery would not be long. Taking the time to explain everything was not an option.

Clank scooped up the fallen child and jogged toward the hidden carriage. The rest followed him, skinny arms pumping, thin chests heaving.

Veronica turned in time to find one of the guards near the alarm bell on the factory wall. As he reached for it, she aimed and threw one of her knives. It landed directly in the center of his hand, sticking it to the wall.

The guard screeched until she rushed over and swung the handle of her Tesla-ray into the back of his head. He slumped, unconscious, still pinned to the wall.

She heard the report of a pistol, twisting just in time for the bullet to nick her shoulder. The guard pinned by the knife, however, was not so fortunate.

"The Eidolon, is it?" the remaining guard asked as he reloaded his pistol. "Not much of an angel, are ya, if ya do stuff like that?" He pointed to his comrade.

She didn't look, but a knot grew in her chest. Another death.

Veronica thought about using her Tesla-ray but drew her sword instead, feeling a twinge in her arm around her stitches. She didn't have much time. The Enforcers were sure to have heard the shot.

The guard, his face smudged with gunpowder, laughed at the sight of her slim rapier.

"Not much good that'll do against the likes of this." He leveled his pistol on her, but she flicked her wrist, her rapier sending the gun several feet out of his reach. He put his hands up in a gesture of surrender and smirked at her.

"You gonna' kill me in col' blood? Eh, angel?" His gaze raked her from head to toe. "You'se a bit small for an 'ero, isn't ya?"

Veronica's skin chilled, and then sweated, remembering the face of the Enforcer she'd burned nearly to ash. He'd worn an expression much like this one. How much more time did she have? Minutes? Seconds?

"Turn around, kneel, hands behind your head," she said in a rough voice.

"No."

"What?" She flicked her sword up and sliced a crooked nick on his cheek.

He laughed and spat on the ground. "Whatever ya plan to do, do's it to my face."

The way he spoke to her made her shake with fury. She should just run him through. The Enforcers would be here any moment anyway.

"Very well."

She whirled and kicked him in the face with the sharpened heel of her boot. He crumpled instantly. She sheathed her sword and ran. Alley after alley, she heard the whisper of the Enforcers' cape. They had to be following her across the rooftops, and she couldn't risk feeling safe. Veronica ran until her lungs burned with a pain sharper than anything she'd felt before.

There. Up ahead. Clank had the children strapped in and the engine running. She leapt into the carriage just as it surged forward.

It wasn't until they'd been moving for several long minutes that she slumped onto the front seat next to several of the children and finally breathed. They hadn't caught her. Had they? She watched Clank steer them through the still streets of the merchant district. The children made no sound on the seats beside and behind her, probably too exhausted to move or question anything.

They were safe.

Safe.

Her heart still felt like it might explode through her ears. She took a breath to give Clank an order but unexpectedly felt the strong fingers of his gloved hand press a cloth on her bleeding shoulder. She nodded her thanks even though she knew he couldn't see it, focused as he was on navigating the dimly lit streets with his free hand.

Nor could he possibly understand the concept of gratitude. As an automaton, he was quite simply designed to follow commands, verbal or non. The first and only of his kind, he had been with her for so long, she had come to think of him less as a machine and more as a companion, steady and strong. He seemed to learn more each time she took him out, understanding her needs and requiring less instruction.

She didn't think, no she *knew*, she couldn't do this without him. As he continued to put pressure on her wound, she wished for a moment that Clank could do more than just process and evaluate; that he could speak, think, feel. That he could strengthen and build her. That he could encourage her to do the unexpected.

She shook her head, wondering if the dizziness she felt from her injury had seeped into her mind.

"You may let go, Clank," she said, still using her rough, deeper voice. He waited until her hand covered the wound and then used his free hand to secure the harness around her waist. She closed her eyes, exhaustion settling in.

The children were silent the entire way to Bridges.

Chapter Twelve

Five years ago…

The duke circled her, his hands clasped behind his back. The low heel of his shined shoes hardly made a sound on the wood floor. Every movement, as always, was perfectly measured and deliberate. His posture was precise. His eyes never left her, searching and finding every sign of weakness.

"Lower, your chin must be lower. You cannot appear to be haughty. You hunch forward too much. Straighten up."

Veronica attempted to comply. It hurt to hold her shoulders so far back. Her muscles ached both across her chest and her back. Sweat dripped steadily down her shoulder blades under her shift. She'd been there for two hours so far, ever since breakfast.

The duke continued to circle her, rapping her on her back when she faltered. "Critchton let you read the article about the robbery in the paper this morning, as I ordered?" he asked.

"Yes, Your Grace."

"Those children, the ones who broke into the bakery, you understand why they did so?" he asked, his tone utterly indifferent.

She wanted to squeeze her eyes shut and think for a moment. He was always testing her. The duke needed a specific answer and she had to provide it or fail. The consequences seemed to worsen with each passing month.

"The orphans have no family to instruct them on what's right and what's wrong. They are thoroughly corrupted and serve no purpose," she answered. Veronica's shoulders started to tremble, but she willed them still.

"What about you and Alec? How are you different from those

children?" the duke asked. He rapped his stick lightly on his hand.

She swallowed. "Alec and I have a parent to show us how to be of service and provide value to society."

He lifted a brow. "Correct. You must always remember that. You are nothing unless you can serve England in some way. That is why I train you day and night to be the perfect lady."

She nearly smiled with relief. Her posture slipped for a moment.

The duke noticed. He calmly motioned for her to hold out both her hands. He slapped his cane across them once.

A tear escaped the corner of her eye. The duke was so very strong.

He slapped his cane down again. And again.

"I only do this to teach you, to instruct you. You are fortunate to have a father who cares for you enough to give you his precious time. My advice is sought throughout EurAsia, yet I dedicate hours upon hours to the instruction of my offspring."

The duke replaced his cane in the closet. Veronica put her hands down by her side, careful to keep them clenched. She dared not get blood on the new teak floor.

The duke sat at his desk without dismissing her. She let the tears dry on her face without wiping them away. To do so would be a weakness she would not admit.

An hour later, Critchton entered the office with a bow. "The colonel to see you, Your Grace."

The duke didn't glance up from his daily correspondence. He sat straight and tall at his desk, pen held at precisely the right angle, the paper in front of him covered in an elegant scrawl. He continued to write as he replied, "Very well. Show him in."

Veronica silently cheered. A guest meant she would be sent away from the duke's presence. Given a reprieve at last.

"Your posture still leaves much to be desired. We'll continue this exercise tomorrow. For the remainder of today, you will practice the pianoforte. The one in the servants' quarters. My guests are not to be assaulted with such mediocrity. Critchton will supervise. Go." The duke placed his pen carefully in the holder to his right and set the paper aside to dry.

She curtsied and left the room quickly. The duke didn't like his guests to see her at all. She constantly embarrassed him. Failed him.

Once out of the duke's sight, Veronica ran to the kitchen in a very unladylike fashion, careful to avoid any servants. She could hardly feel her legs after remaining in one spot so long. It felt good to move freely.

After wrapping her hands to staunch the bleeding, downing a glass of water and sneaking a sandwich from the icebox, Veronica didn't go to the servants' quarters. The duke would have told Critchton, of course, but the old butler moved slowly. She had a few minutes before he made it over there, to the other side of the house.

Instead, Veronica flew into the gardens. The bright, bold oranges and reds of fall encircled her. Usually, this was her favorite time of year. The weather was mild, the world about her on fire with color.

Today, however, she ran until she collapsed. Hearty, wrenching sobs filled her lungs and spilled out her mouth. Surely, surely, she could not endure such a life much longer. Secretly, she envied those orphans. Free to choose. Free to go where they may. They might not know if or when they would eat, but they had the most precious gift of all. Choice.

Veronica, on the other hand, was allowed to do nothing of her own accord. Her meals were chosen by the duke's cook. Her plain dresses and shifts ordered by the housekeeper. She was instructed in Latin and French by a retired military officer, a stern, older man who tolerated nothing from her. After her private tutoring, she practiced the arts of an accomplished lady; embroidery, singing, pianoforte, and dancing. The duke often interceded, adding his own brand of instruction to her many tutors.

Not one of them showed an ounce of caring for her personally. They all taught the duke's doctrine. The orphans were evil. She was lucky. By the time she ate supper each night, she nearly fell asleep at the table.

The times she failed, which happened more and more often, the duke's punishments wore her down. Standing for hours. The cane not just on her hand, but her back. While she might have had the will to resist at one point, she felt it slipping through her fingers. Her will was the last piece she felt was truly her.

Now, she was simply tired. So very tired. She couldn't leave. The duke would find her. Not a single person in the household would help her. There was no way out.

A handkerchief appeared in front of her. It fluttered once. Twice.

She took it and glanced up. A man with shockingly white, thick hair smiled at her. It was a little manic, yet full of warmth.

"Oh, my child. Such tears. How would you like to do something about it?" he asked, sounding very pleased with himself.

"I don't know what you mean, sir," Veronica replied, unsure of how to properly address this man. He didn't appear to be a gentleman. He wore a leather vest riddled with oddly sized pockets and a leather aviator's cap. Several pairs of goggles hung about his neck.

"I mean, dear lady, that it's high time you did something about your circumstances. You're smart, of course, and with all that Latin and science and government, you know enough to be dangerous. I mean to make you much more so." He extended a hand to help her up.

She eyed it warily. "I'm only fifteen. And a girl. How could I ever be dangerous? The duke says—"

The man reached down and pulled her up. He set her firmly on the ground and placed both hands on her shoulders.

"Never mind what the duke says. You and I will outsmart the duke. I assure you, my dear, it can be done."

She used the handkerchief to wipe her face clean. "Outsmart him? At what? Never mind, it doesn't matter. I still don't even know your name." Then, she covered her mouth with her hand. She shouldn't speak so to her elders.

He stepped back and clumsily saluted her. "Dr. Hoch, at your service, my lady. Inventor extraordinaire."

She curtsied. She'd heard of the man, of course. The famous scientist who took the steam engine into the skies.

"Pleased to make your acquaintance."

He grinned again. It looked even stranger this time. She found it a bit charming. "What I mean to do, Lady Veronica, is to give you a purpose. A reason to fight."

"Fight what?" she asked. This man seemed sincere enough,

even if he were an associate of the duke's.

Unless this was another test? She stepped back and straightened her posture. The duke could be watching, even now.

"Relax, this isn't one of the duke's twisted tests." Dr. Hoch waved his hand carelessly.

"You know about those?" she asked.

The man nodded, his smile turning sad. "Yes. I know many things, if not everything, about this household. Don't ask me how."

For the first time, the idea that this man might truly have a solution to offer her entered her mind. Her heart warmed in spite of everything, in spite of the blood that began to soak through her hastily wrapped bandages. "What kind of purpose? And why help me?" she asked.

"Because you, Lady Veronica, can change the lives of many. Your title, your position, your education, you can use it all to do such a work the world has not seen before." His eyes sparkled. He hooked his thumbs into the pockets of his vest and rocked back on his heels.

"What work?" Everything Dr. Hoch said led to more questions. Why could he not answer her plainly?

He lowered his voice. "You will save them."

"Who?"

His features flipped from joy to sadness in a blink, and he suddenly looked much older to Veronica. "It's my fault. Those poor children. You, my dear, will be their salvation."

Chapter Thirteen

"It's nearly four, my lady," Matilda reminded her. "Hale will be waiting. And I must have time to prepare you for the ball."

They'd lingered in the science room of the boy's wing at Bridges, while Veronica demonstrated how to run the miniature clockwork train set. That caught the attention of all the new arrivals, even a boy of about fourteen with hard lines creasing his forehead and a stare that seemed to see directly through her.

Veronica glared at the clock, wishing it didn't perform its duty quite so accurately.

"Time doesn't pass here like it does in other places, does it my lady?" Matilda asked.

Veronica threw one last wistful glance over her shoulder before shrugging and setting a brisk pace toward the door.

"And it's worth every sacrifice I have to make."

<hr>

Veronica groaned. And it wasn't just from the stitches that alternately itched and burned. "I must simply think of the children," she muttered.

"Think hard," Matilda replied, "or you might cry."

The seamstress had outdone herself. Veronica hadn't wanted the gown to be overdone or slightly off color as her others, just tired and outmoded. Something that would draw as little attention as possible. Lacy and fluffy and a bit larger than was fashionable, this ensemble wasn't as putrid in color as her usual attire, though she would hardly be invisible. She'd look like a matron instead of a debutante. The duke might even approve.

As for the prince? A military man like him may not care that she wasn't dressed in the height of fashion, as long as she was modest. Didn't they all believe like her father that women were only useful in an ornamental way?

Veronica's face flushed at the thought of appearing in public in such a relic. Her dresses had always been horrid but nothing so utterly old fashioned and unlike her.

What if she came across the man from the masque? He would not possibly recognize her now. He may know the shape of her face—she shivered remembering the touch of his fingers—but how could he pick her out from the hundreds that would be there this evening? His voice, that lilt, that warmth. She'd likely spend the whole night looking.

Suddenly, Matilda giggled. "You could certainly hide your Tesla-ray in there, my lady."

Veronica glanced down. "Excellent point."

"Perhaps Clank, as well."

Veronica snorted.

Matilda laughed, and Veronica joined in until their eyes watered. She mimed drawing her ray gun from the folds of her skirt. Matilda feigned a hit and fell back on the bed.

Then, an image flashed in Veronica's mind. She turned away from her companion, hiding her reaction. Matilda didn't need to know about the Enforcer, nor that she'd lost control.

She'd done fine since then, kept her actions and feelings under control. She hadn't killed the pinned guard last night, that had been the gunshot. Not her.

Not her.

"Just be careful, will you?" Matilda dropped a wrap over her lady's shoulders. "Perhaps this may, er, cover up those puffy sleeves a bit?"

The wrap simply sat atop the sleeves, as stiff and structured as they were. Veronica looked in the mirror and once again laughed, in spite of her dark thoughts. Matilda snickered. Veronica tossed off the wrap.

"I will preserve some shred of my dignity, if you please."

"Not much to work with, is there my lady?"

They took the servants' exit to avoid Alec. If he saw her, he would *never* cease teasing her.

"Good evening, Hale," Veronica said with a sheepish smile.

To his credit, Hale never blinked.

"My lady."

He offered her a hand into the carriage, but when she tried to lift her dress up the steps, he grabbed her waist and tossed her gently inside.

"Thank you," Matilda said softly to Hale as he helped her inside next.

His hand lingered on hers, as it always did. And as always, she pretended not to notice.

"The prince will certainly get the surprise of his life," Veronica said.

When Hale started the carriage, she opened the window. She certainly didn't need a wrap with all these layers. Matilda resumed her usual posture with her head between her knees.

As they passed carriage after carriage, Veronica fluffed her dress, trying to tame it. "Perhaps the prince might look at me and suddenly find a need to call off the engagement." She pulled on a pair of white leather gloves. "Suddenly, I cannot wait to meet His Royal Highness."

The carriages in front of them seemed to dump their passengers with undo haste, like loads of refuse. As she watched one particular carriage, the gearman hopped down from the driver's box, revealing shortened breeches and a short skirt. The gearman, er, woman, opened the door, one hand on the heavy silver belt around her waist that held goggles, a scope, several wrenches, and other tools. A man with silver-streaked hair stepped out, revealing gold-plated armor underneath a full overcoat.

Would this evening never stop giving? Suddenly, Veronica wished she *had* concealed her Tesla-ray. It was the Lord Almighty Grillett. Several younger men followed. Their gearwoman bowed, shut the door, and followed the empty carriages around the back of Almack's.

The footmen standing at the bottom of the stairs did not bow or acknowledge the new guests in any way, they simply stared after the gearwoman.

Maybe the youth of the New Era did not care where their steam-tech came from, but they had no problem flouting convention. Perhaps it was a step, albeit a strange one, toward change.

The line started to move again, the gearmen apparently recovered from the shock of a gearwoman.

Veronica inevitably turned her own thoughts toward the prince. She could hardly credit that he would be different from the privileged men of her experience. He would most likely expect her to return to his homeland to live, since her feelings would not bear consideration. He might be old, wrinkled, ugly. Perhaps even so crude she could not bear his touch.

But what could she do if he *were* any of those things? Veronica had no recourse, save a vague idea to get out of this trap any way she could.

When Hale steered them up to the entrance of Almack's, Veronica guessed at least two hundred people had already arrived. The duke had left their townhome long ago, likely ready to discuss Russia's newest airship strike with his generals or to stand like a giant sword beside the queen.

She leaned down and grasped Hale's fingers tightly. Walking in this dress took all of her concentration and at least some of his strength.

He led her over to the steps and bowed. "You look quite… modest this evening, my lady."

Veronica glanced down ruefully. "By chance, can I interest you in some grease rags, Hale? After tonight, I believe I will be retiring this ensemble."

He chuckled. "I'd be the prettiest greaser on the block, with that swag hanging from my belt."

"It *would* improve your appearance," Matilda muttered.

Hale tipped his hat to her and said, "You've been lookin', then?" His amused gaze met her flushed one for a moment, and then he leapt up in the carriage and drove off.

"Well. What a horrible man." Matilda sniffed.

Veronica attempted to gather her skirts and tackle the stairs.

"Of course," she said with a grin. One day, perhaps when Veronica didn't need Matilda so much, Hale would step out of Matilda's peripheral vision.

Hale held the single exception to her rule about men. Of course, he had neither title nor means to spoil his watchful, caring, and genial disposition, but she wanted to believe that even if he did, he wouldn't change. If she had to relinquish Matilda to a man's care in the future, Veronica might not flinch at Hale.

After tripping nearly a dozen times, Veronica finally made it inside the ballroom. She threaded her arm through Matilda's. The crush of people made it difficult to move, let alone find the duke. Yet some women, like the fashion goddess Lady Ambrose, still managed to float through the room in her colorful silk gown, much like a butterfly in a steel cage, wearing a diamond necklace whose value could feed all her orphans for a month. Some people could move like that, parting crowds as a breeze through tall grass.

Veronica was not one of them.

She and Matilda pushed their way past several debutantes, each holding court with men that elbowed each other as they vied for the prized girl's attention. The suitors' metal cuffs clinked, scuffing others as they jostled the weaker men out of the circle. Veronica glimpsed one man knock another's goggles off his head and then apologize profusely as he "accidentally" stepped on them in the confusion. Thank heavens she'd never been the center of such a melee.

Veronica stepped past them and promptly saw one member of the *ton* who embodied everything she despised.

She groaned. "Hide me."

Matilda glanced over. "Not her! Criminey."

Though she attempted to shelter Veronica from view, the feat proved impossible, thanks to the appalling dress. Once Lady Clarissa Prine spied Veronica, she leaned to her nearest companion and whispered. A chain of muttered conversation dispersed through the room like a foul wind. Noses crinkled. Eyes widened. Eyepieces fell from fingers. Hands flew up to cover open mouths.

The mystical music coming from the odd-shaped guitar and the violin in the corner paused.

Veronica took a deep breath and then smiled as though proud

and a bit shy about wearing such a dress. She waved in a friendly fashion while Lady Clarissa approached, wishing someone, anyone else would engage her in conversation. Now. But Lady Clarissa wouldn't be deterred. She thought tact a method of the weak, the dimwitted.

Of course, Veronica had to remind herself Lady Clarissa had not been raised among the *ton*. Her father's money bought her the hand of Lord Prine, and a place in this overstuffed room.

She fairly screeched to a halt in front of Veronica, her necklace bouncing on her chest a few times before settling. "Has your seamstress taken ill, Lady Veronica?" she asked.

Lady Sarah Hoover drifted close to Veronica, the cream silk on her dress fluttering about her neat figure as if imbued with the grace of its wearer.

"Now, Clarissa, I'm sure Veronica does not take your meaning," she said, but her tone agreed with the other woman. As the daughter of one of the three sponsors of Almack's, she had learned early how to say one thing and mean another thing entirely.

Veronica twirled. "Isn't it just divine?"

"You'll never catch a man with that hideous—" began Lady Clarissa.

"Lady Veronica doesn't need to marry," Lady Sarah said with a placid, bitter smile. "Half of her papá's fortune will pass to her. Her mother, you know."

"Is that right?" Lady Clarissa asked. "You do not have to choose a husband? You're free to well, be free of men?" She shot a glance at her own plain husband, already well in his cups.

Before Veronica could respond, Lady Sarah said, "Clarissa, dear, I'm sure she doesn't take your meaning."

Veronica tucked her mother's butterfly necklace inside her gown, needing to feel the cool metal on her skin. She spotted the duke standing by the queen on a raised dais and swallowed.

"Please do excuse me, ladies," she interrupted.

Lady Sarah paused mid-word and simply stared at Veronica. Like a true lady, her eyes said what she had not. That Veronica was an embarrassment, a ridiculous nitwit, and a waste. She not only wasted a night of Almack's on that dress but a potential position of power as an heiress.

Veronica grabbed Matilda's arm and moved forward, each step echoing in her mind. She'd seen and overheard such nonsense a million times. Her disguise at these events proved extremely tiresome. Yet some small part of her felt giddy at so completely fooling them all.

"Do you see *him*, my lady? The prince?" Matilda asked.

Veronica turned and scanned the room. She could not decide which was worse, wondering if the pot-bellied man in a sagging red turban or the baby-faced boy in over-large robes was her intended, or actually meeting the man to whom she'd be tied for life. Before she could panic, Matilda pushed her gently forward.

The queen's bulky guards moved aside to allow Matilda and Veronica to pass. Both of them curtseyed deeply before Her Highness.

"What an unpretentious dress, Veronica." The queen sounded thoroughly amused.

Had she overdone it? Veronica glanced at the duke, who had started to answer, but the queen cut him short with a wave, her thick, diamond bracelet reflecting shimmering light through the room as she moved. Her hand settled on the chair as she eyed Veronica with a gaze that performed the same such appraisal on a daily, perhaps even hourly basis. Her shrewd, brown eyes locked with Veronica's. It felt like a blast from a Tesla-ray. There was power in those eyes, as though the queen were something more than human, a higher intelligence, evolved through generations of the fittest, the most attractive, the conquerors.

The orchestra quieted. Dancers' arms fluttered to their sides. Veronica's knees quivered.

The fact that the queen was more than sixty did not weaken her effect, for even the youngest of men watched her as though bewitched. The women appeared to bristle at the men's reaction but could not hide the awe in their submissive posture. Veronica simply wished the queen would release her before she somehow pried into the dark vaults of her mind.

Her Majesty finally smiled the smile of one used to setting others at ease, lifting her cheeks and crinkling her eyes.

"I like her," she said. "And I'm sure Durad will introduce her to the styles of Sombor soon enough."

The duke bowed his head as though humbled. Veronica didn't understand if she'd just been humiliated or gained approval. Blessed saints, she might have miscalculated.

"She is a modest child," the duke said.

Veronica couldn't tell what he was thinking. It'd been years since discipline of the physical sort had happened, but she would never underestimate him. He may threaten or take something else dear to her instead.

While her expression betrayed nothing, she felt ill.

"Prince Durad, come!" Her Majesty called out, her strong voice cutting through the chaos.

The crowd parted to allow a broad-shouldered man through. Not the one with the belly, nor the youth. He wore a white turban wrapped around his head, covered in jewels and matching white robes, making him appear much larger and more imposing a man than Veronica had ever seen. He strolled through the crowd with purpose and bearing, his eyes fixed on the queen. As he drew nearer, Veronica noticed he appeared not much older than her, perhaps in his mid-twenties, though his swarthy skin made it difficult to tell.

A man dressed similarly, in a white turban and robes, appeared at the prince's side, the bottom half of his face covered with a scarf. Veronica's eyes fell to the sword at his side and guessed this was His Highness's bodyguard.

The prince knelt before the queen. "Your Majesty," he said in a clipped, deep voice.

The same type of musical accent as the man she'd danced with at the masque.

Surprisingly, the queen flushed and said, "Prince Durad, may I present your future bride, the Lady Veronica Clarke." Her arm swept toward Veronica.

Prince Durad straightened up and fixed his gaze on Veronica. Deep brown, piercing eyes widened at the dress but stopped at her face. He bowed and lifted her hand, placing a kiss on it she felt through her glove.

"I am honored and very pleased to meet you at last," he said.

The sincerity in his tone and his manner startled her into simply replying, "Your Highness."

He nodded with a grave expression.

She stared, unable to move. This man was not old, nor wrinkly, nor ugly. In fact, even the queen had nearly swooned.

The accent. The charm. It couldn't be.

It was the man from the masque.

Chapter Fourteen

Emil's pulse raced as he followed the prince up to the dais. Why would *he*, Emil, be nervous? This was a mere girl, one many people considered crackers, not to mention the daughter of a man he knew to be an unconscionable killer. She held no significance, save as a means to Richmond.

So then why did he feel so hot? *It must be these dress robes. Or this blasted scarf.* He stifled the urge to rip it off and take deep breaths.

The crowd of idiots parted, focused mainly on the strong figure of the prince. He'd slept off the effects of the night before, his eyes without shadow, his face unlined and smooth. No wine left Durad stumbling the next day. They'd tested this talent on many taverns. Strength, confidence, bearing, he'd always had these. Even at the end of a guard's stick while operating a widget cutter for eleven hours.

The prince's turban made soft clinking sounds as he moved, the beads of his rank and his royalty proclaiming his status. Durad strolled toward the queen as though he'd been born a royal, not earned it on the field of battle.

At Her Majesty's feet, below the raised dais, stood a girl in a blue dress covered in lace, looking like one of those round, fancy, white things women put all over tables. Not a tablecloth. A doily, or some such ridiculous word. The ripples, waves, and layers reminded Emil of one, as though her entire body were submerged, her head floating just above it. He recognized the lift of that chin, the shape of that face. But not the vacant expression.

This woman might never cease to surprise him. What was she doing, wearing a thing like that when meeting her intended for the first time? She hadn't dressed this way last night. Her style had been arresting, at the very least.

But this thing, the pond dress, and her now blank face… what was she playing at? This had to be the reason society considered her "touched."

The queen and Durad exchanged words, Her Majesty quite obviously taken by Durad's accent and his mysterious looks. Emil watched Lady Veronica during the exchange, searching for any sign of what she thought of her engagement.

Her blank expression didn't waver. For a moment, her shoulder twitched, along with a corner of her mouth, as though it caused her pain. Her companion, who stood next to her, cast a worried glance at her lady.

Last night, she'd been indignant for a cause no one cared for. Angry at society. Compassionate to a damaged stranger. Now, she was careful to hide whatever had injured her shoulder. Nothing about Lady Veronica added up. Other than the fact that she hid behind a mask as real as his.

He couldn't decide if that fascinated or repulsed him.

When a man standing next to the queen spoke, Emil glanced in his direction. The voice was strong, arrogant. Emil mouthed several curses.

You fool. It's him… the duke.

Here he'd been giving Richmond's daughter too much consideration, *again*, when he should've been watching her estimable papá. He turned his full attention to the man, watching as he placed a steadying hand on the queen's shoulder, helping her from her chair. He leaned forward to speak into her ear while they paced slowly toward the exit.

Emil glanced from Durad to the slowly disappearing duke and back. He longed to follow them, but he didn't feel comfortable leaving the prince on his own. The ballroom was palpitating with hundreds of the youth of the New Era, along with the older matrons and gentleman of society, all most likely eager to meet their royal guest from Sombor. One knife could slip by unnoticed, or even a pistol, amidst all the steam-tech dripping from men's belts and strapped across their ample girths. Even women wore leather pouches large enough to hold a derringer.

He cursed again. He couldn't follow the duke. Not now.

Durad offered Lady Veronica his arm, and they headed toward the doors leading into the gardens. Emil remained close behind, placing himself near enough to deflect a blade or shot. Several ladies pressed in, and Emil shoved them away without ceremony.

Lady Veronica's face appeared animated as she spoke with Durad, her body leaning toward the prince. She stumbled over her pond dress, but Durad caught her easily. She flashed him a grateful expression.

Emil realized his jaw had clenched tight and begun to ache. He should be going after the duke, but he was forced to watch Durad spew charm all over this female, and her turn to a cloying puddle at his feet. Surprisingly, Durad appeared to all the world as though he actually enjoyed talking to her. He scented a hint of genuine interest.

Whatever she hid behind that tinny laugh and calculated clumsiness, Emil intended to find out. It was quite obviously something of great importance, perhaps even something that would embarrass or hopefully destroy her. Almack's matrons were not very forgiving.

A lover? No, that did not seem likely, not when she trembled so innocently at his touch last night. Debt? That could make sense, for who would expect a "nitwit" to understand money. No matter her secret, she'd gone to great lengths to conceal it. It had to be significant.

He continued to watch. Observe. Catalog. As he did, his mind formed a picture. Every gesture, every word illuminated another feature. It felt, just a little, like looking in a mirror.

Chapter Fifteen

"Lady Veronica's papá, the Duke of Richmond," the queen said to the prince, nodding to the uniformed man at her side.

Veronica sighed as the entire room turned in rapture. There'd not been such great entertainment in London since Grillett unveiled the *Terror of the Skies*, the pride of the British air fleet, at last year's Steam Expo. The duke rarely ventured out in broader society, much less to an inconsequential place like Almack's. Not many had actually met him, though plenty claimed an acquaintance.

It seemed *no one* had failed to hear the stories of the duke's impressive victories. Up until now, that was all they had been, a collection of stories, legends, and shocking tales told over whist tables or punch bowls. Plenty had asked Veronica about the duke, only to give up in a few minutes when it became clear she never actually answered the question asked of her. Veronica preferred to change the subject entirely, bouncing from one topic to the next until her audience simply stomped off mid-sentence, utterly frustrated.

Now, here stood the hero of England before all in full red military dress, adorned with so many gleaming medals that she'd long ago stopped counting. Or caring. There were times she was tempted to steal one off his uniform, just to see if he counted them each night.

The prince paused for a moment before snapping to attention and bowing.

The duke bowed in return. "Prince Durad."

Apparently still speechless and having lost some of his wits, Prince Durad bowed again.

"Your Grace." Veronica curtsied.

The duke nodded but didn't look at her. Instead, he turned to the prince. "I've heard report of those lightweight frigates you used to outmaneuver the Turks. Quite brilliant."

Durad bowed again, cleared his throat and said, "Thank you, Your Grace."

"The battle on your southern border, a single ship held the west end of the line against half of the Turks when they attacked unexpectedly in the middle of the night?"

"Yes, Your Grace. The captain in question, *Kartal*, they call him, strung several smaller boats out so that our force appeared much larger than it was. Then, he doused the lights on his own ship, snuck behind the Turks, and took out three of their finest cruisers. The Battle of Heroes marked a key victory."

The two men conversed, one hesitant, the other acting more like an indulgent father to the stranger beside her than to his own daughter. Veronica listened closely. She loved the *Kartal* stories. She hadn't realized the self-same hero fought for Prince Durad. If he could inspire such heroics, he might not be quite as bad as others of his station. Possibly.

Veronica kept trying to glance at the prince's wrists, checking for the scars she both dreaded and hoped were there. If they were, her orphans might be safe.

If the scars weren't there, she'd be back where she started. Marrying a stranger. Wondering who in Hades she'd danced with at the masque.

The prince remained annoyingly still.

Restless, Veronica examined the man beside the prince, the one she assumed must be his personal bodyguard. He stood the same height as most men, perhaps a bit taller, though his shoulders were wider than the prince's. She could glean nothing else with that covering on his face and his loose robes, save the color of his eyes. She wouldn't call them simply *black*. A more dynamic description would suit, like the obscurity of a rainy night or the chill of a wine cellar. He stood so still beside the prince and in such a way that one might never think to notice him or give him a moment's thought.

She admired that. It was exactly what she herself had been aiming for, and what she'd come to achieve to a degree. Look at how the duke ignored her.

Matilda poked her side and whispered, "The prince is quite striking, isn't he?"

Veronica's gaze shifted back to the royal by her side, and she found herself nodding.

The queen rose and said, "I think you should take Lady Veronica for a walk, Durad, and get to know your fiancée." She appeared to have lost interest in the military conversation. "The duke and I have matters to discuss." She left the room once more with the duke's hand on her arm.

Prince Durad bowed and offered Veronica his arm. His sleeve slipped, revealing a perfect wrist.

"Would you care to join me, my lady?"

Veronica's smile faltered. She shouldn't have expected such a miracle. She should've learned by now that destiny didn't favor her, preferring instead the most powerful and the cruelest among men. Happiness in her life was only to be found between the walls of Bridges. And she felt blessed with such a wealth.

Veronica placed her hand delicately on the prince's flowing sleeve. "It is the queen's command," she answered lightly.

She gathered up her many skirts in her other hand and walked slowly with him through the parted crowd and onto the terrace. No one seemed to dare snicker or mutter about her as they passed. Perhaps because of her frightening father. Or perhaps because the man next to her seemed to have a mystery about him that left the *ton* respectfully speechless. As she took one careful step after another, she began to suspect it was because they'd ceased to see her when Prince Durad's presence eclipsed hers so thoroughly.

They exited into the damp evening, and Veronica tried not to be obvious as she drank in the fresh air, untainted by fear, expectation, or ridicule. She couldn't relax, not with the prince so close, but at least she could think more clearly.

Prince Durad led her deftly down the garden path and to a clearing containing a single stone bench. With the lamps covered in a shroud of steam, she could hardly see the ground, let alone navigate in this dress.

Blast. How was it that she could leap over the side of the bridge and fend off several grown men but not manage to traverse a simple garden path in a ball gown? The prince steadied her more than once and then seemed to give up, wrapping his arm around her waist until they reached the bench. She half-collapsed, not entirely feigning her role as the weak miss. Walking in this dress took a good deal of concentration and skill that she doubted any woman could possibly possess.

She huffed and wiped her brow. "My apologies, Prince Durad. I seem to be defeated by my talented seamstress."

His gaze flicked down to the dress. "You handle yourself quite gracefully. The fault is entirely my own for leading you down this rough garden path." He gestured back to the smooth, flat walkway, entirely free of debris.

She followed his gaze and raised a brow.

"Your dress, it is lovely. You look like an," he glanced at his bodyguard, who would not meet his gaze, "ocean."

She flushed and tried to shift in her seat, but the fabric of one of her skirts caught on a nearby bush. Prince Durad leaned over to help her at the same time she yanked on the material. Her hand caught his cheek in a loud slap. He staggered back and rubbed it with a startled look in his eye.

"Blast! I'm so very sorry! Please, let me get some help…" She tried to get up but stumbled again and would have fallen if the prince had not caught her arm to steady her.

"No, my lady. I do not think you should attempt to move for the time being." He set her back on the bench with exaggerated care.

She watched him move his jaw back and forth and declared, "This dress is utterly hideous!"

The prince suddenly laughed, a deep, wonderful sound. "I think *dangerous* would be a better word."

How true. She glanced down woefully. She'd rather change the pistons in a steam engine than wear this dress another minute.

The prince squatted before her, looking earnest. "Forgive me, I meant no insult," he said in his clipped tone.

She smiled. "I would mean it, if I were you. Just look at this thing. I'm sure we could come up with some splendid names for it."

He tapped his chin. "Perhaps *the Silken Steamer.*"

"*The Maid's Delight.*"

"Forever Blue."

They both laughed.

Several snorts sounded in the corner where Matilda and the prince's guard stood. The prince himself rocked back on his heels as he laughed, losing his balance. At the last moment, she reached down and pulled him up, making her arm ache like the devil. He brushed off his robes and sat next to her, his eyes sparkling.

"Thank you, my lady, for saving my best robes." His eyes darted to her arms.

She followed his gaze. She'd forgotten for a moment that a society miss shouldn't have muscles like hers, nor a grip that could pull a large man off the ground.

"How embarrassing. I don't usually go about assisting gentleman. I ride excessively, Your Highness. We have a manor house in the country," she lied. Not about the house, which was true, but about riding. She'd never been on a horse in her life.

"I did not know that debutantes still considered horseback riding an accomplishment."

"Papá is rather traditional in some areas."

"One cannot help but see."

She laughed again.

He reached over and took her gloved hand in his bare one. "Lady Veronica." His accent made her name sound foreign and glamorous. "I am sure you did not envision yourself married to a foreigner, nor the ruler of a small country like Sombor. Your queen offered you to me and I could not refuse. Nor did I want to. It is a smart move for Sombor. It will ensure support for my people when the Ottomans move against me, which they assuredly will again someday. It will also provide financial stability." He squeezed her hand. "But I am a good man, my lady. I will endeavor to make you happy not only to keep England satisfied, but because I want you to find contentment with me."

She stared down at his hand. Whether it was browned by the sun or his natural shade, she could not tell. It felt strange to touch a man warmed by foreign lands, by places she had never been.

It reminded her of another man's hand, strong and reassuring in hers. She pulled away gently, wondering if all men used such a ploy to gain a woman's trust.

Did men speak like this often in his culture, so boldly, so straightforward?

No. He could not possibly mean what he said. Her pleasure at their earlier banter died as she realized she'd slipped in every way since she met the prince. She'd forgotten to guard her conversation, not to mention revealing her unusual strength for a genteel woman. With this man, as with all others, she would play the part she'd chosen; the one that kept her secrets safe.

"I thank you for your kindness, Prince Durad," she said in a shy whisper.

"Please, call me Durad."

"Veronica." She giggled and squeezed his hand. "I think we'll have grand adventures together, Durad."

He gave her an assessing glance that she returned with a vacant smile. He must think her mad.

Good.

"Yes, we will, Veronica." He lifted her hand and kissed it. "My first order of business is to see London. I haven't been here since my days at Cambridge, when Mr. Marcovic here," he nodded at his bodyguard, "and I would sneak away for several days at a time to the big city. Will you take me, *sultanim*?"

An exotic endearment. Oh no. Veronica suppressed a shiver. Durad's charm was deadly, but nothing she couldn't combat with fluttering eyelashes and absurd comments.

"Of course! It would be a pleasure, Your Highness."

After helping extricate Veronica from the bench, Durad led her back into the ballroom. The sound of violins alongside drums and a guitar led the ladies and gentlemen in the room in a slow, sensual rhythm that appeared to shock two of Almack's patronesses. The most fashionable men dragged their fingers across their partner's arms and down to clasp their waists in an intimate movement while the older gentlemen mimed the motion, clearly uncomfortable with the dance but unwilling to be considered outmoded. A few debutantes of the Season blushed, their eyes bright. It was a popular, new dance, one that men approved of and women would not admit to enjoying.

The music stopped a moment later, and the lights seemed to brighten as if awakening to a new day. Durad stepped forward and the ton slid up to them in waves, as though this, too, were part of their dance.

Remembering the duke's threat, Veronica smiled, curtsied, and chatted inanely with several gentlemen and ladies who approached her. She gushed about Durad, his generosity and charm, and tried to appear flushed at the mention of the wedding. She'd never had to hold court in such a manner before, with the exception of her debutante ball, where she'd smiled until her head throbbed, hoping the duke would see her as the perfect lady.

Now, the tension of keeping up such a vacuous act made her want to scratch someone's eyes out. How could anyone believe her so dimwitted? The men paid her almost no mind, their gazes constantly searching just beyond her left ear as though the duke might reappear. The women were worse, speaking to her only when Durad was already occupied, their eyes never on her. She felt like a screen, both useful for concealing what lay beyond and annoying for doing so.

She laughed for the billionth time, her throat aching with dryness.

A wine glass appeared in front of her. "My lady? I think you need this." The voice that came from beside her was scratchy and painful to hear.

She took the drink absently. "Why thank—" She turned, and the words died on her lips. She dropped the glass, shattering it on the floor.

One of Durad's admiring set snapped at a nearby servant and pointed to the mess. She gave Veronica a glance that told her exactly what she thought of Veronica's suitability as the prince's bride.

Veronica paid the woman no attention in return. She turned first one way and then the other, searching for the man who had given her the glass.

A gentleman appeared before her and bowed, giving her only a glimpse of the hideous, yellow cut on his face. "Lady Veronica. We haven't been properly introduced, but I hope you won't mind if I present myself to you. My name is Mr. Ophir Blackthorne."

Lady Clarissa and two of her friends turned when Mr. Blackthorne spoke, as though drawn to any deep, male voice. He didn't look directly at them, but his gash was clearly visible. One lady, it might've been Lady Green, swooned, falling directly into Durad's arms.

Veronica watched the spectacle and wished for the wine glass she'd just dropped. She wished for anything to give her a moment to think.

Blackthorne said, "I apologize for frightening you. Please, allow me." Taking her arm, he moved her away from the mess the servants were now cleaning up. She concealed her gasp at his touch by biting her lip.

It was her training that saved her, the endless balls she'd attended and lunches she'd endured. The hours she'd spent with a mask so vague, it'd nearly become her natural expression. Veronica smiled, feigning indifference, and swallowed her fear as she extended her hand. She watched him bow and raise his face up for her inspection. She pulled her hand back slowly, though it nearly killed her not to yank it from his grip.

"Thank you, Mr. Blackthorne," Veronica said politely, as though she'd never seen him before. As though the last time they'd met, she hadn't burned him with her Tesla-ray and fled, leaving him there alone, dead at her hands. She wanted to both congratulate herself for her fine acting skills and sink through the floor.

"You are most gracious, my lady." As he spoke, the single, raw, yellow gash running from his ear down to his mouth pulled up the corner into a hideous half-grin. Stitches still crossed half of the wound.

He turned his face so that she could only see the unmarred half. "I apologize. A recent accident during routine fencing training. I know it's unsightly. I hope I've not caused you to become ill."

"N–no, not at all, Mr. Blackthorne," was all she could manage. Every smell in the room seemed stale and her stomach churned.

Mr. Blackthorne couldn't know who she was. Yet there wasn't any way he could simply be one of the crowd of well-wishers. *Was there?* She clamped the lid down on her frenzied thoughts before she ripped away from him, fled, and caused a scene.

"Over here, my lady." He led them to a corner of the ballroom.

She tried to breathe normally, in and out. This could not

happen. A part of her felt relief that Blackthorne lived, yet the greater part admitted a shame and guilt she thought she would never feel. *She* had done this. Turned a man into the horror that stood before her. She thought for a moment she might be dreaming, but this man and the newly scabbed wound on his face was not just something out of a nightmare. He was a walking spirit from the darkest part of her soul.

"May I congratulate you on your engagement?"

"Wh-why thank you."

He nodded and rested his hand on his rapier, his gaze roaming the room.

She cleared her throat. "Do we have a mutual acquaintance, Mr. Blackthorne?" She kept her tone light.

He grinned at her and the sight stole her breath yet again. It transformed his face into an even more hideous reminder of the damage she'd done. The unmarred side of his mouth rose higher than the other so that his smile appeared lopsided and cruel. He watched her reaction with knowing eyes.

"We do, in point of fact. A Lord Grillett?" he said.

The name grated on her ears. "You must be mistaken. I've never met Lord Grillett." His eyebrows flew up in a macabre gesture. She barely concealed a shudder. "I've heard of him, of course. The man who makes those lovely dirigibles and carriages." Veronica tried to smile but couldn't.

"Oh? My mistake, my lady. Nevertheless, I am glad to meet you," he said.

"How kind of you," she replied with an empty titter.

His eyes finally freed her, focusing instead on Alec, her brother, who had just arrived. He stood by the door, wineglass in hand, searching the crowd.

"Your brother is looking for you."

"You know him?" she asked, startled.

"Your whole family is well known, my lady."

"Of course. I must go to him. If you will excuse me." She stepped forward, but Durad appeared in front of her with an apologetic grin. He bowed over her hand.

"Please honor me with a dance, my lady. I promise to move slowly." He winked.

Her fingers unwittingly tightened on his. "Your Highness, this is—"

She turned to introduce Blackthorne, but he'd vanished. She searched the milling crowd, still numerous even at this late hour, but he'd disappeared as quickly as a breath on a cold day. She waited for a sense of relief at his departure, but instead found herself even more nervous not knowing where he was. Why had he left so quickly?

He must've been playing with her. He knew who she was. Somehow, he knew.

"Veronica?" Durad asked.

"Nothing." She smiled through her lingering horror. "Have you met my brother? He just arrived."

"There will be plenty of time for that later. First, can we dance? I've waited all evening for this opportunity."

He smiled, but she could see weariness etched in the creases around his mouth. He must've been overwhelmed this evening, but he'd borne it well. No court in the world, much less Sombor, could possibly host such vipers.

She squared her shoulders and tried to set aside the last few minutes of the night. "You will have to carry me most of the time."

He laughed and swept her onto the floor for the cotillion that had just begun.

The footsteps she'd heard in the alley yesterday as she visited Bridges. It could've been Blackthorne. He might have traced her identity through her visit. What did he intend to do with that knowledge? And the way he mentioned Alec didn't seem coincidental. She felt trapped inside an hourglass, with her future streaming down on her, one thin lie at a time.

"I will arrive at your residence at ten o'clock tomorrow. Does that suit you?" asked Durad.

They'd stopped dancing. When had they stopped? She must be more agile than she thought to have remained upright during the number. Veronica nodded in response to his question and threw in an extra giggle for good measure.

"I simply cannot wait."

They now stood on the edge of the ballroom, the bodyguard looming close behind them.

Prince Durad wasted no time encircling his arm about her waist as he navigated through the milling crowd to the front steps. Sighs followed their departure.

She felt cold, as though she should be shivering, but she had to wipe perspiration from her forehead. Her entire body ached with contrasts, trying to be still when it wanted to break free, trying to cool itself when it felt like ice, and trying to maintain composure when it wanted to shout and cry until it slept.

Yet, for the first time, as Prince Durad led her through the crowd, ignoring the calls of many, she felt support in a man's touch. His hand was wide and warm on her side, steadying her, grounding her. When the doors opened and the cool air reached her lungs, she coughed over and over.

"Veronica, are you well?" Prince Durad asked. His hand gripped her shoulder, his face searching hers.

No. But she swallowed, eyes tearing, and nodded.

"Can I fetch you a drink? Are you sure you are well?" Durad persisted.

She dabbed her eyes with a handkerchief and forced a laugh. "How silly of me. I'm in quite excellent health, I assure you."

"I'm not yet certain that *I* am not the cause of your sudden indisposition." Prince Durad smiled.

This time, she did not have to force her laugh. "You couldn't possibly have that effect on any woman, Your Highness. It must simply have been the damp air."

"I'm glad, because, Lady Veronica, it was indeed a great pleasure this evening." Prince Durad bowed, the jewels on his turban clinking.

She curtsied.

The mist thinned suddenly, and Hale appeared out of the gloom. He steered Veronica's carriage right up to the bottom step, the machine humming like a tame tiger. Hale patted it and hopped down.

The bodyguard, a Mr. Marcovic, whom Prince Durad had introduced earlier, was closer and offered his hand to Veronica. She took it and raised a foot. Her slipper tangled in her skirts. Before she could fall or even stumble, a hand appeared on her waist to steady her, and a man's warm breath fanned her exposed neck.

Shock, either from her clumsiness or the bodyguard's quick reflexes, made her freeze.

"Steady there, little princess," he said in a mocking, clipped voice.

She twisted her head to meet his gaze. His eyes were as dark as agate, rimmed by thick lashes, shimmering like a crystal catching a ray of light. The hint of foreign places in his gaze and the scent of turmeric made her head fog.

How many moments passed, she could not say, until he placed both hands on her waist, lifted her the two steps into the carriage, and abruptly released her. Then, he stepped back into the mist and disappeared.

She waved a weak goodbye to Prince Durad and escaped inside the cabin. Matilda slid in next to her and instantly drew the curtains. Heavens, that bodyguard, Mr. Marcovic. He had quite the presence. Utterly rude, though. Veronica would have to get used to him, she supposed. He appeared to be a fixture by the prince's side.

She glanced over at Matilda, wondering what she thought. Oh no, Matilda's hands were fluttering.

Veronica recognized the move. Her companion always looked a hummingbird when she had something to say.

"The prince…"

Veronica glanced away. She'd made a ninny of herself with that man. Hopefully, enough of one to support the ongoing rumors about her.

It didn't make her feel as good as she thought it would.

Matilda did not speak for several moments. Perhaps she recognized the rigidity of her lady's shoulders and the way she would not meet her eyes. Matilda sighed and sank back against the cushions.

"Is it such a far-fetched idea that you might be able to find happiness for yourself?" she muttered.

"Happiness?" Veronica whispered.

She never considered such an outrageous idea. The word seemed to suggest a freedom of self and a lightness that she would never have. Happiness was the ending to the story of good-hearted Melilot in the fairytale Veronica told over and over to the orphans. She hoped they believed it, but she never would.

"With the prince, you goose," Matilda sighed.

Matilda could never understand such an ending would not be possible for Veronica. There were no fairies in disguise waiting to give her a cottage of her own, means to provide for herself, and a man with a pure heart to watch over her. Durad might seem to have all the trappings of romance, but she didn't believe any of it was real.

Her orphaned children were her happy ending. And she had work yet to do.

Chapter Sixteen

Emil couldn't keep his eyes off Lady Veronica. She suffered through the most difficult of conversation partners, most of whom appeared to only be paying their dues to the fiancée of the man who'd become an instant success. Many checked timepieces while nodding absently at Lady Veronica. Some even ignored her altogether. Through it all, she smiled as though nothing mattered in the world.

The more he watched her, the more she grudgingly impressed him. She didn't fit into this world, where she was expected to act in her own self-interest and twirl among women who dressed themselves as meticulously as one of Fredrich Church's landscapes. Instead of making herself into something she didn't believe in, Lady Veronica made herself so pale, she was nearly invisible. Her persona had every single person in this room believing her to be no one of consequence and with nothing to say.

One man approached her, his entire face red and puffy from what looked like a recent, nasty burn. When Lady Veronica saw him, she dropped her wine glass, and someone motioned a servant to clean it up while steering her out of the way. He spoke to her for several minutes while her mouth tightened into a thin line and the hand holding her fan shook.

The man's clothes were clearly worn, his boots scuffed, not to mention the burns on his face, which would horrify any gentlewoman. Emil had just set on approaching them when Durad abandoned his admiring set to dance with Veronica.

Curious, Emil slipped away from the prince and followed the man. Ugly slipped through the crowds, head down, the brim of his top hat hiding most of his facial injury, a scarf the rest. No one appeared to notice him, even as they stepped aside to let him pass. He moved like a dance instructor, graceful and fluid.

Ugly vanished through the doors to the gardens without gaining one person's notice. Emil managed to follow, though under the gaze of several suspicious stares. He wasn't used to this much attention, curse Durad and these white dress robes. Emil could hardly blend in, dressed like this.

When he stepped outside, he loosened his belt and tore off the robe with a swift motion, barely taking time to consider what he did. He tossed it over a brace of evergreen bushes along with his turban. He replaced his scarf with the black mask from the previous evening, which he'd concealed in one of the several pockets he always had sewn into his clothing. He secured his rapier at his waist. The chill of the air instantly cooled his heated skin as he headed in the direction he'd seen the ugly man go.

Emil continued moving as he always did, without sound, a habit he'd learned as a child in the factories. Ugly stepped crisply, navigating the gardens as one who knew them well. Night had long ago settled in, heavy with moisture and a fog that obscured any but the brightest of lights.

Ugly stepped around a corner and saluted another man, this one dressed in red and gold armor, and adorned with several pieces from the New Era. A complex set of goggles with several levers and lenses hung at his neck, a watch with three faces wrapped around his wrist, a scope had been clipped to his belt, along with several closed leather pouches. He stood with feet regulation width apart, his hands clasped behind his back. A Smith & Wesson pistol was strapped to his side, underneath his coat. When he lifted a hand to adjust his leather aviator cap, Emil glimpsed a head of thick, silver hair.

Under cover of the thinning brush in the gardens, Emil crept closer. Silver Hair stopped speaking and held up a hand. Two sets of eyes darted in his direction. Silver Hair's arm disappeared inside his coat, probably gripping his gun. Ugly had his hand on the hilt of his sword.

Emil ceased breathing.

No one heard him. Ever.

Ugly waited for several moments before bowing to the admiral and continuing on the path away from the house. Silver Hair drew his Smith & Wesson pistol and pointed it several inches to Emil's left.

He shot. The sound echoed, painfully loud in Emil's ears.

A bird flew from the bushes. Emil remained still, even though his body ached to scramble away. If he moved, he'd reveal his location.

If Lady Veronica had a connection to Silver Hair and Ugly, Emil and Durad had a problem. The stakes were high enough that these men were willing to kill without hesitation.

Silver Hair laughed while he re-loaded the pistol. "Could have sworn there was bigger game in there." He aimed once again, just to Emil's right.

And shot.

This time, Emil could no longer remain immobile. Whoever these men were, Emil didn't want them to feel safe, as though they could conspire against Lady Veronica or fire a pistol at a ball. From his hiding place, he flung both his wrists, one after another, releasing the triggers on his wrist sling. One poison dart bounced off the man's chest, deflected by some unseen body armor. The other bounced off the side of Silver Hair's neck. Neck armor?

Impossible. Those darts had never failed Emil. The shock kept him immobile for a moment.

Silver Hair finished loading his gun and pointed it dead center at Emil's chest. He fired.

Emil dove to the side just in time, the shot barely missing his shoulder. He rolled and sprang to his feet. The man stood before him; the tip of his rapier pressed to Emil's chest. He brushed it aside and swept his foot out, clearing Silver Hair's feet from under him. Emil leapt up and drew his sword.

The man raised his blade, but before he swung, the sound of screams broke the intent stillness between them. They both froze. Someone must've heard the shots.

Emil didn't take his eyes off the gilded Silver Hair, poised to strike at him. He appeared to be waiting for something. A shout rang out, closer this time. Emil's gaze flicked in the direction of the sound for a moment, but he didn't see anyone. When he turned back, Silver Hair was gone.

Emil glanced from side to side, trying to see in the weighty darkness. He listened. Nothing.

Why had the man left? Perhaps he feared getting caught. His appearance had quite obviously been of import to him, with his dandified armor and polished boots. That concern might extend to his social status. Murder at Almack's, after all, is not something English gentleman did.

Nothing else made sense. The man had proven to possess many advantages over Emil. He'd worn armor far superior to Emil's. Emil had never encountered the like.

Footsteps sounded, the next hedge over. Emil sheathed his sword and headed back toward the ballroom through the brush, listening for signs of the uncanny Silver Hair and Ugly.

He'd get Rosseau and venture into the taverns for more information on an officer with full body armor and a quick blade. Emil had a feeling Silver Hair was somehow connected to the Clarkes. He hated that the man had nearly bested him.

Emil snatched his dress robes from the bushes, wrapped them about him in a few swift movements. He then strapped his rapier back on, and re-entered the ballroom, humming the tune they'd played when he'd waltzed with Lady Veronica.

Emil and Rosseau stumbled through the door of The Flighthouse, the supposed hub of gossip in the West End. They were both dressed as English airshipmen, from leather breeches that made Emil's legs itch to an unbearably hot cap with earflaps. No wonder the poor sods were always so miserable. Emil covered the lower half of his face with a nondescript scarf, like those that many airshipmen used to protect their skin from the wind.

Local tradesmen and enlisted military men mingled at a dozen large, wooden tables spread throughout the room. Loud, boisterous chatter flowed in waves, filling every corner of the room. The stale, unwashed smell assaulted Emil, reminding him how much he hated these places. He tried not to detest those that hid their problems behind a mug of tasteless ale, but he rarely succeeded. Whether these men fought for the crown or swept the streets, few of them possessed any conviction for their work.

Flames simmered in the corner fireplace, while several barmaids sashayed to and fro, hands filled with brimming mugs. Paintings of famous dirigibles, both military and pleasure cruisers, covered the walls, their frames made of gears and cogs. Lamps hung low over each table, the light glowing enough to illuminate faces, while still concealing much.

Rosseau pointed to a darker corner, where several miserable-looking men sat clutching mugs of beer. They sported long, dirty beards and dark circles under their eyes. They could be wearing their only set of clothes, with how threadbare the fabric appeared and how it molded to their thick arms and wide chests.

A barmaid smiled at both of them as she approached, revealing yellowed teeth. Still, she was pretty in an ordinary kind of way, and Emil wished she didn't have to work in a place like this.

"Your order, gents?" she asked.

Emil gave her a coin and then said, "See those men over there? I would like to buy them a round."

She nodded, shrugged, and then left. Emil and Rosseau approached the weary men. Rosseau, who could be good with accents when the circumstances required, took over. Emil gladly let him do so. It'd been a long evening already at that insufferable ball. The sooner they got information on Admiral Silver Hair and got out of here, the better. He sniffed. He now smelled of sweat and spirits. Wonderful.

"We've had a long day. Could we join you?" Rosseau asked.

One of them waved as if it didn't matter either way. He rubbed his hand over his brown beard and said, "Name's Carter. This 'eres Jones and Dutton."

Rosseau plopped down with a sigh of weariness. "Evenin'. I'm Taylor and this is Walker. We just enlisted. Airfleet. Used ta be Cleaners. Got tired of those nasty factories."

Carter raised his mug and saluted Rosseau. "God love ya. We're all Sweepers here. Nasty job, especially in the Grave."

Jones nodded. "Right foul stuff."

"Really?" Rosseau asked. He sounded only politely interested, as though humoring the men.

The barmaid finally delivered new mugs. The Sweepers

accepted them with nods of thanks. Jones downed half of his in several gulps and then glared at the rest, as though wishing more might appear. Emil longed to pick up the cups, dump them on the Sweepers' heads and demand they quit whining. These men were exactly the kind Emil detested; lazy and rotten to the core.

Dutton said, "After that Eidolon fellow comes, it's wors'. Those Enforcers get after the guards wot failed."

"What's an Eidolon?" Rosseau asked.

Dutton glared at Emil and Rosseau. "You not from aroun' 'ere? What chap doesn't know about the Eidolon?"

Rosseau shrugged. "All we do is work. Don't get out much, ya know. Bosses are tyrants. Work, sleep, sometimes eat. That's it. Not much of a life."

Carter leaned forward, eyes clouded, words slurred. "The Eidolon. The Angel of the Grave. A gentleman of sorts, wears a cape and top hat. Sweeps in and steals them useless orphans from Lord Grillett. The womenfolk gave 'im the name. Ridiculous, if ya ask me. Kids need a purpose. We all remember hows it used ta be. Before Grillett cleaned up the streets."

Rosseau shook his head in sympathy. Emil took a sip of the foul ale. Astonishing. Someone with the guts to stand up to this Lord Grillett, the man that ran the factory district in the Grave. This Eidolon stole his orphans right out from under him. This bit of gossip was worth the several baths he'd need to take to wash out the stench of this place. First Lady Veronica, and now a gentleman soldier, both shared his sympathies, his conscience. An odd feeling came over him. Something light and airy. He wasn't alone in this fight.

Jones chimed in. "Ever seen 'im? Lord Grillett? Wears golden armor, can't miss 'im."

Emil choked on his drink. Rosseau thumped Emil on the back and said, "Nope, not in person."

Several pieces clicked into place for Emil. Lord Grillett, a man with a powerful enough title to gain admittance to London's highest society, ran the factories. The duke controlled the factories, so he must control Grillett. Grillett, therefore, must work for the duke. Emil had no idea why, yet. Money, influence? In the end, it mattered little.

It seemed that once Emil killed the duke, he would also have to remove this Lord Grillett, or the factories would remain and Emil would have only succeeded in one part of his plan. Ruin the duke.

He'd still have to destroy the work of the Grave.

Dutton pushed aside his mug and pulled a knife from his breast pocket. He ran his finger along the handle. "If I ever meet that Eidolon, I know what I'd do. Gentleman or no."

"He's a gentleman wot steals kids?" Rosseau asked, rubbing his forehead as though baffled by the concept.

They all nodded. "It's that Admiral Lord Grillett wot deserves our thanks. 'E's the angel," said Carter.

All three of them finished the last few swallows of their ale and then bid Rosseau and Emil a good evening. They staggered to the door, holding on to each other for support.

Rosseau smiled at Emil and raised a brow. They'd gotten what they came for.

Light filtered in through the windows. It was early morning, and nearly closing time. Emil and Rosseau were the only two customers left in the tavern. A large, muscular man approached their table. He wore an apron with several rags hanging out of the pockets. His eyes were bleary, as though just finishing a long work shift. To Emil's surprise, he took a seat at the table.

"Name's Giles. I'm the proprietor of this fine establishment. You two are new 'round 'ere." He leaned forward, with his hands clasped in front of him on the table in a friendly manner.

Rosseau answered for them. "Nice place you got. Good ale. We'll be back, you can count on that." He took a long drink, set the mug down, and wiped the foam from his face.

Giles grinned. "Not much else is there, in this 'ere life we got? Good drink. Good company."

Rosseau nodded. "Those fellows that just left. They were telling some tale about an Eidolon. Never heard of such a thing."

The tavern owner rubbed his large chin and leaned back in his chair. "Carter and his lot don't think much of the Angel. Wot you think of it?" He folded his arms across his chest as though the answer mattered little to him. As though he were simply passing the time with two friendly customers.

Emil exchanged a glance with Rosseau. Giles was good, but he couldn't quite hide his sympathies. This was definitely unexpected. A man that believed in the Eidolon's work. In spite of the anomaly that Giles presented, a member of the working class caring enough to support change, Emil became a little irritated. The Eidolon even had his own fans. Emil had never heard of such a thing, nor encountered the like when he did the same work throughout EurAsia. Sure, his persona *Kartal* had fans, but only on account of his war heroics. Not his work with the factory children.

"We think the Eidolon is brilliant," said Rosseau with a grin.

Giles's whole face lit up and he smacked the table. "I knew you seemed like respectable chaps." He waved at the barmaid, who rolled her eyes and disappeared into the back. "We'll have a drink to the Eidolon. The only brave man left in London."

Emil sighed inwardly. Once he took care of the duke and Lord Grillett, he needed to find this Eidolon and figure out his secret.

Chapter Seventeen

Veronica settled her mold-colored dress about her legs as she sat down to the breakfast table. Her head throbbed from nightmares she could not remember, making her movements shaky and slow.

Alec whistled cheerfully as he entered the room and picked up a plate. "Lovely dress, as usual."

She lifted her chin. After his behavior at the masque, she was determined to show him nothing but contempt.

"Prettier than your face, to be sure."

"So, I hear my little Peanut is to be married off to a man that could make butter out of you."

Veronica picked up her knife and began spreading jam on her toast. At least he hadn't confronted her about it at Almack's. Though would he have bothered? He hadn't had any interest in her life since his return. She supposed the novelty of their childhood relationship had faded, withering like autumn leaves, once he'd found brighter pastures at Eton.

She almost didn't answer, but he prodded her with his walking stick.

"Butter? Me? When have you ever seen me swoon over a man? You're being ridiculous."

"Sources tell me the prince is," his hands fluttered to his face, "sooo dreamy. Tee-hee."

Veronica scowled. "He was extremely cordial."

Alec swaggered over to her chair and patted her arm. "Cordial? For my darling little sister to use any kind word about a man, this is the dawn of a new age! No longer are you running around in leading strings. You are finally a woman, taking an interest in men!

Aye, me, how the years have flown." He dabbed a fictional tear.

She snapped her napkin at him. "You know this is all your fault. If the duke could have found anyone willing to take you on, you'd be engaged, not me."

"I cannot help it if I'm simply too much for any one woman to handle. The prospect would be daunting for any person, royal or no."

"Daunting is not the word I'd use."

"Come, Peanut, it seems to have turned out smashing in the end, has it not? At the very least, you are simply doomed to look at your handsome prince's striking visage for the rest of your long days." He pretended to swoon. "How terribly wonderful!"

"Are you saying that any part of me finds this situation desirable?"

Alec laughed. "You find nothing desirable but your fencing lessons and books. I wasn't even aware until now that you knew you were a woman."

She patted her purposely frizzy hair. "Let me be clear, dear brother. Cordial prince or no, I am not a romantic."

Alec shrugged. "If the idea bothers you so much, then don't do it. Don't marry the dreamboat."

That comment made her drop her toast. "B-but what about the duke? And the queen?" And Bridges?

He plopped down beside her. "I didn't say there wouldn't be consequences. We'd both be disinherited. Since Papá passed me over for the title, I'd say he'd choose one of those horrible cousins of ours. The ones that dress up like airshipmen and attend those steam-tech conventions."

She felt her shoulders slump. For a moment there, she thought he might have had a solution to all of this. Sometimes, admittedly very little, her brother had surprised her since his return. A glimmer of strength, a hardened resolve, that showed him to be more than a man bent on gaming and women. But these past few weeks, she'd seen it less and less.

An arm slid across her shoulders. "Is the prospect truly so horrible, Peanut?" Oddly, the question sounded more real than anything else he'd said recently.

Yet she stiffened and didn't answer. She didn't blame him for not looking out for her. Who could, when faced with the duke? But Veronica wasn't daft, and she wouldn't let herself hope he'd be the brother she needed. Especially now.

After a moment of awkward silence, Alec sighed. "You know I could fight him for you," he said in a very non-Alec voice. There it was… the rare glimmer.

She closed her eyes for a moment, gathered her strength, and opened them again. Even if her brother said nothing but those fictional words, they still meant something to her and lent her courage. He might not be capable of truly protecting her, but he probably meant well. "The prince isn't so bad, Alec."

"Even though he is a man?"

She nearly smiled but sniffed instead. "But I will miss all *this* terribly. The dark, stuffy rooms. The constant chill in the air because the duke doesn't order fires to be lit. The depressive silence of it all."

Veronica motioned toward the thick walls that hid the horrors of their childhood. Neither of them had ever felt at home here, the duke had made sure of that. No comfort or kindness either, except for with each other, when the duke was off at the battlefront.

Alec grinned. "Must you leave right away? I thought these things took months to arrange. Posting the banns, the parties, the wedding?"

"I have no idea. I'm sure the duke will want it all done properly." The more time she had to devise a way to continue to fund Bridges and escape the marriage noose, the better.

Alec popped a grape in his mouth and chewed while he watched her, waiting. He was doing that thing where it seemed as though he saw through her. She snatched two more pieces of toast off the table and averted her eyes. "You'll meet him tonight at dinner. Please, Alec, let's change the subject."

"If you wish."

He sauntered over to the sideboard and piled a plate with cake. As though her brother needed any more vices.

She noticed the morning paper from *Lloyd's of London* on the table and opened it. The headline read, "Masked Man Kidnaps Children." She turned so Alec could not see it, her chest constricting as she continued reading silently.

It couldn't be. Could it?

A mysterious gentleman dressed in a black cape, unusual goggles, and a top hat, entered the factory district several nights ago and kidnapped twenty children walking home from their shift. The victim, a Mr. X, said, "His gun shot fire and he had a bleeding giant of a manservant. The bloke wielded two leather whips. He would 'ave killed me if I 'ad not got help!"

Chief Inspector Marwick of Scotland Yard assures this reporter that the kidnapper, who has been identified as the same man known as the Eidolon by residents of the East End, will be caught. Chief Inspector Marwick, backed by an unknown donor, is offering a reward of one thousand pounds for any information leading to the identification of the Eidolon. In the meantime, the police are implementing tighter security in and out of the factory district.

Notify the authorities immediately if you hear anything about the whereabouts of the dangerous criminal known as the Eidolon.

Veronica read the article again and again, not trusting her weary eyes.

Several horrible words ran through her mind in rapid succession as she considered what this article meant. The Eidolon had never been mentioned in print before. It'd been merely a name whispered on the streets.

Some part of her thrilled to see her actions reported in *Lloyd's*. Her missions seemed more real to her in this moment, now that her other life crossed into this one. Her life as the Eidolon was becoming less a dream. Of course, her visits to the children were substantial enough, but now, now all the world knew who she was and what she'd done.

Her masked crusader persona had lost any anonymity, which did not bother her. She would much sooner London know that someone was trying to make a difference. What did bother her was the manner in which she was reported; a villain, a child stealer, a thug. The very type of person she'd been trying to fight. As a result of this horrible article, she'd lost any chance people would support her cause. It was all some sort of horribly brilliant lie interspersed with bits of truth.

Who was Gentleman X? Who would dare contact *Lloyd's*? Nothing, not in the many months she'd been doing this, had ever been reported. She'd assumed Grillett hadn't wanted to be exposed like this, with his child-funded operations open for public discussion.

Gentleman X must be one of the guards from the factory, perhaps the pockmarked one. He had been rougher and meaner than the others. She knew men like him, men that never took the blame for anything. Men that could spin a story any which way so that they ended out on top.

Grillett would be furious. The man had probably already been identified and disposed of. He wouldn't want *Lloyd's* or any other paper looking too closely into his affairs.

The Eidolon must not become a subject *on dit* in London. On this one and only point, she and Lord Grillett must surely agree.

She scanned the article again and noticed one other key point. One that would bring fortune hunters to the doors of the factory district.

One thousand pounds reward for her whereabouts.

The Eidolon would be hunted, no longer sheltered by those who closed their shutters and dimmed their lights when she and the children rushed past. Veronica knew better than to expect loyalty even from those who bestowed the name of 'Angel' upon her. One thousand pounds could change a person's life, especially when they lived, crowded thirty to one room, in the East End.

How long would it be before someone found something about the Eidolon? Or worse, before they fabricated a stream of evidence leading to the wrong person?

"Peanut? You look peakéd, darling. Did you make it into *Defunct Debutantes* again? You know, if you'd just let me help…" he trailed off.

She turned to look at Alec and blinked.

His gaze dropped to the paper and he snatched it up before she could stop him. He read for a minute and then said, "Just another article about that pirate who steals from the Russians. Ah, it's the children, isn't it?"

She swallowed her cold tea and asked lightly, "Have you heard of the Eidolon before?"

He shrugged. "A whisper here and there at the track. No one puts much stock in it. Seemed to me like the Eidolon was a character from one of those Radcliffe novels you women all swoon over, you know, underneath the covers at night. Or like that supposed *Kartal*. Likely story. Take on a hundred Turkish ships indeed."

"And what do you think of the Eidolon now?" She pretended not to watch him closely.

"Kidnapping twenty children from under Grillett's nose would be nigh impossible, not with his Enforcers. What would a gentleman want with those scraggly little orphans anyway? Nah, it's all rubbish."

He tossed an apple in the air, caught it, polished it on his sleeve, and bit into it, spraying juice into her face.

She wiped her cheek and pushed his elbows off the table. "Well, Alec, your refined and elegant lordship, don't you think people might start asking questions about Grillett now? And his child-laborers?"

"Unfortunately for your sake, Peanut, no. You know he is one of the Untouchables, like Papá. Without Grillett's airships, England would have long ago lost her lands to Russia, France, or the Turks. I don't know anyone who wouldn't sacrifice an appendage to be held in his favor." He reached over and flicked her nose. "Twenty children? It only makes him a more tragic and romantic figure, not a man under suspicion. You know how he sends all those orphans to school and gives them a living. He dotes on them."

She forced her mouth shut. They'd had this argument, she and her brother, many times. He believed the photographs of Grillett and a dozen, fat children printed in *Lloyd's*. He didn't think to question the reports of families with a parent or two killed during wartime, whose remaining sons and daughters sought refuge in Grillett's orphanages, never to be seen again. He saw what everyone else saw. A man with gold-plated armor, slicked silver hair, fancy goggles swinging around his neck, and a confident smile that only nobility seemed to possess. Why did she persist with her questions, thinking Alec might change?

"Peanut, honey, quit your worrying. Chief Inspector Marwick is a solid chap. He'll get the job done. Those children will be back in their beds before the week's out, just you see."

"Back in their beds! Alec, you dolt, I don't want them back!

The Eidolon—"

"Veronica, lower your voice. The Berkleys will be able to hear you next door," the duke said as he entered the room.

He wore his full, red uniform again today, all his medals polished to high shine, making his shoulder gleam like Lady Ambrose's décolletage. He sat at the head of the table without looking at either of them.

Had he heard the discussion of the Eidolon? Or simply her rant about the orphans? If the latter, he would not give it a second thought. If the former… well, it would soon be all over London. And the duke was about as likely to associate her with the Eidolon as Alec was to stop pouring whisky in his orange juice.

Veronica froze when the duke picked up the paper, but he only glanced at it and tossed it aside.

He could still be angry. About her dress last night. She glanced down, feeling ever so alone.

"Your presentation last evening was quite terrible. I discussed it with the queen afterwards. Luckily, she was amused." The duke laid out his morning ration of pickled meats and fruits. He arranged his napkin and said, "In fact, Victoria and I agreed that the banns are to be read this week for your engagement. You'll be married one month from now."

Veronica masked her panic as she always did, by concentrating on keeping her face completely blank. Her movement unhurried as she took a bite of toast that threatened to choke her. "Wonderful," she said

"You will handle none of the details. Lady Ambrose is taking care of everything. Your sole responsibility is to keep the prince and his party entertained and see to their comfort." He cut his meat into even pieces, forked one and chewed meticulously.

"Lady Ambrose?" She kept her voice even.

Anyone but her. Even though it made sense to have the help from the daughter of an Almack's patroness, since Veronica's mom had long ago left, she couldn't imagine worse torture. The duke had outdone himself.

Alec interjected. "May I propose an alternative?" His tone was lazy, but Veronica saw the slight tremor in his hand as he wiped the corner of his mouth.

Shock must be the only reason the duke didn't respond.

Alec continued. "As you may know, Papá, I am experienced in both spending money and high fashion. I saw Lord Morris married off last year to that sweet little thing, do you remember? Their wedding was the event of the Season. All my doing, I assure you."

The duke polished off the last of his food. After several moments, he spoke stiffly. "Very well. I concede your foppish ways, Alec. I will allow you to work with Lady Ambrose to plan the wedding."

Alec nodded. Only Veronica saw the surprise in the loosening of his jaw.

"You are to stay away from the track and gaming houses during all of this, or I will reverse my decision." With that, the duke swept from the room in his measured, military strides.

Veronica instantly turned to her brother. "Alec—"

He waved his napkin like a dainty handkerchief. "For you, my Peanut, I will restrain myself. Besides, I will have no time! We have a wedding to plan. For once, you will have to listen to my advice on your wardrobe."

She reached over and patted his arm. He laughed once and patted her back.

It had taken much for Alec to concede ground to the duke. She'd never seen Alec do so since his return. If Alec dared speak, the duke would not hear it, no matter the subject. He made it clear he did not care for gurney races or the latest gossip at White's. After a while, Alec ceased talking, and the only noise at mealtimes came in the form of orders, given from a general to his men, without a response required.

The glimmer had grown into a full beam of light that warmed Veronica down to her toes.

"Together?" he asked quietly.

Always.

She couldn't quite bring herself to say it. The response she'd given dozens of times over the years. As much as she appreciated Alec's intervention, she would still try everything she could to stop this marriage. She hated the thought, Alec left with the wedding dangling in ruins, and the duke's meager trust in him with it.

Particularly now, when the darkness surrounding him lifted momentarily, revealing an Alec that might have been without the cold, suppressing hand of the duke.

Chapter Eighteen

As he rapped on the front door of the Clarke home, Emil told himself to focus on the task ahead, and not on the escapades of a gentleman who had, of all things, a nickname. Yet he couldn't help himself.

Three beers in, Giles had opened up. Wept, in fact, over the Eidolon's work rescuing children. Admitted how powerless he and the wife felt to do anything. Lamented his guilt about how he lived, when so many had so little. Sobbed over how much his own two children had compared to the orphans trapped in the Grave.

Emil and Rosseau discussed the contrasting opinions, Giles and Carter. They both agreed that the different sentiments that existed in the Grave and the Merchant District were alarming. In other countries, they had similar dichotomies of wealth and living conditions, but nothing like this. Barbaric. They didn't plan to sit still. These were the scales they'd helped balance in other countries across EurAsia. They would not leave London without doing so.

Then when he saw *Lloyd's* this morning, Emil knew everything would change. One thousand pounds. Pennies to steam barons like Grillett, but life-changing for a man in the Grave or a man in the dozens of workhouses dotting the south end of London, making only enough to feed and clothe himself. How many were there who would now unclog their stuffed ears and scrub the film from their weary eyes to find out what they could of the Eidolon? Who would now awaken within them some kind of frantic hope that they alone would be the one to find him?

They would not hesitate to turn against the one man who'd not only recognized their plight but also stood up to their oppressor.

Emil should know. He'd seen it happen in France with a good-hearted merchant who tried to stand up against steam barons. Parts of Italy. Need, in the end, would always trump the defense of anything, good or evil. Even, perhaps, for kind pub owner Giles and his family.

A hunched butler in an impeccable uniform opened the door. His eyes traveled upward. And upward. When they reached Emil's scarf, he said in a bland manner, "I see. Your name and purpose, sir." His words suggested the answer would not matter, as a man like Emil did not deserve entrance.

"Mr. Marcovic. Here to collect Lady Veronica for her outing today wither fiancé, His Royal Highness, Prince Durad Jurinic of Sombor," Emil answered, making sure to exaggerate his accent.

The butler stared, the heavy wrinkles around his eyes unmoving. He blinked once. And said, "I apologize. Your words are muffled through that scarf. Her fiancé, you say?"

Emil nodded slowly, as though the man were daft.

The butler opened the door and led Emil across a shiny marble foyer and into a dark drawing room. He left without a word, closing the double doors behind him.

Emil settled into a comfortable leather chair near the fireplace and glanced about the room. A roll-top desk with nothing on it, no papers, pens, correspondence. Several framed portraits of notable airship battles, most of Her Majesty's victory over Germany, when Duke Richmond was the key player. The colors were all sober and muted, very masculine. It appeared to Emil as though no female had influence here. Surely, this would be the place Lady Veronica received visitors, callers. Where were the bright sprigs of flowers? The delicate settee and other such furniture that baffled men?

Surely, she did receive. A lady of her standing must do so.

"Mr. Marcovic. How kind of you to pay me a visit this morning."

Lady Veronica entered the room, skirts the color of rotten green apples swishing about. She wore that same idiotic smile she'd featured so prominently the night before at Almack's.

He didn't bother rising. "My lady. The prince requests your delightful presence this morning at the Steam-Tech Expo. He would be so happy if you would join him." He delivered the promised invitation in a flat voice.

Slight color rose in her cheeks and her eyes widened most vacuously. "Yes, yes, of course I accept. I've been hoping he meant it. When he said he wanted me to show him London." She giggled.

He wanted to roll his eyes, but since they were the only feature anyone could see of his face, that gesture drew a lot of attention.

"I have his highness's conveyance here, if that would suit you?"

"I'm sure it's quite grand! Just allow me to get my wrap and call for Matilda." She turned in a flurry and was gone.

Her wrap? So, she was planning on going out in public in the rotten apple dress. He supposed she had already established her tenacity at this role she played.

He noticed he was tapping his foot, as though impatient for her return. He stopped.

In a matter of moments, she was back. Her "wrap" looked like it had been washed too many times and the color scrubbed out of it. It might have been yellow once, he supposed. Emil couldn't help staring.

She offered her hand to him, her chin lifted in confidence, as though she wore the very height of fashion. He extended his forearm in exaggerated diffidence. Lady Veronica placed her hand on him, the strength of her grip surprising him.

He felt a smile grow beneath his scarf at how she exacted her revenge for his coldness as they exited the Clarke townhome and headed toward the royal steam carriage. She squeezed his arm with each step they descended. He might actually bruise. Matilda followed them silently, not nearly as outrageous as her employer in a sensible muslin.

Lady Veronica paused in front of the machine. It wasn't what she would be expecting. The design was wholly original, Durad's idea. The engine and the driver's box were the same as a traditional machine, but the cabin had been placed above the driver. Draped with curtains and filled with pillows instead of benches, it rather looked like something that would have been carried on the shoulders of massive slaves in Egypt. It had been made in one of Sombor's own factories, staffed by legitimate workers, and would never be mistaken for Grillett's work.

Emil loved it.

He led Lady Veronica around the back, where a staircase with a rail wound up to the cabin.

"My lady." He gestured for her to ascend. She squeezed his arm one last time before gathering her skirts and climbing up. Matilda tilted her head sideways, like the concept baffled her, before following her employer.

Emil bounded up behind them, rubbing his arm. He found the two ladies looking quite lost.

Lady Veronica pursed her mouth and asked, "Where are we to sit? There are no benches, sir."

He sank down onto one of the cushions, his black robes lifting slightly as he did so. He cocked his head, waiting for them to do the same.

Her ladyship smiled and copied his position, crossing her ankles and adjusting her skirts.

Emil was glad she could not see his grin as he tapped on the floor and shouted at the driver to go in Turkish. The carriage lurched forward. Lady Veronica near fell into his lap. Her hand was not wrapped around the rail as his was. Her side brushed his. The scent of roses assaulted him.

She threw an elbow into his stomach and said, "Oh my apologies, Mr. Marcovic! I'm not used to the movement of this conveyance as of yet." She lowered goggles onto her face and turned away.

This woman would leave him more damaged than any of his missions so far. Still, some part of him wanted the driver to continue to have an unsteady hand at the wheel, forcing her back into his arms.

Rather than bother with what was sure to be the most inane conversation he'd ever had, as the lady proved she wouldn't drop her veneer for him, Emil faced the street and enjoyed the view of London's streets from their elevated height. Durad's vehicle kept them out of the fog and away from the continual bursts of steam from passing carriages. Thin streams of air occasionally tickled his face from the jutting pipes of tall buildings, but not enough to annoy him.

They passed older townhomes now converted into steel-plated structures with swags of iron décor. As with anything new, Emil wondered where they had been made. As far as he could tell, Grillett was the only supplier of such things in London. He was looking forward to this Steam-Tech Expo to learn if there were other players in this game that children never won.

When they arrived at the Crystal Palace, the Expo venue, Emil rapped once more on the floor, and the carriage stopped at the front steps. As they descended from the carriage, he noticed a large banner hung across the door to the Palace. It was not made of fabric but of a thin steel. The letters hammered into the material proclaimed this to be the "19th Century Steam-Tech Expo." Several large corkscrews held it in place, though it appeared precarious to Emil.

What caught his attention, though, was a group of raggedly dressed urchins shouting from across the street, Her Majesty's soldiers keeping them there, chanting "Nick the Eidolon! Kill the bloody toff!"

Women with faces thick with grime spit on the ground and joined in just as loudly as the men. Some men brandished clubs as they spoke, waving them about as they chanted and raved. Emil thought he recognized Dutton, one of the rotten men from the pub, among them, ragged and filthy.

"Good heavens," Matilda said. Her already pale face appeared as white as freshly fallen snow.

Lady Veronica said nothing. She stared at the group, her expression completely unreadable, except that her eyes no longer held the wide witlessness he'd seen all day. The glow inspired by the prospect of meeting Durad had vanished, replaced by a dullness he saw most often on the faces of factory children.

Emil watched her closely. Her façade had slipped, revealing the woman from the masque. One of her eyes twitched and she rolled her shoulders back as if preparing for battle. Her face flooded with color all at once, making her invisible no longer. Whatever regard she felt for the Eidolon animated the society corpse.

Emil waited. Watched. Had an impulse to take her hands, as she had his at the masque. He did nothing, of course, but he wanted to. *Remember she was the duke's. And Durad's.*

Matilda whispered something to her lady and pulled her gently up the stairs of the Crystal Palace. After finally tearing her eyes from the spectacle, Lady Veronica followed. With each step she took, she seemed to shake off her heavy thoughts. By the time she reached the front doors, the real Veronica was gone.

Emil waved the carriage away and followed them inside. Whether Lady Veronica simply admired the Eidolon, or knew the fellow personally, he would find out.

When they entered the exhibition hall, they joined a crowd of gentleman and ladies gawking at the sight before them. The ceiling soared several stories high, made entirely of glass, lighting the room with the bright sun and making him feel as though he weren't actually inside. Several platforms supported by steel girders rose in each corner, one atop another.

In the center of the room, anchored in place, floated a dirigible the likes of which Emil had never seen. The bottom half of the ship appeared to be of traditional construction, with several glass portholes. The top was encased entirely in a sturdy-looking glass. As he stared, a man inside the machine cranked a lever and the glass retracted back inside the ship, leaving it as open as Emil's frigate.

"Oh, my," Lady Veronica whispered softly. He glanced sideways at her, but her face did not show the same sense of wonder as her tone. In fact, she looked scared for a moment, before her features smoothed. Her hands clutched and unclutched, mangling her hideous wrap.

"Quite a sight, isn't it, my lady?" he asked.

"What a simply gorgeous craft. I cannot wait to have a ride!" She fluttered lashes at him. "Do you think Prince Durad would ever buy such a vessel?"

And there she was again, the imbecile. He thought his eyes might be crossed from how quickly she changed from one moment to the next.

He nearly denied her right off. *Durad would never buy such a monstrosity.* Then he reconsidered. Would he? He could, this new Durad, who refused to speak of where they'd been and what they'd always wanted to do.

"I am certain he would do whatever his, er, beautiful lady wished," he replied, fluffing her wrap with his hand.

Lady Veronica stepped forward, rising on her toes. "Where's Prince Durad? Is he here yet? Can I see him?"

"He is to meet us at the booth of the fellow that invented the dirigible. Some German who went loony during the wars. Hooch or something."

"Dr. Hoch?" Matilda asked immediately.

Emil pulled out a timepiece. "I believe so. In a quarter hour. Shall I take you ladies to see that magnificent thing in the meantime?" He gestured toward the dirigible.

Lady Veronica flashed him the simpleton smile, though it seemed harder around the edges. He enjoyed this other side of her so much more. From here on out, he'd do everything he could to goad her out of Lady Crackers and into the passionate woman he met the night of the masque.

"What a marvelous idea," she said.

He raised a brow and offered his arm, uncaring that she might not be gentle. He simply wanted to feel her touch.

Chapter Nineteen

Veronica shot glances at Mr. Marcovic, focusing her thoughts on how much better he'd look on the other end of her sword. She tried not to think about what she'd seen outside, how the very people she'd helped had so thoroughly turned on her. She was their one champion, was she not? Who else but the Eidolon did something about Grillett's factories?

At that moment, Grillett himself appeared on the deck of his new dirigible. His golden armor caught the light at every angle, nearly blinding her. He removed a plumed helmet, revealing white hair pulled back and fastened at the nape of his neck with a metal clip. A red cape attached to his shoulder plates swayed as he raised one hand into the air.

Cheers, so loud they might have shattered the glass enclosure above their heads, assailed her ears. She glanced at Mr. Marcovic, silent and stiff beside her, before applauding in a proper, reserved manner. She watched her hands, wishing they didn't have to join in this abominable celebration. The pressure in her chest mounted as the cheers grew and grew.

Clap, clap. *I wish I had my Tesla-ray right now.* Clap, clap. *I would show Grillett how vulnerable he really is up there.*

Finally, *finally,* Grillett lowered his hand. The crowd hushed as though it were Christmas Mass, and the pope himself stood before them about to sermonize. Veronica wanted to snort. And shoot him.

"Together as a nation, we've accomplished great things. We beat the Germans back when they thought us too weak to fight their slow and weapon-laden dirigibles. We proved that speed and bravery are more important than firepower time and again. We showed them *who we are.*"

Smart. Implying that any of these people here had something to do with England's victory. Pat their backs, now tell them what they deserve. Veronica wished at that moment for Mr. Marcovic's scarf, so that she might let her mask slip for a moment and show how she truly felt about this slumlord.

"And who are we? We are the smartest steam-tech engineers the world has to offer. We are the highest producing factories. We invest in our future and in the defense of our borders.

"My team continues to design a faster, stronger fleet of airships. Of course, the first models go out to our military, as always, and now I'm proud to offer *you* the benefits of your continued support. Named after the patron of soldiers himself, I give you the *Saint George.*"

Amidst more nauseating cheers, a dozen of Grillett's men stepped forward holding a large panel of glass, about ten feet long by five feet tall. They stood between Grillett and the crowd.

He held up a hand and dropped it, silencing the masses once again. "This may appear only to be a vessel of pleasure, made to enjoy the skies in any weather, but it does serve another purpose. This glass is the same we've installed on all our new dirigibles."

He whipped out a Smith & Wesson and fired at the glass. As one, the entire mass of people flinched and ducked, gasping. Some ladies screamed, while several appeared to swoon, but the bullet ricocheted and appeared to lodge into the deck in front of Grillett. Veronica couldn't see clearly from her viewpoint, about halfway back in the crowd. She produced a fan from her reticule and waved it in front of her face as she made what she hoped were incoherent sounds of fear.

A glass strong enough to repel bullets. How in the devil had Grillett managed to manufacture such a thing?

The concept was frighteningly clever. These dirigibles could transport any type of cargo without fear. Most airships had long since abandoned heavy artillery, opting for deck-mounted semi-automatic rifles, or slings to launch explosives. As the Germans had so aptly demonstrated, weight could be trumped by speed.

This glass would not be limited to this application alone. Grillett would soon be putting it in steam carriages. Homes. The uses were endless. If Grillett's factories had been busy before, the workload would surely double or triple now.

No one, after all, would want to be outdone.

"Land's sake, my lady," Matilda whispered to her. "They won't be able to get enough of that glass. Those poor children!"

Veronica nodded, while raising her eyebrows in a way that silenced her companion. Matilda should know better than to make such comments in public, even as troubling as this situation was.

Grillett motioned for silence once again. "Many of the war orphans in my factories have recently graduated from their studies and have volunteered to stay on to work for me. As a result, our production capacity has doubled.

"I'd like to urge each of you to continue England's legacy of greatness, to continue to show the world who we are. We travel in only the safest, best-engineered dirigibles. We can and we must afford the best protection for our families and ourselves. Especially with creatures like the Eidolon on the loose."

Boos sounded through the room.

Even though she was used to such propaganda with the Grave "orphans", and now the Eidolon, Veronica still couldn't believe what she was hearing. How deeply selfishness, ignorance, and the desire for convenience and easy solutions ran within this city.

"We neither cower nor covet, for we, England, are the most powerful nation on Earth!"

Grillett raised both arms and the crowd reached a new level of noise, shaking the platforms and booths surrounding the dirigible. After several moments, he saluted the mass of people, crisp and official, and left. As one, several hundred men and women surged forward toward the line of booths with the *Saint George* banners.

One group of ladies, however, remained behind. Oddly enough, they looked concerned. Veronica drifted closer, forced by the shifting crowd, and wondered if these women would hate her, too.

"More orphans, he says. I didn't know we were losing so many men in the wars," one woman said. She waved a peacock blue fan for emphasis.

"You'll not hear me complaining about Grillett's cruisers. I enjoy them as much as the next person, but I don't know. Should children be working so hard?" This was said by an older lady in hushed tones.

Another woman carrying a reticule adorned with cogs and wheels replied, "It doesn't seem right. I can't imagine my Harry in a factory." They began moving toward the crowd with seemingly reluctant steps.

Veronica made her way back to Matilda and Mr. Marcovic, her thoughts great bursts of energy inside her.

Those women, women of the *ton* no less, questioned Grillett? While the masses picketed outside, it appeared some orphan supporters were here, among the nobility. If what she heard was real, if those women really believed those things, then Veronica might be wrong. There were others among her set who suspected something wasn't right with Grillett's factories.

Others who might be willing to help her fight Grillett.

Lord Grillett. He had mentioned the Eidolon. But why, when he had every reason not to draw attention to the children's plight? With the masses on his side, he must feel empowered, placed once again on that pedestal from which she could not seem to shake him.

The thought made her pull her awful wrap tighter around her shoulders. She'd been wrong about Grillett, thinking he wouldn't want anyone looking too closely at the Eidolon's work.

Mr. Marcovic cleared his throat. "Is your wrap not sufficient, my lady? Or is the excitement simply too much for someone of your delicate sensibilities?"

"It's all simply thrilling." She projected a more than adequate amount of high-pitched fervor into her voice. It made her want to gag.

"Indeed, my lady. Should we find our wayward prince?" He checked his timepiece, swept an arm out, and bowed.

Veronica declined to take Mr. Marcovic's arm this time. She had likely left him bruised enough. She thought his eyes might have lightened in relief when she didn't. He led them past the teeming booths and into the southwest corner of the exhibition hall. They stepped into a lift that took them past several brightly lit, colorful platforms featuring an array of new tech, from goggles and quizzing glasses to watches, to another one that was dark and sparse.

Mr. Marcovic stepped off the lift and offered his hand to Veronica. When she took it, he clasped his fingers over hers. His grip was reassuring, strong and firm. She glanced up and made the mistake of meeting his black-as-stormy-midnight gaze. She tripped over her skirts as she stepped forward. Quicker than she could right herself, Mr. Marcovic swept her into his arms and stepped back from the platform.

Veronica looked up. She was a breath away from his face. He barked out a laugh as his eyes softened around their hard edges. She didn't move, fascinated by how the darkness lifted from his expression. She smiled.

Then he set her down abruptly, his hand remaining on her arm until she straightened up and put several steps in between them. He turned to help Matilda as well.

Something about Mr. Marcovic made Veronica not only incapable of stepping in and out of things but oddly mute and jittery when he got too close.

Mr. Marcovic led them past a heavy curtain into a room with a single chair and a small table. Durad, standing to the side of the chair, rushed forward upon seeing them. He lifted her glove for a kiss.

"My Veronica! How lovely you are today," he said as he looked straight at her. His brown eyes lit the room and his smile was unfeigned.

To her dismay, her cheeks warmed. "Good morning, Durad. How pleased I was by your invitation."

He squeezed her hand gently. "I'm so glad you could come. I enjoyed our time together at Almack's last night and had no thought today but to spend more of it with you. I had also hoped to meet this man, one of whom so many stories have been told." He gestured toward the chair.

Dr. Hoch, white hair limp amidst a complex set of goggles, raised sharp eyes to hers. In public, they were nothing more than mere acquaintances through the duke, but seeing him always brought back the memory of the first time they'd met in the gardens of the duke's country home. When he'd told her they'd change the world together, believed in her and animated her, when she'd only been a breath away from complete despair. He patted his leather vest, produced a set of spectacles and placed them on his nose.

Prince Durad nudged her forward several steps. "Have you met this remarkable person, Veronica? I just arrived and had the pleasure myself."

She nodded and extended her hand to Dr. Hoch. "Do you remember me, doctor? We met once when you called upon my papá."

Dr. Hoch shook her hand like an American, pumping it up and down. "You'd think I'd remember such a pretty face, but I'm sorry m'dear. Age and all that."

She inclined her head and giggled. "Of course. You must've had the chance to meet so many important people!"

He coughed and wheezed. "Some of them filled a little too much with their importance, but yes."

The prince picked up a small airship model, the only item on the table. Veronica recognized it as the first Dr. Hoch had designed. Boxy and cumbersome, it was a miracle it had flown.

"Will you tell me about this, good doctor? How did you come up with the idea?" Prince Durad knelt by Dr. Hoch. With his eyes wide like a child, he looked truly fascinated and hopeful.

The doctor's eyes glazed when he saw the ship. "I'm sorry, lad. I don't remember." He patted his vest again and then abruptly stood. "I wish Her Almighty Majesty wouldn't make me come to these things. What I've forgotten far outweighs what I know now. Useless, I am."

While Dr. Hoch stormed out through a door at the back of the room, Veronica saw he'd left a slip of paper behind in the chair. She slipped it into her reticule before anyone could notice.

The prince sighed and muttered something in Turkish. Mr. Marcovic nodded. Then, Prince Durad turned toward Veronica, smiling once again.

"Shall we enjoy the rest of the exhibition, my lady?"

Veronica began to nod, but the idea of staying and feigning excitement any longer made her sick. "How about an English ice instead, Your Highness?" She glanced around the dark room. "I feel in need of some revival."

He grinned. "An excellent idea. I haven't had one since my graduation day at Cambridge."

"Your English is impeccable, Durad. Is that where you learned to speak it so well?"

He nodded. "I do prefer my native language though. It inflames, like spices on your tongue, *sultanim*."

She giggled, though it took quite a bit of effort to do so. Her persona settled stale and flat in her mind. She longed for fresh air and a moment alone. Since she could only have one of those, she shut away her heavy thoughts and tried to enjoy the sound of Durad's crisp English, and the way he couldn't stop looking into her eyes.

Veronica's gaze kept straying to her reticule. What message had Dr. Hoch left her that could not be delivered through his normal channels?

When their party reached the bottom floor of the Crystal Palace once again, she excused herself to use the powder room while Matilda followed close behind.

"Are you all right, my lady?" her friend asked, as soon as they reached a hallway that appeared vacant.

Veronica sagged against the wall and immediately removed the note from her reticule. "Dr. Hoch left this behind."

"He did?"

Veronica waved her companion into silence as she read.

E. is no longer safe. Stop immediately. You must obey me in this. Wait for my word and don't do anything.

The last sentence was underlined three times. She passed it to Matilda without a word.

In spite of his mad scientist act in front of Durad, Veronica knew Dr. Hoch to be mostly sound of mind. He'd been proud of what they accomplished together. He *lived* for it. If he wrote this note, something wasn't right. It sounded desperate. Pleading.

"He's right, my lady. It's not safe. Not with that article in *Lloyd's,* and now his high and mightiness Grillett inciting the crowds against you. Not to mention the protestors. We'll find another way to help."

Veronica pressed her palm against her forehead and closed her eyes. She couldn't give up the Eidolon. How could anyone ask her to? She was no longer certain who she was without that part of herself. It had taken her over completely, leaving the meek Lady Veronica far behind. She no longer thought of herself as a titled noble, but as the masked fighter. There would be nothing left without the Eidolon but a hollow, vacuous, horribly dressed, and aging debutante. A person no one cared for, and little remembered.

She'd always obeyed Dr. Hoch. He'd given her Clank. Her Tesla-ray. Her fencing lessons. Self-worth. Kindness.

The children.

He couldn't take this from her now. He'd created her and he couldn't power her off or hide her in an armoire like Clank. With the reveal of the *Saint George*, he couldn't expect her to wait and do nothing.

"I cannot give up, Matilda."

Her companion placed a hand on her arm. "I know, my lady, but there must be another way. You've got Grillett after you, along with the rest of the world. It's time to switch tactics."

"What would you have me do? Picket outside the Grave's entrance? Toss food through the bars?"

Nothing could be more effective than the Eidolon. At least nothing she personally could do. Knowing how many more children remained, knowing they waited for their Angel… she closed her eyes, picturing them, shuffling through the factories, wondering if they should hope for rescue anymore.

"I've no idea, but you and Dr. Hoch are the smartest people I know. You will figure something out. Preferably something that won't leave you with any more scars." Matilda sniffed and Veronica was dismayed to notice actual tears on her companion's face.

Veronica handed a handkerchief to her friend and pulled her in for a hug. "No one has ever shown such faith in me. Thank you."

As Matilda continued to sniffle and occasionally sneeze into Veronica's terribly old wrap, Veronica realized that whatever happened to her in her marriage or with the Eidolon, she had to make plans for Matilda. She would not suffer for her lady's choices.

Chapter Twenty

"Everyone is talking about how you're such a hero, stealing Sombor back from those nasty Ottomans. You simply must tell me how you did it."

Veronica was trying to be flighty. Ridiculous. Uninteresting. She was probably succeeding even more so than usual, since she was so distracted. Veronica crushed her spoon into her dainty bowl, wishing it were Grillett's meticulously groomed head.

Durad gently took the bowl and spoon from her hands. "Am I correct in thinking you're done with this?" He appeared to be fighting a smile.

She sighed. "I have horrid table manners, Prince Durad. My apologies."

He laughed. "I quite enjoy your manners. To answer your question, it's a long story. You're sure you want to hear it?"

She leaned forward, clasped her hands together in front of her, and said, "I would love to, if you don't mind telling it. I'm sure you were so brave!" She fluttered her lashes.

He laughed again, then sobered. He rubbed his chin with his hand. Crossed his legs and hunched forward, as if sharing a confidence.

"My people, my soldiers, gave me the strength to do what needed to be done. Mr. Marcovic and I gathered them from the darkest, forgotten corners of Sombor; places where hope had fled, where life was suspended in an unending reality of work, pain and misery. We stole these young people away, re-lit their fires and gave them a cause they embraced of their own accord."

Young people. Unending work. Dark, forgotten corners. Prince Durad's soldiers sounded like factory orphans. Surely, it couldn't be... another person caring enough to do the Eidolon's work. In a small, conquered country no less.

"Young ones? They were not trained soldiers, then," Veronica said. She creased her brows as if worried for Prince Durad's safety in this story.

The prince glanced over at his bodyguard then back at her. "No, they were not. Mr. Marcovic and his men took care of preparing them. He made sure they could fight in a way that made sense for their size and strength. We didn't allow anyone younger than the required age of your own military to enlist; fourteen years.

"We kept them hidden at Mr. Marcovic's family farm, in a small village razed by the Ottomans and left as embers to wither and eventually burn out. When the villagers—still alive, through many small wonders—saw what we were doing, I witnessed a miracle." Durad reached out and placed his hand over hers. His touch matched his words, sincere and heartfelt.

"They gave what they had, which was so very little. They'd just enough food to keep from starving. Just enough shelter to keep safe from the cold and heat. Just enough clothing to remain protected. They risked it all to join us. Men, some with hair white as snow. Women, some so weary with work they walked doubled over. Nearly grown children, malnourished but ready to save their families and their futures."

"Poor people?" Veronica widened her eyes as though astonished. Secretly, she loved that Prince Durad allowed women and men of any station to join him. The prince clearly didn't share the duke's opinion on the roles of women.

He chuckled softly. "Yes, they were very poor. One, a girl not much younger than you, had a little babe of her own. She fought alongside us all, dressed like a man, never asking for a single thing. Strong, quick, lethal. One night, a terrible one during a chilling winter, she lost her child to what you would call an ague. Some passing Ottoman soldiers forced her and her family outside while they searched their home."

Veronica dropped her persona for a moment. She couldn't help herself. "What happened to her? To all the villagers who helped you?"

He squeezed her hand and gave her a sad, half smile. "Some

of them survived the war. We will always remember those we lost. And those we now protect. Every day. With every decision we make."

She couldn't help also asking, "What of *Kartal?* Does he exist? Did he really help you win the war?"

Prince Durad's eyes flicked once again to his bodyguard and then back to her. "Unfortunately, dear lady, *Kartal* is nothing more than a story. One brilliant enough to terrify even the roughest of the Ottoman soldiers."

That was rather a disappointment. She'd enjoyed those stories. *Kartal* and the blockade. *Kartal* and the three-armed soldier. *Kartal* and the ship that shot fire. She'd told them to her orphans. They loved how strong he was, how undefeatable in the face of any foe.

She pulled her hands away from the prince and stood, ready to leave. Like the Eidolon, he'd done something no one else could. He'd risked much to save many, and he'd succeeded.

Once again, she found herself asking if she might be wrong. Wrong about how alone the Eidolon was among the nobility. Yet it seemed awfully convenient to find all this out at once. First, the ladies at the Steam-Tech Expo, and now the prince. She found she didn't trust any of it. Nothing had ever been what it seemed, especially when it was too good to be true.

Veronica tossed her wrap on her bed and sneezed. Blast that old thing. She'd need to replace it soon, even if she had enjoyed watching other ladies' scorn for so many years.

Durad had been charming today, all white teeth and shiny, flashing brown eyes. His heart-twisting story made it ever harder to stop thinking about that note from Dr. Hoch.

She sat on her bed, pressing her fingers to her temples.

It is not safe.

What changed Dr. Hoch's mind? Was it the protestors? The article in *Lloyd's?* Growing support for Grillett?

Veronica removed the offending note from her reticule and laid it flat on her desk. A review of its contents revealed exactly the same message as earlier.

She held it above a candle until a corner lit, then tossed it into the glowing embers of her fireplace. No matter the meaning of Hoch's orders, several facts remained that couldn't be ignored.

One, Grillett's factories had increased capacity to accommodate new orders for the *Saint George.*

Two, Grillett hadn't hired any new workers. Grillett didn't advertise, he never had. Thus leaving the existing crews more shifts. Unless he'd found another source, another place that cared little enough for their young and helpless. It was possible.

Three, there would be casualties. As far as she'd observed, Grillett cared for the children just well enough. They had adequate energy to make it through each shift, fed with a clinical precision. Grillett wouldn't dare allow them to grow stronger to manage the increased work. He would simply increase the influx of children to cover the losses.

Fourth, the protestors, the article, the note from Dr. Hoch… it all meant little compared to the drumming of her heart as she thought about facts one through three. Yes, she'd have to be much more careful than usual. Change up her disguise. Approach from a different gate. Take the children at a different time.

From now on, she had no intention of involving Matilda. Perhaps not even Clank. No one, not even an automaton, would be hurt as a result of what she planned to do.

Chapter Twenty-One

Several hours later, after staring so hard at Dr. Hoch's maps of the factory district that she earned a painful headache, Veronica shoved aside the paperweight holding them down. She cringed when the object thudded heavily on the floor.

Bugger, someone would have heard that. Just then, a knock came at the door.

"Peanut, dearest, are you quite all right? I hope you're not doing anything drastic. I've been out making calls all morning, and I think we can easily make this wedding less torturous than you might imagine."

Alec sounded quite unlike his usual droll self. He was downright cheerful, in fact.

Veronica sighed and stowed away the maps. "You might as well come in and tell me about it, because I know you'll stand there chattering away about nonsense until I admit I'm here."

Her brother tossed the door open with a flourish and sat on her settee. He swung his walking stick from side to side without looking at her. "Do you at least like him a little? Will life with him be so miserable?"

Her thoughts, to her dismay, turned to Mr. Marcovic first. His dark, beautiful eyes. His strength. The moment he'd swept her up into his arms when she'd stumbled off the lift. His amusement, his mocking words.

Shoving those ridiculous ideas aside, she turned her thoughts to Prince Durad. To this afternoon. The security of her hand tucked in his elbow, how he'd ordered her a second ice after she'd polished off the first. She remembered the shine in his eyes as he spoke of Sombor. When he'd turned that beam on her, how she couldn't help getting a little caught up in his passion for his country.

Even if most of the conversation eventually steered toward dirigibles and Grillett's latest glass. The prince's enthusiasm over the potential protection of his soldiers and military was endearing enough to overshadow her hatred for the manufacturer of the product. In that particular moment, anyway.

"No, Alec. Life with Prince Durad would not be unpleasant. He seems to be a very amiable, caring, and generous person. He's never been less with me."

Alec leaned forward. "But?"

But she didn't plan on getting married. Perhaps not ever. Especially not while she had work to do. Anyway, a content marriage… Who'd ever heard of such a thing? Certainly not for a lady of her rank, who must choose among so few qualifying candidates. Marital bliss existed only in theory, in the minds of those men who proposed and women who accepted. Even if there was a chance for it with Prince Durad, how could she take it and leave her children? The thought that so many remained behind would surely haunt her.

"But I don't want this right now."

"You don't want him? Or marriage?"

She shrugged.

Alec tilted his head to the side and observed her for a moment. "I think you're right on one count. For some inexplicable reason, you really don't want to marry anyone. Whether it be some sort of twisted guilt at grabbing any chance of happiness—thanks to the life-long misery you wear as neatly as my cravat—or whether Prince Durad's failed to inspire you, I'm not sure."

She didn't reply.

"Either way, this entire thing could be much worse. You could be married off to one of Papá's wrinkled, old generals or a twit that cares for nothing but the track, like me. So, let's make the best of this, shall we?" Alec tapped his stick on the floor.

"I'm sure you already have a plan and care not for my feelings on the matter."

He grinned, looking much like the brother she'd always wished for.

"Did you hear about the protest today?" Alec waved a hand carelessly, knocking her dessert fork onto the floor. Supper was ever an adventure when the duke wasn't around. She'd endure this circus over the terrible, silent meals between the duke and herself in the past.

"Of all the important matters of our time to object to, why did it have to be that fascinating Eidolon chap? Just when I thought all conversation at the club would forever center on war, we finally got an interesting subject to discuss. And now we want to get rid of him?"

Veronica placed a delicate bite of smoked salmon in her mouth at that particular moment, so she'd be spared from responding. Alec's attitude toward the Eidolon had certainly changed. Of course, the gossip on the streets and through Hyde Park was nothing *but* the Eidolon. How that monster stole those poor orphans! And poor Lord Grillett! How could he be expected to defend all of those children against such a sneak thief? Bless my soul, the man should be caught and hanged straight away! And of course, when speaking of Lord Grillett, have you heard of his new glass ship?

She chewed slowly, trying to keep her temper in check. At least Alec wouldn't cart the Eidolon off to prison, even if his reasons were not what she could hope.

The duke entered and sat precisely straight in his chair. "The queen has assigned her top men to the job. She's formidable when opposed, you can count on it," he said. He picked up his fork and pointed it at Veronica. "Enough of this nonsense. Veronica, have you been spending time with Prince Durad?"

With the duke's sharp eyes focused directly on her, Veronica had to answer in a demure, polite manner, but it had not been a good day. She ached all over from the restraint she'd shown so far. Somehow, the ache felt worse than usual, and her thoughts entangled in briars.

"Yes. We attended the Steam-Tech Expo," she responded in the neutral tone she always used around him. The effort consumed her, so she could not even take a bite of food.

The duke nodded. "In light of these current events, I would like to move up the wedding. Say, to next week?"

Veronica could only stare at her plate. *Next week.*

Alec dropped his fork with a clatter. "Impossible."

The duke looked impatient. "You have unlimited resources. Make this happen, Alec."

Veronica wanted to open her mouth for once. Let her thoughts tumble out and entangle. *Next week. She couldn't possibly. No. Not yet.*

The duke spoke, his words cascading in a cultured and bitter flow. "Child, you are to obey me in this. There will be no discussion, no bargains. In spite of my best efforts, I've raised a simpleton who is only capable of speaking to children and cares nothing for anything important. I tire of the endless gossip about your inability to dress yourself or carry on the most basic of conversation. I will be rid of you once and for all. And for heaven's sake, for once in your life, you will do something worthy of the Richmond name. This is your final test, and for once, you will pass."

When Alec opened his mouth to speak again, the duke slashed his hand through the air. "I hear Lord Grillett needs more volunteer workers to help him with his increased orders. I could, perhaps, take him by the Bridges to enlist?"

There was no air. Breathe. *Breathe!* Veronica swallowed the words she longed to say, laced with anger and sadness.

No. She simply couldn't. She averted her eyes down to her lap in a show of submission. Now that her children at Bridges felt safe, secure, now that they felt *hope*, she could not let Grillett anywhere near them. He'd recognize them. It wouldn't take him long to link Veronica to the Eidolon. Everything she'd worked for would be gone.

She'd do whatever the duke said to avoid such a fate. Even if it meant marrying Prince Durad and losing her freedom. *Even if.*

How could she have thought, for even a moment, she could escape the duke's orders?

The duke tossed his napkin on the table. "Saturday next."

She nodded, not daring to speak.

And then he left.

A set of arms lightly pulled her to a standing position. Alec embraced her, his chin resting on her head. He felt surprisingly strong in the areas where she expected him to be soft. "Now there, sister. We'll figure a way to make this work. You'll still have a smashing wedding. And those little orphans of yours will still be safe as houses."

She wanted to laugh and cry all at once. While Alec encased her in a security she rarely felt, it was not nearly enough to soothe her worries, her fears. Still, she leaned her head into his chest.

"I don't have a choice," she whispered.

Alec patted her back and squeezed her tighter. "I don't know what kind of deals you've made with Papá, darling sister, but perhaps it's time you enlightened me."

Over Alec's shoulder, Veronica saw Matilda's head appear in the doorway. She motioned Veronica out of the room with a frantic wave of her hand. Her pale face then vanished, leaving Veronica even more unsettled.

She eased out of Alec's embrace and placed both hands on either side of his face. "Thank you, Alec," was all she said before she dropped a kiss on his cheek and left the room.

In the hallway, Matilda tossed Veronica's wrap around her shoulders and headed toward the barn, her shoes barely skimming the floor. Veronica kept pace close behind, her mind moving as fast as her feet. Where were they going? What else could go wrong this morbid evening?

Hale waited by the steam carriage, which already hummed and jittered, much like Matilda.

"For heaven's sake, Matilda. What's the matter?" Veronica couldn't help her sharp tone.

Matilda shooed her into the carriage. "It's Agnes, my lady. She's doing very poorly. She may not last the hour."

Veronica settled down on the bench, a pressure squeezing her chest and weighing her down until she felt as heavy as the bundle of coal Hale had just shoveled into the engine's firebox.

"What's the matter with her?" she asked quietly, even though she already knew. Agnes's mind, much like a refined metal, had been heated too hot and then beaten with a heavy hand until it broke apart. It was too young, too tender to see all she had seen, no matter that her body survived.

Matilda simply stared at Veronica, her eyes wet. Tears dripped down her cheeks each time she blinked, yet she made no sound. She'd been particularly fond of their little doe-eyed new girl.

Veronica spent the ride to Bridges with thoughts that circled and circled with no resolution in sight. *Marriage. One week. Bridges. Eidolon. The children. Funding.*

When they reached the block before Bridges, Veronica leapt out of the carriage and scurried down the alleyway. Matilda followed without her usual complaints about the undignified conditions of the route.

Mistress Phillips waited by the servants' door. She ushered them inside and then shut it tightly behind them, flipping the lock. Her stern face had little remaining color, save the red that ringed her eyes.

"Come, hurry. She's nearly gone."

She led them up the stairs to the recovery wing, worry hastening her usually deliberate, methodical movements. Inside the Peach Room, Agnes lay on a small cot, a pink blanket embroidered with daises covering her tiny frame. The skin on her face had stretched even further until her cheekbones jutted out in sharp relief, and her eyes were impossibly large. She appeared to have aged a hundred years in the week since Veronica had last seen her.

"She took a turn a few days ago. Vanished inside herself. Wouldn't talk, wouldn't eat. We can't get her to drink anything, either." Mistress Phillips blew her nose into a handkerchief. "Just decided she would have nothing more of this world. Going on to join the angels, she is."

Veronica took Agnes' hand, remembering how small and trusting it had felt the first time she met her. It now seemed so cold.

"Grab another blanket," she ordered.

Mistress Phillips started at her sharp tone.

"Please," Veronica added.

She stroked Agnes' cheek. Such a sweet light, such innocence. Veronica had borrowed her name. That shy smile when Agnes realized Veronica wanted *her* help, was asking for it. The delight in her eyes when she heard the ending of the Melilot's story.

And now, like Melilot's parents, she would soon lay in a cold grave, instead of celebrating the rebirth of a new life.

This, *this* fueled the machine that slaked the *ton*'s lust for steam-tech and the EurAsian wars. Surely, Grillett did the devil's own work, for how could suffering like this ever be justified? Just because England could not see the truth did not make it a lie.

Matilda now sobbed softly on the other side of the bed. Her eyes were so filled with tears she looked as though she could hardly see.

With one last sigh, Agnes fell still. At least God had eased her passing from this world, a small yet significant mercy. Veronica dropped one more kiss on her forehead and stood.

Mistress Phillips rushed back into the room, her arms laden with blankets. "My lady, this is all I could find."

When she saw Agnes, she dropped her bundle and cried out, the sound so heavy with agony, it seemed as though it, too, fell to the floor with a horrible thud. The bundle of cotton flew everywhere as her hands rose to cover her open mouth.

Veronica turned to face Mistress Phillips, placing a hand on her arm. "Mistress, you did all you could. This is *not* your fault. Do you understand me? You're not to blame yourself."

Mistress Phillips sobbed, unable to reply.

Veronica hesitated and then pulled the mistress in for a hug. The mistress stiffened and then hugged her back fiercely. After a moment, Veronica released her. Mistress Phillips's eyes were still filled with anguish, yet around the edges, they'd hardened, black as night.

"Go, my lady. Get them all. Bring them to us. I won't lose another one," she said in the same voice she used to order the children about once they felt comfortable enough to misbehave.

Veronica glanced at Agnes' corpse.

"Yes."

The word was harsh, flat.

The mistress nodded once, sharply. "I'll take care of arrangements here."

She turned to the bed, pulling the cheerful blanket over Agnes's lifeless face, her movements stiff and deliberate once again. She paused and bowed her head, her lips saying a silent prayer.

Chapter Twenty-Two

Steam streamed from the pipes jutting out from the factory buildings like a high-powered waterfall, shrouding the streets in a thick, white mist. Yellow spheres floated in the air, the gas lamps glowing with a sooty light. The factories hummed a tired song, churning hour after hour.

Emil crouched on the guard roof by gate thirteen just as the massive clock in the nearby tower rang three times, signaling a quarter to midnight. Rosseau waited nearby, their ship hovering above a nearby clock shop, cloaked in black sails and lights extinguished.

Watching the scene before him, the night of his and Durad's escape from the factory rose to the front of his mind. The bond they'd formed during those few, eternal hours created an unbreakable trust between them. Even though Emil had left for a time last year, Durad forgave him; it could not end otherwise. They'd risked it all for each other once, their lives were now forever intertwined. Even if Durad temporarily wore blinders, Emil would see them removed.

Emil turned to the gate in front of him. From what he'd gathered from his reconnaissance flights a few days ago, it proved to have very little activity. All the others creaked back and forth, ushering in and out steam carriages that pulled trailers, locked and bolted. For some reason, this gate sat quietly, with barely one shipment leaving every hour.

It made him wonder if the Eidolon had noticed the anomaly, but even if he had, would the Eidolon dare show, after the demonstrations and the bounty on this head?

Emil rubbed the scars on his wrist. No, the Eidolon wouldn't cease his "rescues." If the man dared enough to dress like a thief and wield a Tesla-ray, he probably wouldn't chafe at a little bad publicity. And if he did? He wouldn't be the first person to abandon the children.

Emil glanced down at his scars and lifted them up into the light. The raised skin circling his wrists brought back memories of another night as well. Slim, strong fingers rubbing his skin. A soft voice filled with conviction and righteous anger, and then compassion after hearing his story. A kiss that nearly happened the night of the masque.

He wanted to smack himself. What was he thinking? Veronica had the ability to plague his thoughts like, well, the plague.

His ludicrous line of thought nearly made him miss the opening of the gate for a large, ancient, traditional carriage, its wheels protesting on the cobbled streets. He lifted his scope, examining the vehicle. As it passed through, he caught a flutter of fabric on the far side. A cape.

He snapped his scope back together, slid it into his pocket, and leapt down from the roof. He'd been right, of course.

The Eidolon was here.

Veronica slipped her hands from her gloves and dusted them with the chalk she kept in a pouch on her belt. She knew she shouldn't be out in the Grave tonight, full of anger and grief. Not when all of London searched for her, her head marked with a price.

Yet here in quiet darkness, shrouded by the warm, thick steam, was where Veronica belonged. Even if she could see the futility in what she was about to do.

She couldn't *not* do it.

She would do what she always did; steal those children right from underneath Grillett's nose. And when she felt their trusting hands in hers, she would be at peace for a few moments.

Perhaps for the last time. With her marriage coming up in a few days, little enough time remained. She didn't bring Clank along, and though she felt the empty air by her side and her heart ached for the wonderful machine, she couldn't bear to put him at risk.

This gate had seemed like the safest bet. Little activity lately. When a lumbering carriage creaked by, it took no effort to slide underneath. After it passed through the gate and down the street, she rolled out and slipped into a side street. She adjusted her trousers and checked the charge on her Tesla-ray. Full.

The factory was just ahead. Time: five minutes to the hour. She jumped and swung up onto a nearby ladder, scaling it to the next story. She ran softly to another ladder, then climbed up again. She reached her desired position on the roof closest to the factory.

Veronica heard the flutter of fabric behind her. She whirled around, Tesla-ray raised.

Clank, eyes whirring, stood there. He raised his hands in surrender.

"What are you doing here? Oh, Clank," she whispered as she holstered her weapon. "It's too dangerous."

He placed a hand on her shoulder and lightly squeezed. God bless him, but she wanted to reach out and hug his metal frame.

"Who sent you?" she asked. "Matilda?"

Clank nodded and then pressed his hand over his heart. Even after she and Dr. Hoch asked Veronica not to continue her dangerous missions, Matilda knew Veronica couldn't simply stop, so she sent Clank to protect her mistress. Veronica patted Clank's glove, the one over his heart.

The clock chimed the hour. Veronica turned, waiting for the line of children to stream from the doors, with their hands clasped behind their backs and their chins wavering with weariness.

Nothing happened. The pipes continued to blanket the streets in steam. The factory continued to hum its ominous song. Veronica checked the clock again. Midnight. Time for shift change. The guards were never late. Something must be wrong.

She hurried down to the street level, palms damp once again. Clank followed. Had Grillett changed the shift times? Or had he lengthened them?

She flattened herself against the alley wall and peeked around the corner. Not a guard in sight. Odd, usually at least two patrolled the doors. A sharp pang pierced her chest and the sense that something had gone wrong multiplied until she felt sick.

Could this be some sort of trap? After all those nights of

surveillance and rescues, one thing was certain. Shift times never changed. Still, no children appeared.

Her gaze darted all around her. She heard nothing. Her inner sense told her a trap had sprung and her enemies were nearby.

Clank. She couldn't let him get hurt or taken. Veronica turned and whispered, "I'll distract the guards when they get here. You leave and return back to Matilda as soon as it's safe. Do you understand?"

His head turned from side to side, as though he worried. As though he wanted to reject her command. He finally met her eyes, his whirring faster than she'd ever seen, and he nodded.

A distraction. She didn't have her fogger to take out the lamps. What did she have?

Ah, yes. Something much more powerful. She lifted her Tesla-ray and pressed the trigger. The beam held for several moments on the lamp until she heard a small pop and the shatter of glass. She waited until her eyes adjusted to the milky darkness and crept forward.

Rough hands grabbed her shoulders. She nearly panicked but sagged to the ground just in time, forcing her assailants to drop her. She rolled, kicking as she did so, and then leapt up to her feet, her Tesla-ray still in hand. Several more men waited for her. She swept the beam of her gun in an arc. One, two, three dropped to the ground, stunned.

She heard the steel slicing through the air before it hit her shoulder. She rolled to the side, drawing her sword. A tall, thin man wearing the Enforcer's red cape came at her again. She blocked him this time and dodged to the right. She brought her Tesla-ray up and shot him. When he fell, another Enforcer took his place. This one wielded two shorter swords.

She needed Clank, but she'd been right to order him to stay in place until it was safe. This was a battle she couldn't win, even with his help.

Veronica calculated as both blades advanced and spun at the last minute, knocking them aside. The Enforcer spun and advanced again. She blocked one, then the other blow, but she couldn't hold him off forever. She was outmatched.

Veronica scanned the area for an escape, but since she'd taken out the lampposts, she couldn't see. Her Tesla-ray didn't have much charge left.

When the Enforcer swung at her again, she reached for her Smith & Wesson pistol. She pulled the trigger, catching him in the shoulder. He dropped one sword and came at her with the other. She spun and kicked him in the face. He fell.

Footsteps, shouting. There were more people coming, but how many? *Run, Veronica.* She had to get out of here.

She turned, plowing straight into steel armor. A hand knocked her Tesla-ray to the ground while another encased her arm in a tight grip. Veronica lashed upward with her now free hand, but before she could connect with the man's face, he spun her around and forced to her knees. Burning, she smelled fire. The man yanked off her mask, pulling out a clump of hair as he did so. She brought up her free hand to hide her face while craning around to see who held her.

Two lights appeared in front of her, illuminating the courtyard. A voice, damaged and deep, yelled with triumph. Others answered, echoing.

"All hail the 'Angel!' "

Veronica closed her eyes against that voice. She didn't need to see his face to know who it was. A point pressed against the side of her head, her Tesla-ray.

"I've always wanted one of these," Blackthorne said, his voice as reasonable and polite as it was the night of the engagement ball. "My compliments to the Eidolon for such a fine gift."

She focused on her breathing. In. Out. Did she have any advantage? Leverage? Could she escape from his hold? No. He had her firmly.

He leaned forward, his warm breath on her ear, "They cannot see you are but a woman, Lady Veronica, or they would be yelling for more than blood."

Blackthorne tightened his already firm grip on Veronica.

"If you will excuse me, my fine gentlemen, while *Angel* here and I have a word in private about his eternal soul."

Blackthorne yanked Veronica to her feet amidst shouts and cheers. They reverberated through her chest, one after another, rising like a tide until she drowned in the noise.

She forced down her panic. She was the Eidolon, for heaven's sake. There must be some way out of this. She refused to believe otherwise.

At least she couldn't see Clank. He must be safe, thank heavens.

Blackthorne held her close to his chest. He smelled of oil and sweat, as he dragged her along the street toward a waiting carriage. She thrust her elbow into his stomach, but he laughed and squeezed the trigger on the Tesla-ray. Her body tensed, stiffened. She tried to move but couldn't.

Blackness rose in her mind, but she fought it, years of experience lending her strength. She pushed at the edges until her vision cleared. If she passed out, Blackthorne would have complete control over her. The thought made her frantically will her body to move, from her fingers to her toes. Nothing happened.

Blackthorne tossed her onto a seat inside the carriage and sat down opposite her. The carriage lurched forward, slamming her into Blackthorne. He laughed again and tossed her back onto the seat. Without any way to brace herself, she collected bruises at every bump and turn, each one making her want to rage at her helplessness.

The man hummed to himself, jaunty tunes she didn't recognize. Most likely with lyrics she didn't want to know. His cheerfulness darkened her rage even further until she could barely breathe.

It couldn't have been more than a few blocks before the carriage stopped abruptly, throwing her off the seat again. She landed face down in the layer of dirt and grease covering the floor.

Blackthorne spit on the ground and then hoisted her up by her armpits and slung her over his shoulder. "Not passed out yet, my lady?" He clucked. "Pity. You won't like this part."

Chapter Twenty-Three

Emil saw the ambush. Heard the triumphant shouts. The man with the scarred face took the Eidolon, stunned him, and tossed him into a carriage.

He rubbed his wrists, wondering why they'd begun itching so much lately. Must be the climate. Curse this city.

Emil padded quickly across the roof, following the carriage's progress. Down a ladder, to another roof, so he didn't lose sight of it. After several blocks, the carriage stopped. The scarred man leapt down, humming a bawdy tune. He reached back inside and swung the Eidolon out and over his shoulder. He entered a nameless building, no sign, no markings. It was large, ten stories, like the rest of the buildings in the district.

Good riddance to the Eidolon, that ridiculous fop with an even more ridiculous name. This wasn't Emil's battle. He'd fought enough for several lifetimes. Now wasn't the time to get involved, with Sombor's future basically in his hands. He couldn't afford to risk that. What if he got caught?

Emil almost laughed at the absurdity of this line of thought. He wouldn't get caught. The last time he did… well, it hadn't happened again. The question remained though; did he want to help?

For the next several minutes, he couldn't escape the memories that assaulted him. His days in the factories, when he helped no one, spent all his energy on his own survival.

Aman Tanrım. It would not do, to leave the misguided Eidolon in the hands of that Enforcer.

Veronica did the only thing she could do, breathe in and out. She tried to organize her frantic thoughts into a plan of escape. She told herself she'd find a way out of this. After living nightmare after nightmare in the duke's home, facing demons of any sort was familiar territory.

Blackthorne took her through a doorway into a building. She could see nothing but the gray floor below until she was flipped face-up onto a gurney.

While he strapped her down, buckling thick leather across her chest and legs, Blackthorne said, "Thanks to you, this place is now empty. We don't have enough brats coming in to replace the ones you stole, but that also means you get an entire wing to yourself, my lady. First class accommodations. Top notch." He chuckled to himself again as he pushed the gurney forward.

Veronica stared up at dusty gas lamps hanging from the ceiling as she passed down the hallway. Large. Empty. This must be an orphanage. Brilliant. No one would think to look for her here, not that anyone *would* look.

Blackthorne shoved the gurney into a large room at the very end of the hallway. There were no windows. No one could see what Blackthorne would do to her. She didn't think he would kill her right away, since he'd had plenty of opportunity to do so. He might burn her, the most poetic type of revenge.

"You'll pardon me, my lady, while I summon the doctor." He whistled to himself as he left, shutting the door behind him. A lock clicked.

Veronica's stomach coiled. Doctor? Would he cut into her?

No. You'll go mad that way. Focus, Veronica.

She began with her hands. Stiffen, relax, stiffen, relax. Each finger, one at a time, until pinpricks jittered through her hand. Second after agonizing second, she focused until she had full movement of her hands.

Next, her feet. *Focus. Think of sweet, little Suzie. She needs you.*

Footsteps. Voices. The door swung open.

"Better hit her with that ray gun of yours again just to be sure. I loathe it when they scream." The new voice was cultured and calm.

Click. A hum. The jolt of the Tesla-ray hitting her again. She wanted so desperately to cry out but could not. Her confidence in her own strength vanished, crushed like a brittle fall leaf. She'd lost the little movement she had, and now her time was up. The doctor, whoever he was, could do what he wished to her and she would be powerless to stop him. The same despair she felt in the gardens before she first met Dr. Hoch threatened to steal whatever presence of mind still remained.

She had no more options. No more time.

Her training had failed her. The Eidolon had failed her. Veronica wished she could escape inside her mind, like she'd wanted to as a child. Something had always held her back; something bright and hopeful. Now, she wished for a way to welcome the darkness. She wished for any way out of out this terrible reality.

A face came into view. A medical mask covered his mouth. Gray eyes appraised her quickly and then flicked away.

"The Eidolon is a girl?" he asked quietly.

Blackthorne's voice, "Does it bother you?"

The man shrugged. "She appears sturdy enough. Knife," he ordered.

The sound of metal slapping into the man's palm. Veronica wished to heaven she could close her eyes, clasp her hands over her ears, do something, *anything*. This time, when the man's hand moved downward, she prayed for the blackness to overtake her.

In the end, she saw it all.

Chapter Twenty-Four

Emil scanned the area; no guards at any of the doors, none on the street. He secured his mask and climbed down. The shadows wrapped so securely around the building, he needed only to quiet his footsteps to completely disappear. He quickly dismissed the idea of entering through the front door. He padded down the alley and around to the back.

He tried the knob to the servants' door. Locked. He paused, listening. It was strangely quiet. While the buildings nearby hummed and puffed steam through the vent pipes, this one stood silent. After several moments of waiting, Emil heard voices through the walls, echoing as if in a large space.

He wasn't sure what might be happening to the Eidolon, but Emil expected the Eidolon to put up a fight. Thought he'd hear shouting, sounds of a scuffle. Certainly not two voices conversing as though strolling through Hyde Park. It didn't feel right. Emil's gut told him something was horribly wrong. He grabbed his whip from his belt and cracked it through the nearest open window. He leapt through and took off in a run toward the voices.

Emil heard a shout from the room at the end of the hall. He drew his rapier and charged forward, whip in his other hand.

The door burst open and light shot through. Emil rolled, the beam cutting through the edge of his cape. The beam followed his movements as he dodged, ducked, and rolled until it abruptly ceased.

Emil stood just outside the door. He waited long moments before peeking around it into the room. A lone gurney sat motionless with the Eidolon strapped in. Blood dripped from the nearest side onto the floor.

A flutter of movement and the door swung violently toward him. He leapt to the side and lashed out with his whip. A man yelped, a high-pitched noise. Emil moved forward, lashing out again and again. He caught the man's foot and dragged him forward. Without ceremony, he swung his fist into the man's head, knocking him out. As he kicked him off to the side, he glimpsed the man's face.

Ugly. From Almack's. Grillett's man. Emil kicked him again for good measure.

"I will leave peacefully. Violence is unnecessary." A voice came from behind the gurney.

Emil glanced up. A man in white doctor's robes and a facemask stood with his hands up in the air. His manner appeared calm, amused. On a table beside him lay a saw, red with blood, and what looked to be a mound of flesh.

Emil rushed over to the gurney and leaned forward, checking for breath. "What have you done to this man?" he demanded.

The doctor chuckled.

Emil looked down again, this time up to the Eidolon's face. Long hair spilled out, obscuring the features. His stomach tightened painfully. A woman? He brushed the hair gently back from her face. The shock of seeing familiar, terrified eyes jolted him. His breath came in great gasps. He cursed. Clasped her face in his hands.

"I am here, *sultanim*. Everything will be okay. I'll get you out."

He should've figured this out earlier. He was blind. A complete idiot. A dozen clues appeared in front of him, signs he hadn't seen, recognized. He whispered her name over and over as he released her straps. He reached down to help but she didn't move.

Something was wrong.

He could tell she saw everything, but why did she not move? Why did she not answer him? Her eyes flicked toward the scarred man. He glanced over. Scar-face still lay there unconscious, the Tesla-ray clasped in his hand.

The Tesla-ray. Of course. She'd been stunned. He moved to pick Veronica up, but her eyes registered pain. He ran his hands lightly down her side until he saw her hand.

By all the gods, the flesh was so mangled he couldn't make

sense of what he was seeing. He'd never witnessed such a sight, not in all his years of war. The hand had been removed entirely, leaving a mess of tissue that bled in a steady stream.

He raised his gaze instantly to the doctor and growled, "What did you do?"

The man removed his mask and smiled. He might mean to look reassuring, professional, an expression he might use when explaining a standard procedure to a nervous patient.

Emil drew his sword.

The doctor shrugged. "She was to be the first of her kind. It was for science, you understand."

Emil roared. "This is torture! This is—"

The doctor raised his arm, a long, wicked knife in his hand.

The long cattail end of a whip came out of nowhere, knocking the blade out of the doctor's hand. Emil stepped to the side and turned, just as the whip cracked again, this time wrapping around the man's neck and yanking him to the ground.

A figure, dressed in a gentleman's town coat with hat and mask, stepped forward and twisted the doctor's neck, causing a loud crack. The assailant then swung his foot back and kicked the doctor clear to the other side of the room, a good twenty feet.

Emil stepped forward, placing his body in between the assailant and Veronica. Waiting, he watched to see what the man would do.

The man dropped to his knee, head bowed, hand over his heart. He said nothing, simply remained submissive. After a moment, he raised his head and removed his hat.

Emil drew his sword. This was not a man… it was a machine. It was made of metal and gears. Its eyes spun, faster and faster. It pointed at Veronica and then to itself, over and over.

Emil glanced at Veronica. Her eyes seemed lighter, brighter in color as the machine frantically gestured at her. He certainly couldn't ask her about the machine, whether or not it posed them any harm.

He turned. He could ask *it*, though.

"Do you serve the Lady Veronica?"

The thing nodded vigorously, as it patted its chest where a heart would normally be.

At least it was on their side, whatever it was. It moved with a machine's precision, but Emil would swear the way it communicated was nearly human. As though it cared for its master.

Emil turned back toward Ugly, sword still in hand. Clank had taken care of him already, in a similar way as the doctor. Emil only wished the thing had gotten here earlier.

Emil grabbed a long length of cloth from the surgical table and wrapped it tightly over Veronica's wound and around her wrist. He then lifted her into his arms. The machine followed him, completely silent. They left the same way Emil came in. He didn't know what to say to Veronica, though his mind continued to propose ideas. Thoughts of comfort? Apology? Sympathy? Nothing felt right.

He knew she had secrets, he'd learned that at the masque. But this? Dressing as a man and fighting Grillett's thugs? Rescuing street rats she clearly cared for?

Emil stumbled. A member of the most powerful gentry in the world, saving children of uncertain parentage. Not only that, *no one knew*. She didn't claim credit, of course. No one among her set would care. She would've had no one to confide in. Instead, ridiculed by all, Veronica had quietly endured it in order to deflect suspicion and do what she believed in.

Veronica's eyes blinked and her fingers brushed his shoulder. He glanced down at her. She seemed to be trying to tell him something, but the stun from the Tesla-ray hadn't worn off yet. He couldn't take her home. He needed to get her back to his ship. Find help.

He headed toward the entrance to the district. As he merged with one shadow and then another, dodging the street guard, once again, his thoughts wandered back to the masque. His first society event and he'd danced with a woman who donned a mask to save children from the Grave.

He glanced down at Veronica. Everything he dreamed of in a woman but never thought existed in all the world he'd seen and traveled—passion, fire, a drive to make a difference—lay in his arms.

Lay *bleeding* in his arms, broken at the altar of greed and cruelty. He'd been sacrificed on that altar long ago. *Aman Tanrım*, he'd do everything he could to make this right.

The gate opened and he slipped through. The alarm hadn't yet been raised. Hopefully, Ugly and the deranged doctor wouldn't be discovered for a while. Emil slipped down the remaining streets to the spot where Rosseau waited.

His friend eyed the bundle in Emil's arms, then stared at the machine that had followed Emil from the workhouse.

"A stretcher please, Rosseau?" Emil asked.

Rosseau scrambled up the ladder on the side of the building until he reached the top where the airship lay in wait. It took several long minutes for him to return, while Emil kept shifting Veronica's weight, hoping to somehow make her comfortable. After they managed to strap her onto the stretcher, Emil covered her in a light blanket. He didn't want the crew knowing he brought a woman aboard, much less the Eidolon.

They got her aboard. The machine man followed, concealed once again in a mask and hat. Emil carried her to his cabin. Rosseau followed, closing the door behind him. He helped transfer Veronica to Emil's bed.

"She is paralyzed?" Rosseau asked.

Emil nodded. "Some type of stunning ray."

"A surgeon must be fetched, *capitan*. This is beyond the basic stiches I perform for you."

"I trust no one in this city," Emil said as he eased off Veronica's shoes and adjusted her into a position that he thought might be the least uncomfortable.

He examined her left hand more closely. A piece of metal jutted out from the stump. The pain must be excruciating. What purpose the metal served, he couldn't tell. He didn't dare touch it for fear of doing further damage.

Veronica tapped her good hand on the bed. When she saw she had Emil's attention, Veronica moved her lips, but the sound hovered too quietly on the air.

Emil leaned forward, hoping to catch the sound before it vanished.

"Hoch." The words emerged in a stream so faint, he nearly missed it.

"That loony professor?" Emil shook his head.

Dr. Hoch wasn't a medical doctor. What would she want with him? Hoch had been all over the place at the Expo, muttering to himself, avoiding any type of eye contact. Rather like those factory kids who became institutionalized. Been too long at the same routine, the same deprivations, same tortures. Their minds snapped and broke into pieces, scattered on a foul wind. Hoch appeared to be a grown version of them.

She blinked several times, then whispered, "Fake."

"Fake? Dr. Hoch is a fake?" Emil searched her face for clues, but her deep blue eyes couldn't speak except to register her pain. Fake at what? Emil tugged at his scarf. He needed to think. Faster.

Her brows wrinkled. She took a breath and exhaled, "Like me."

"You? Ah, you mean he was faking it? The loony bit?" Emil asked.

Her chin dipped down and then up very slightly in what must have been a nod.

Of all the idiots she'd met, he must seem the worst of the lot. Of course, if Veronica could convince the world of her insanity, so could Dr. Hoch. Like her, he played an excellent part. Emil cursed his stupidity for the second time tonight. They might have been in on this together from the start. Dr. Hoch with his genius in mechanics, maybe the source of the Tesla-ray? And her with unlimited means and unmatched intelligence.

The machine stood in the corner all the while. Eyes spinning fast enough to make Emil dizzy. When he heard Dr. Hoch's name, he stepped forward and pointed to himself, jabbing his chest.

"You can fetch Dr. Hoch?" Emil asked.

It nodded and then simply vanished, moving faster than anything Emil had ever seen. He thought it might've gone through a window, but he couldn't be sure. He blinked, and then the thing was gone. Thank goodness the machine was on their side.

"I'll fetch some water," Rosseau said. He bowed and then left.

Emil looked about the room. Did he have anything to give Veronica for the pain that she must be feeling by now? His eyes rested on Rosseau's medical bag. He opened it. Powders of all sorts. Ah, opium. That would do the trick. He grabbed the nearby teakettle. Good! The sides were warm to the touch. He poured some into a cup and mixed the opium powder with it.

He gathered clean bandages and a washbasin and knelt by the bed. Emil looked into Veronica's eyes. They stared back unflinchingly. "I am going to clean the wound and bind it, but first, I would like to give you something for the pain."

She appeared to consider this for a moment, then her eyes clouded over and lines appeared on her forehead. Her lips moved, but no sound emerged.

She must be out of her mind with suffering. Emil cleaned his hands and tested the liquid. Not too hot. He trickled it into a syringe. He hated to inject it straight into her, but anything else would take too long. He couldn't risk the injured arm, so he found a vein and pumped the opium into her other one. After a few moments, her eyelids drooped shut.

He began cleaning and wrapping her wound, glancing up at her face every few moments to make sure she rested. Emil wondered at his impulse to gather Veronica in his arms, press her to him and listen for her heartbeat. He couldn't lose Veronica now that he'd just found her.

He prayed to God to send Dr. Hoch soon.

Chapter Twenty-Five

"I should've brought more tools," Dr. Hoch muttered. "This is not a simple surgery." He bound his white hair in a leather tie and scrubbed his hands.

"What do you need? I will have it fetched for you," Emil said.

Dr. Hoch had indeed arrived quickly, but Emil worried at the blood continuing to stain the bandages on Veronica's hand.

"This apparatus my deranged colleague shoved into her without thought, I cannot remove it. The good news is that it will stabilize the new hand that *I* will attach. One of my own design."

Dr. Hoch peeled back the bandage. "See, here, where the metal extends up into the arm. He must have been re-enforcing her bone structure. Such a procedure should be done so much more carefully, with greater precision."

Rosseau looked, horror plain on his large features. "Has such a thing been done before?"

Dr. Hoch shook his head. "There's been much discussion about the possibility, but it's never been attempted. I dare not remove the metal now. It might trigger further bleeding. It's small enough that she can heal around it. I have to get started. *Now.*"

"Of course. Do what you must." Emil's chest tightened.

He could have prevented this, could have saved her this pain, if only he'd been quicker. Instead, he'd taken his time, immersed in memories. He muttered curse after curse in Turkish.

"I see Clank is still in one piece," Dr. Hoch said as he began sterilizing his tools.

"Clank?" Emil asked.

Dr. Hoch pointed at the machine man. "An automaton. My invention. Brilliant one, too."

"What's an automaton?"

"A machine made to move and look like a man. A bodyguard for the Eidolon. She has become quite attached to him. And, oddly enough, he to her." Dr. Hoch smiled like a proud parent.

Emil studied Clank. The automaton had removed its hat and mask. It had a normal, human-sized nose. Metal lips. Gears for eyes. Its face was oval, chin more strong than aquiline. The shoulders spread wide, narrow waist, thin legs. It stood a few inches under six feet, a bit taller than Veronica.

"How can he act so human?" Emil asked.

"He watches. Imitates. He's designed to act like one of us. He's capable of learning but not of disobeying orders. Unless his master becomes incapacitated," Dr. Hoch replied, his tone cheerful.

"Fascinating," Emil muttered.

The doctor set out his tools. They looked sharp and scary, every single one of them.

Emil asked, "She won't wake, will she? Should I administer more opium?"

Dr. Hoch shook his head. "Only if she begins to stir. We don't want to overdose her. I have a tisane that you can give her as soon as she wakes that will ease her pain."

Emil laid a palm against Veronica's cheek. She didn't move. Her skin felt warm and soft, in spite of her pallor. While Dr. Hoch worked, Emil kept his eyes on Veronica's. She had to survive. *He* did, after all. Surviving was never the easiest option, but she wouldn't give up easily. Emil would be there to make sure she had the best chance of doing so. There wasn't another woman like her in the world, and he would not let her go.

Unless… Durad's easy grin rose in his mind. As he pondered his options, his heart twisted over and over, wrung out like a wet sponge.

Maybe, before he handed her over to Durad, Emil would share just a few moments with the one woman in the world for him.

Chapter Twenty-Six

The instant Veronica awoke, memories of Blackthorne, the doctor, and Mr. Marcovic flooded her mind with a force nearly painful. Her eyes flew open, and she looked at her left arm. It was covered in a sparkling white bandage and rested on a silk pillow. Someone had put a glove on her hand. Hadn't that terrible doctor removed her hand? Had she dreamed that? She tried flexing her fingers.

White, blinding pain hit her. Her entire body convulsed. She couldn't think beyond what she felt. Blackness threatened, and she tried to embrace it.

A cup pressed to her lips. "Drink. It will help." Mr. Marcovic said in his deep, softly accented voice.

Veronica willed her body still and took a few sips of the drink he offered. The liquid was smooth and warm, but even swallowing hurt.

"It will take but a few moments."

A cloth, warm and smelling of rose water, pressed against her cheek. She shut her eyes, the dim light in the room too bright for her senses. The numbing from the Tesla-ray had certainly worn off. She could feel everything. The slippery smooth sheets, the cold, damp air on her face. Her left arm burned as though a giant splinter wormed its way up to her elbow. She wanted to yank it out, to see if it would ease the pain, yet feared removing the glove would make her nightmare reality.

For the next few minutes, she focused on the simple task of drawing air into her lungs and expelling it. She winced with even that small movement, the upward and downward motion of her chest. Mr. Marcovic muttered something to himself in Turkish. She didn't understand the words, yet she recognized the tone as bitter, angry even.

In the next instant, a warmth flooded her senses and the pain lifted, evaporating as though it might have only been an illusion. She opened her eyes and immediately shifted to a sitting position, using her right arm as leverage.

Mr. Marcovic moved off the bed quickly; one moment he was there with his scented cloth, the next, he was across the room. Oddly, Veronica had the presence of mind to be impressed by his quick reflexes.

"The tisane worked?" he asked.

She nodded, feeling a smile nearly break her face in half. *Blessed relief.* "Will it last?"

He shrugged and held up a small leather pouch. She wanted to snatch it from him. The thought of enduring that pain again made her more than a little mental.

"I don't know, but Dr. Hoch left plenty. How's your hand?" He asked quietly, nodding at the blanket.

The manner in which he stood, so stiffly, nearly made her wonder if he blamed himself for what lie underneath.

That would never be true. Even now, moments after awakening, she knew she owed him her life.

Veronica steeled herself and lifted the sheet. Her gloved hand lay still, an accessory but not part of her. She flexed her fingers. They moved, awkward and stiff. She tried again, this time using a bit more force. Her glove tore at the seams and fell away.

For several moments, she couldn't speak. Perhaps this was a dream. The one of Blackthorne had certainly felt real. She glanced up at her surroundings. Wooden desk. Large canvas map. Sextant. Globe. Small dining table. Several hanging brass lamps. Curios, like tribal masks, rolled papyrus, and satchels of spices. She must be in an airship.

Mr. Marcovic could be an apparition. She remembered the flash of his sword, how he'd knocked down Blackthorne with an efficiency she'd never seen before. She remembered how he'd carried her, smelling of saffron, and his strong arms erasing her terror at being utterly helpless.

And Clank. He killed the doctor. She glanced around the room frantically.

"Where's Clank?"

"He is fine. Dr. Hoch sent him back to your companion," Mr. Marcovic said.

He approached her with slow, deliberate steps. He must see the fear in her face. What did he think of this misshapen, inhuman contraption she now wore? What would Durad think? The duke? Alec? Though the metallic joints matched the length of her fingers, flexing and moving at her command, they felt awkward and stiff. Unnatural. Ugly.

She trembled as Mr. Marcovic knelt beside her. He spoke her name softly, his accented voice familiar and calming.

"My lady—"

"What happened to my hand? Is this Dr. Hoch's work?"

She lifted it from the pillow, barren, now that she'd torn through the glove. She didn't really want to know what he would say to her. The words would be falsely comforting or brutally honest. Either way held little appeal.

Mr. Marcovic nodded, the scarf around his face fluttering. His black eyes stared into hers, soft and sad, as if trying to apologize for whichever path he would've taken.

"That other doctor," Emil spat the word, "did not leave anything whole enough to save. Dr. Hoch preserved your arm, and then, by some miracle, produced this hand and attached it to your nervous system. Is it… do you have control over it?"

Dr. Hoch had done that for her? He saved her arm, and then restored function with this hand. The thought of being without a hand *did* seem infinitely worse… even if it were not the prettiest thing she'd ever seen. But then, Veronica was used to looking less than her best.

She glanced down at the glove. With a proper leather one, the hand could be hidden. She should feel grateful, yet some part of her wanted to grab her sword and test out the strength of this new hand on Lord Grillett and his blasted golden armor. Or on the duke. They were both to blame, after all. She'd always wondered at the need for a woman to do the work of a man, and now she had paid the price to do so. It seemed a little enough blow to her vanity, yet her heart twisted and ached.

Veronica dragged her new finger along the pillow, tearing a clean rift. She had to merely think of doing so and her hand responded, but the action caused a little jolt of pain up her arm, stopping at her elbow. She felt a muscle in her face twitch.

Mr. Marcovic noticed. He seized her arm with gentle hands and examined it. "What? What happened?"

"I'm not sure. I can move it, but…" She didn't want to continue. She really shouldn't complain.

"He worked without ceasing, you know. All night. He saved your life, I am certain of it." Mr. Marcovic said. "I would have never known the man had so much skill about him. His charade had me completely fooled."

Veronica looked away from her hand, down at the sheets. "He's quite brilliant, always has been. When Grillett appeared on the scene and wanted Dr. Hoch to design war ships, he refused. Grillett built his factories anyway. Dr. Hoch believes the fate of the children to be his fault."

Mr. Marcovic muttered in Turkish again. She recognized a few of the words from his prior bitter rant.

After a moment, Veronica continued, "Of course, it was not entirely an excuse. He talks to himself and forgets things a lot. He's been disappearing often for a while now. When I saw him at the Expo, it'd been nearly six months since our last visit. I'm surprised he came, and even more surprised by his success with this." She lifted her hand and the pain sharpened, steel on bone. Hopefully, it would ease over time. "Where is he now?"

Mr. Marcovic stood, the distance between them leaving the air feeling cold and empty. "Dr. Hoch is resting in my first mate's cabin. Rosseau, you may remember him. He was here last night."

She thought back, cringing at the memory of the previous evening. "The fellow with the black mustache? French accent?"

He nodded and then picked up her top hat, turning it over in his hands. He glanced up and met her gaze, the question in his black eyes making it impossible for her to look away.

"My Lady Veronica, Dr. Hoch is not the only master of deceit among us."

Panic, sharp and sudden, made her sick. He knew her secret. In the mess of what had happened, she'd nearly forgotten the implications. Who else knew?

"You mustn't tell anyone. You won't, will you? Please."

She let herself beg, laid herself open and raw for his inspection. She'd come all this way. She'd survived. She couldn't lose everything now.

Mr. Marcovic leaned forward and adjusted her covers where they had fallen away, his eyes unreadable, but his voice soft. "*Aman Tanrım*, I will not tell. I have to admit, though, I thought the Eidolon a man, just like the rest of the masses."

Veronica relaxed a little. For some reason, she trusted the man. He seemed capable enough of keeping a secret. One had only to wonder at what lay behind the mask he never removed. She smiled and scoffed at his words.

"A man could not do what I have done."

He laughed, his scarf fluttering high enough that she nearly saw the lower half of his face. She watched it, hoping it might reveal a glimpse of something, anything. Yes, he seemed to keep secrets, and now he would keep hers.

"Indeed," he said.

"Did you see me fight?" she asked.

The thought made her oddly proud, yet self-conscious at the same time. She'd seen *him* take out Blackthorne with seemingly little effort. She must seem a child, playing at soldier. His opinion mattered to her now, after all that he had done for her.

He nodded, his scarf lifting, perhaps hiding a smile. "I would not want to face you in a fight."

Veronica couldn't determine if he spoke seriously. Between them, there would be no contest. She was lucky indeed she'd never met the likes of him in the Grave. He'd brought Blackthorne to his knees and then knocked him clean out with one hit.

"How did you happen to be there in time to save me?"

"I was at the same gate and followed you. I did not realize who you were until I found you in that room in the empty orphanage. No one, save Rosseau and I, knows what passenger we carry aboard this ship."

"You can trust him?"

Mr. Marcovic nodded and turned to leave. "You should rest, my lady Eidolon," he said, his low voice vibrating through her.

She felt her eyelids droop and wondered at the power he had to influence her. Saffron and a crisp, accented voice now made her feel safe. Secure.

He paused at the door. "Does anyone besides the men I dispatched at the orphanage know who you are?"

She thought back to Blackthorne's threats. *If they knew you to be a lady, they would be yelling for more than blood.* "Matilda knows. Other than that, I don't believe so."

He nodded again. "You are safe here, then. No one will harm you while you're under my protection."

Protect her? The idea seemed strange. That was *Veronica's* job, after all. To protect others. To protect Claire and Suzie and all of the other children. She felt a warmth begin to grow in her chest that she was helpless to stop. Warmth in places that had been cold for so long, frosted over by the duke.

Before he could turn the knob, she called, "Wait! The duke. I must write to him. Matilda can only plead a headache for me for so long before he become suspicious."

Mr. Marcovic's brows furrowed. "What difference would one night make? You have slept the day away before, after your nights as the Eidolon."

"Yesterday, at supper, the duke ordered me to move the wedding up to Saturday next. He's worried about the protests, about how London must look to an outsider like Prince Durad." *And about me. How fickle I am. And that I might find a way out of this wedding, which I very well planned to do. Now that I have this metal claw attached to my skin, I might not need any further plans.*

The idea created complex thoughts inside her. After all, she liked the prince but hated that the duke was forcing her to marry him and leave England and the Eidolon's work behind.

"Saturday next? Does he not care about Durad's opinion on the matter?" Mr. Marcovic turned and crossed the room. The man seemed to have two states, supremely still or supremely restless.

"The duke always gets his way. He will talk the queen into it, and then there will be no going back. She simply adores him."

"You cannot go through with it," he said with what sounded like a frown.

Veronica crushed her sheets in her good hand. "What do you

mean? He's your prince, after all. Does he not want to marry me? I thought he didn't find me too repulsive."

Or perhaps he would, now that she wasn't whole. Of course, no one saw her as a desirable woman anyway. Her face was too plain, her figure too strong, and she met most men at their eye level.

"Of course he does not find you repulsive! He likes you, in spite of your ridiculous persona. Durad has always had a talent for looking beneath the surface." Mr. Marcovic tapped his foot. "I thought it might not be what *you* wanted."

His words caused her to miss a breath. Why wouldn't she want to marry Durad?

"Is there something about His Highness I don't know? Is he a rake? A thief?"

Mr. Marcovic's voice lowered. "Be careful what you say about my friend."

She held up a hand, a little frightened of the way he stalked across the room without a sound. "I meant no offense. I'm simply asking, if he is all you say, why should I not want to marry him?"

He covered the distance to the bed in a few strides and sat, careful not to jostle her. He planted an arm on either side of her, leaning in until she swore she could hear his heartbeat. In her mind, it thumped in time with hers, strong and quick. Up close, his eyes were as dark as a moonless sky. She wondered if they'd ever been light.

When he spoke, his words were sure and confident, flowing through her senses into her heart. "Why not?" he laughed, short and quick. "Because you do not ever do what you're told. Because you have always wanted more, my lady, and that, *that* has been your problem. You have wondered why you could not fall in line behind Lady Ambrose, like the rest of the witless debutants. You have thought your brain wired differently and maybe even wrong."

"I never *felt* wrong," she whispered.

"You took risks that made you wonder at your sanity, but still, something compelled you onward. The feeling of finally being free to be yourself. *That* is why you put on this costume. *That* is why marriage to Durad would drive you insane. You not only want more, you *need* more."

She felt her mouth gape open. His insight was so utterly

correct, tears welled up in her eyes. No other man had seen beyond her moldy dresses and idiotic remarks. Indeed, Veronica thought no male capable of such perceptions. Mr. Marcovic surely harbored darkness of his own, one had only to listen to him speak and watch him fight. Was that why he could summarize her life so perfectly?

His voice dropped, nearly to a whisper. "I only say this because I see the same fate in the mirror every day."

"If you are not the Eidolon, then who are you truly?" he said.

It was obvious from his tone that he didn't expect an answer. Mr. Marcovic pressed his forehead to hers, his skin soft and warm, yet anything but comforting. Her breath quickened. Her thoughts scrambled and fled. She felt lightheaded. Exposed. Was it the opium he'd given her? The warmth in her chest spread.

The only other time she'd felt so emotionally exposed was at the masque.

She couldn't stop that warmth now, not with a hundred Tesla-rays. And she was not even sure she wanted to.

In the next moment, Mr. Marcovic was up off the bed, across the room and by the door.

"I will write to your companion. Rest, my lady."

This time, Veronica awoke more gently. The light streamed in the windows, soft and dim, a warning that soon, night would fall. The gas lamps hanging from the ceiling swayed, the flame in them barely enough to illuminate the person sitting beside her bed. He wore a leather vest littered with pockets so stuffed that items of a random nature appeared to spill out of them. Spools. Wheels. Nails. His top hat lay on the chair beside him, leaving his thick, white hair sticking out at all angles.

"My dear," Dr. Hoch said. "How do you feel?" He lifted her arm and examined her hand.

Veronica winced. "The tisane helped, but a little of the pain has returned. Could I have some more?"

He nodded and handed her a cup, already prepared. She drank deeply and relaxed on the bed to wait for the smooth liquid to work its way through her system.

"Your hand, dear, how is it?" Dr. Hoch couldn't remain still, his foot tapping the cabin floor, hands fidgeting with his pockets.

"There's some pain when I move, but it's manageable. How on earth did you do such a thing?"

She flexed her metal hand, ignoring the now familiar jolt of pain, trying to get used to the motion. Most likely forgetting her entire body was sore, he reached over and patted her leg.

"You know me, Veronica. I'm always experimenting. I knew grafting metal into flesh to be a possibility, but I couldn't stomach the thought of what I would have to do to prove the theorem." His eyes flashed to and fro, unable to settle.

She watched his behavior, nervous for what it meant for the operation he'd performed. Though more lucid than at the Steam-Tech Expo, he still appeared half mad.

"You just happened to have a spare metal hand lying around?" she asked.

He smiled, the sad smile she'd seen so many times over the years. For a moment, the light in his eyes reappeared and he stilled. "Has the tisane worked? Do you feel any pain anywhere?"

It had indeed worked, she realized, spreading relief like a heated blanket. She nodded.

Dr. Hoch ran his finger along the bone on the top of her arm. "The doctor who operated on you. He placed a thin but very strong metal rod here. I've connected your hand to the rod. It should strengthen your grip exceedingly, but it will take time for the bone and muscle to bind with the rod. Luckily, the mad sod remembered to drill holes in the metal, so the bone should graft around it. Eventually, it will heal, and you will have no pain. It will take, however, several months at the least. Take the tisane as often as you need it, the contents will not harm you. In fact, they may speed your recovery." He patted his vest, produced a pocket watch and handed it to her.

"Squeeze this. Not too hard, mind you."

Veronica gingerly formed her metal fingers into a fist around it. The watch popped open, parts flying everywhere.

"Magnificent," Dr. Hoch said. He nearly sang the words, so obvious was his glee. The mad glint had returned, making her shiver.

"What have you done? I'll hurt everyone I touch!" She lifted the metal monstrosity up and asked herself for the dozenth time whether she would rather have it or nothing at all.

Dr. Hoch's eyes, laden with wrinkles, yet sharper than she'd seen them in a while, looked up at her.

"That, my dear, is exactly the point."

Chapter Twenty-Seven

Emil nudged open the door, carrying a tray with dinner for two, courtesy of his cook. The delicacies of his country had been carefully chosen: m'jadarrah, a lentil stew, a tangy fatoush salad, and, of course, kompot for dessert. They were all his favorite dishes, their aromas tickling his nose and his mind with happier memories of his youth. It was awkward to eat around Veronica, since he hadn't removed his scarf, but she seemed not to mind. She seemed to understand his need for a mask, even without knowing why.

Her worst days had passed, and she moved easier now. Her face, which had once been vacant and plain, now glowed with life and beauty. She didn't speak shyly with him, and he quite enjoyed their lively debates on the economy and the wars. Most of all, he loved prickling her ire about gender roles. He silently agreed with every point she made, but it fascinated him to watch her cheeks flame, her eyes spark, and her passionate words fill his senses.

"Hungry, my lady?" he asked as he set the tray on the table. He'd included a single sprig of peppermint, which grew abundantly in the fields surrounding his home farm.

"That smells like foreign places I've only imagined."

She shifted off the bed and rose. Her white robe outlined a figure strong in every way. Instead of the awkward gait of Lady Veronica, she moved like the Eidolon now, smooth and steady.

He helped her into her chair. "These are some of my favorites from home. I will take it personally if you don't eat every bite."

She picked up her spoon and tasted the stew, feigning a look of disdain. "Not enough salt."

He smiled and lifted his scarf to sip it himself, careful to keep the lower half of his face concealed. The dish was perfection, and she knew it. He scooted his chair closer to hers and dipped his spoon in her bowl.

"Hmm. I think your tastes run too glamorous. Do not the English prefer their food plain and simple?"

She waved a hand in a gesture typical of a member of the *ton*, dismissive and arrogant. "But of course. Nothing too out of the ordinary for us. Don't upset the apple cart. Back straight, chest out, hands folded. Keep the discussion to weather. The neckline of Lady Abbot's gown. The latest in *Lloyd's*."

"What of you, then, Lady Veronica? Surely you are far too rich a taste for London."

Her mouth quirked up slightly. "Me? I've made sure I'm too plain, even for our standards."

He lifted the mint and rubbed the leaf in his hand, letting the pieces fall into her glass of water. "It is a lesser known fact, my lady, that what may appear plain may yet have a brightness to be uncovered. Not all men care for the smell of a sharp intellect." He sniffed the mint-laced water, then took a sip and set it in front of her.

"I've never known another type of man." She seemed to be asking a question.

Without another word, he let the honesty in his eyes speak for him. She'd heard all the wrong words from men. He wouldn't add any more.

After dinner, Emil stood and offered his hand to Milady Trouble. "Would you care to take a stroll around the deck, Lady Veronica? It is dark enough that my crew should not be able to tell who my lovely guest is."

A half-smile crossed her face and she placed her right hand in his. She rarely used her left. It hung by her side, awkward and unwanted.

"I'd be delighted, dear sir."

He picked up one of his scarves and began wrapping it around her hair, neck and the lower half of her face. His fingers brushed her skin several times, causing a pleasant jolt to run through him. She smelled wonderful, like always. Clean, fresh.

"A good soldier never reveals more than he, or she, should," he said.

Veronica cleared her throat. "Right."

He reached up and secured his own scarf. "I hardly notice it anymore."

"When do you take it off? You bathe, I presume. You don't smell too terrible."

He laughed. "Come. The stars await."

Emil opened the door and exited first, leaving her to follow. He couldn't treat her with the same manners and respect in front of his crew, lest they suspect. They had too keen of an eye some days.

Emil and Veronica passed Kasun and a few other crewmen on the way to the helm. None spoke or called out. They knew better. They had docked again on top of the Imperial, with several other ships nearby. Emil remained here so he could keep a close eye on Durad and Veronica both, though they hadn't seen each other since Veronica's kidnapping.

Veronica sent word that she had fallen ill and was recovering at a friend's home. Her companion, Matilda, had written several times. Durad wanted to send flowers and visit, but Veronica asked not to be disturbed. Emil didn't mind having the time with her, this suspended reality between both worlds.

When they reached the captain's box, he lowered his voice and explained some of the controls; the com-piece, altimeter, extendable scope, and wind-powered navigation system. She listened, touching each piece curiously.

"You love it, then?" she asked after he finished, matching his hushed tone. "You're very good at it, I'm sure."

He shrugged. "Do you fly often? I have seen the luxury cruisers that always seem to hang about London's skies. Or do you travel in your father's military escorts?"

She shook her head. "I've flown a handful of times. Short trips to and from our manor house in the country. Only when the duke insisted, when I could not refuse him."

"Why?" he asked.

Veronica lifted her gaze out into the black night. "I know where these crafts are made. How could I?"

He wanted to pull her into him, hold her close. He wanted so many things he couldn't have with her.

"This ship and all of Sombor's are made at legitimate factories, staffed by paid adults only. The business is nearly profitable. After what happened to Durad and I, we made several promises. The one to keep children out of the factories was the most important to me."

She turned to look at him, a smile in her eyes. "That's wonderful."

"I've tried to encourage the same thing across EurAsia. I meet with factory owners to help them understand, but it's a dark, twisted business. When no one listens, I do what I have to," he admitted.

She lifted her hands as though she might take his but turned to lean on the rail instead. "Why does it feel as though the world has gone mad? That we're the only sane people left? The only ones willing to do something about it?"

Emil joined her at the rail. "I have thought about that. Every day when I worked in the factories, and every day since I escaped. I believe that most people are average people. They get up, go to work, and come home. They struggle to feed their families. They get by the best way they know how."

She nodded.

He continued, "Those in positions of power, like your English gentry, have much more complicated lives. They might still worry about money. In which case, the only acceptable solution is to marry into it. Which means they have to appear acceptable to the largest number of wealthy suitors.

"Those that don't have to worry about money are focused on power. They play in the political arena. Right now, war is profitable on every front. For those like Lord Grillett, who manufacture supplies. For those in government, like the duke, who gain power by proving he alone can keep the country safe."

She continued nodding. "Right, right. What about the poor? The lower classes that suffer the most?"

He sighed. "They have nothing, and everything to lose. They

might run a street sweeper in the Grave. They might clean the factories between shifts, or even during shifts. They all know what goes on, but what does it profit them to speak up? Who would listen to them? They are uneducated and unimportant."

She tugged at her scarf. "I can answer for the group you've left out."

"Yes?"

"The women. Wouldn't we see these children, beaten and starving, and our hearts not be moved? How could we not show some compassion?"

He tilted his head to the side. He had his theories, of course, but he was anxious to hear her answer.

"Those of the lower classes are too hardened. They see suffering every day. It's a fact of life for them. They might want to do something about it, but they're simply too tired. Those of the middle class, the wives of the merchants, aspire to greater than their station. They see the pleasure cruisers, the steam-lux carriages, and they believe it within their grasp, if they can only be introduced into the right circles. They believe themselves above the sweepers and the cleaners." The words came out fast, hard, bitter. She gripped the rail tightly.

"Agreed," he said softly.

"And those of the upper crust? They're the worst of the lot. They're too smart not to know what's happening, but they feign vapors at the idea. They pretend it's all nonsense until they believe it themselves. Those children are given a legitimate purpose in life. After all, look at what happened before Grillett cleaned up the streets. All those thefts? He's a saint." He inched closer to her, trying to show support. "After Dr. Hoch found me, he warned me not to discuss my opinions with anyone. That it'd be dangerous. Someone might identify me with the same sympathies as the Eidolon. Still, I wrote letters directly to Queen Victoria, hoping one might get through to her. Hoping she'd listen. I was a right idiot. She never returned one missive." She gestured out into the night. "So much for queen and country."

He wanted to take her into his arms, press her cheek into his chest, and feel her relax against him. Instead, he leaned forward and took her arm, leading her back to the cabin.

Chapter Twenty-Eight

Once back inside his quarters, Mr. Marcovic shut the door and took her good hand in both of his. "The rest of the world might be too selfish or tired or afraid to take on Grillett, but you were not, *sultanim*."

The feel of Mr. Marcovic's rough and calloused hands sent an uncensored thrill through Veronica. She tried not to move. Since she'd boarded his ship, he'd taken her arm, pressed a guiding hand to her back, but he'd never touched her so deliberately. The same hands she knew to be efficient and brutal held hers in a grip that could have been comforting but seemed to be so much more.

Mr. Marcovic released her, and she nearly sighed. He turned his hands over and uncovered his wrists.

"I told you once how I got these scars."

She stared at the puckered skin. She wanted to trace it, make sure it was real. Just as she had that night at the masque. The foreigner. She'd pushed aside the memory, afraid it was too good to be real.

"It was you? At the masque?"

Mr. Marcovic tilted his head to the side and waited.

A silly, light feeling rose in her. It felt unnatural and insubstantial. Not just a weight lifted but something more. It felt like the look on Claire's face when she saw Lady Flowers. Or Matilda's smile when she thought Hale wasn't looking. It was a feeling that shouldn't exist within her darkness. It was so bright and free.

He was the one. The one she felt so comfortable talking to. The one with an energy, a pull she nearly couldn't resist. The one she'd wanted to kiss and had guiltily dreamed about since that night.

Veronica hesitated, then said, "Then I thought…"

"That I did not want you?" he asked gently.

Yes. "You didn't? Of course you didn't. You barely knew me," she said.

"I had never wanted anything more." His tone was simple and straightforward.

As the seconds ticked by and neither of them moved, Veronica's thoughts whirled. This didn't feel the same as anything she'd experienced before. Her love for her orphans or Matilda. Her fear and hatred of the duke and the *ton*. Her thoughts seemed to calm around Mr. Marcovic, and every moment she could, she wanted to be with him.

But Prince Durad was her fiancé.

And Mr. Marcovic's prince.

The lightness faded, shoved aside by the greedy fingers of her darkness. She couldn't ask such a thing of Mr. Marcovic, could she? To betray his prince for her and… what?

The horrible part of her, the part that reminded her she was her father's daughter, wanted to ask him to choose her. They had a ship, and both of them had a talent for evasion. She imagined how it would feel, his scarred hands on her cheeks as he seized her for a kiss, exciting and beautiful. How it would be to feel that lightness all the time. It was Melilot's happy ending.

But not hers.

She brushed Mr. Marcovic's cheek through his scarf, and then turned away.

Veronica awoke to the sound of swordplay, metal crashing against metal and the quick scuffle of feet. Were they under attack? What was happening? It'd only been a few days since her capture, and Mr. Marcovic's rescue. Every unexpected sound had her twitching.

She rose from the bed, squeezing her eyes shut against her momentary lightheadedness. Her clothing had been laundered and her shirt replaced. She donned them and then tied on her cape. She strapped on her mask and added the top hat for good measure. The crew didn't know Mr. Marcovic hid a woman aboard.

She opened the door just far enough to see the deck before her. Mr. Marcovic stood in the center of a ring of men, all members of the crew. He'd stripped to the waist, and his loose, black pants hung about his hips. His dark hair, short and spiked atop his head, moved little as he blocked his crew's thrusts and parries. His face, however, remained covered, the scarf tied into place like the kerchief of a thief.

His crew lunged at Mr. Marcovic one after another, their swords singing with skill. He moved almost faster than Veronica could follow, remaining untouched. He wielded two swords, neither arm weaker than the other.

He was magnificent.

When he turned to parry a blow, she saw his back. A gasp escaped her. Ugly, raised scars crisscrossed his flesh. Not one part remained untouched. Lands, were those from his time in the factories? She thought her scars told the story of her life, but his? How many stories did Mr. Marcovic have?

The tenor of the fight escalated suddenly, and Emil lashed out with not only his sword but also his fists and feet. Some of the crew managed to land blows, but they all fell in the end. Veronica watched every movement, fascinated by his skill.

Mercy. She'd never seen such a fighter, neither in her fencing instructors nor in the Enforcers she'd faced. He straightened up slowly and met her gaze, his eyes clear and fierce. She quickly shut the door and discovered she was breathing as hard as he had been. She tossed aside her Eidolon props and retreated beneath the covers of her bed.

What must Mr. Marcovic think of her? He'd seen her fight, she had not nearly his skill. His artistry with the sword appeared more like a gift from the gods, a talent of legends.

When he knocked a moment later, she called for him to come in, hoping her voice was steady. He entered, and she noticed he'd donned a shirt, though it gaped open at the top.

Such strength.

"I apologize for waking you," Mr. Marcovic said. He unstrapped the rapier at his side and set it on his desk. She watched every movement. "How are you feeling this morning?"

She cleared her throat. "Fine. The tisane Dr. Hoch sent has really helped. It's miraculous, really. The pain is nearly gone." Was she prattling? Did she sound normal? She certainly couldn't look at him in quite the same way she had before.

Mr. Marcovic rolled up his sleeves and plunged his hands into the washbasin. With his back toward her, he removed his scarf and cleaned his face. She wanted to peek, but she felt she'd already seen quite enough of him for one day.

Instead, she found a clean towel and, while keeping her back to him, offered it to Mr. Marcovic. She waited for a moment, until she felt his hand briefly steady her arm while he took it. The familiar current she felt at his touch shot up her arm.

"Thank you." His smooth voice sounded pleasant and mildly amused.

She huffed and returned to her bed. Veronica picked up a nearby book and pretended to be absorbed, but as he whistled and tidied up his cabin, she knew every movement he made.

Late that afternoon, Veronica lay on Mr. Marcovic's bed after drinking a cup of the tisane, surprised to find herself restless. She had too many thoughts, too many worries to remain still. It'd been five days. Matilda knew where she was and had sent many pleas for her return. Prince Durad only knew her to be ill. Mr. Marcovic hadn't mentioned telling him anything, thank goodness. That subject would break the spell between them, and they both knew it.

Veronica avoided the duke most of all. She'd gotten fairly adept at hiding secrets over the years, concealing them in plain sight. She'd long ago accepted the fact that she could be discovered and was willing to accept the consequences.

Now, as Matilda pleaded a deathbed illness and the wedding date approached, Veronica risked everything. She dreaded the Clarke townhome with a heaviness she'd never felt. It was as though the glimpse of lightness had forever spoiled her. How could she return to that place where misery painted the walls, where she could not escape its chokehold save in a mask?

Mr. Marcovic slipped inside his quarters, the fresh, chill air chasing him into the room. He glanced over at her and raised a brow.

"Something on your mind, princess?"

She rubbed her temples. "Don't call me that, please. It doesn't feel right." For so many reasons, not the least of which stood before her, strong and appealing.

He bowed and mocked her tone. "But call *me* Emil, please."

She flushed and then sighed. "Veronica."

He removed a rapier from the wall and tossed it to her. It fell to the floor at her feet. Her reflexes were not what they had been, and the tisane dulled her mind.

"Tsk. We must get you comfortable in your own skin again. That hand of yours could be very useful in a fight." Emil removed another sword and pointed it at her.

Veronica picked up the blade with her right hand and saluted him. "I might be good with a sword, but you cannot expect me to spar with you."

"Why not?"

She flushed. "I saw you this morning, as you well know. I've not an ounce of that type of skill. It's..." She shrugged. "A little unbelievable."

"I saw you, Lady Eidolon. You are not as feeble as you pretend. Come, I promise not to cut off your other hand."

Veronica sputtered and then laughed. "Very well."

She stepped forward, spun and then thrust. He blocked her ,and then with a flick of his wrist, knocked her blade out of her hand.

"You are uncertain. Again," he said.

She retrieved her sword, reminded of her many fencing lessons with Dr. Hoch's instructor. He was merciless, though not quite as intimidating or alluring as Emil.

Veronica tried once more. He disarmed her within a few blows.

"Your form is not bad, but you lack conviction. Where is the Eidolon's purpose? Her fire? Again," Emil said.

She lasted a bit longer this time. Less on the next. A half hour later, Emil disarmed her, tossing the handle of her blade into his free hand. He flipped it and handed it to her, handle first. She reached out to take it with her right hand, but he shook his head.

"The other hand."

Veronica hesitated. She could hurt him. Couldn't she? She hadn't used her hand since Dr. Hoch showed her its strength.

"Take it. We need to know now. Not when you're in battle again."

She could never be the Eidolon again, could she? She grasped the handle as gingerly as she could. Dents appeared in the wood. Emil raised his sword in a familiar move. Veronica parried it. The force sent Emil's blade flying out of his hand and clear across the room. She dropped the sword on the floor and stepped back.

Emil scratched his head. "Well, then. It will take some practice, but that's a good start. You will send them running for sure."

"Maybe this is a gift," she said softly.

Emil placed a hand on her shoulder, his strong grip electrifying and comforting her. "Of course, it is. You can defend yourself and the children."

She did still have children to defend, no matter if the Eidolon remained. She turned, finding herself very close to his large chest.

"How can I save or protect them after I marry Durad?" she asked, hating to bring it up. Only one day remained until the wedding day, and she had many problems to solve. She dared to hope he might help.

Emil looked away, his voice low beneath his scarf. "We will find a way. The Eidolon's mission is too important to abandon."

The idea that she could remain the Eidolon after her marriage never occurred to her. She'd only ever seen a black hole, swirling with endless state dinners and social obligations among those whose language she didn't understand.

If Emil helped her, perhaps she could plead a headache, stomachache, anything, so she could vanish for a day or two. He did captain an airship. Yet it would be terribly improper to go on secret missions with Emil as a married woman. Not to mention terribly difficult to be around him, knowing the lightness she would no longer be able to feel.

Veronica picked up one rapier and placed it back carefully on the wall. A map caught her eye, one of Sombor. She stepped closer. Open plains with scattered mines. There were a few larger cities, but the country seemed to be mostly rural. Veronica hadn't studied much of Sombor. Her tutors deemed the country insignificant in size and likely to be swallowed by the Ottomans. Which it nearly was.

Emil reached over her shoulder and pointed to an area in the northeastern part of the country. He seemed to be surrounding her, his presence and his crisply accented voice.

"My home. A small, farming village."

"You were happy there?"

"Very. We lived a simple life, off the land. Sold our crops at the market every month. Knew all the neighbors. Very quaint, you English would say."

Her stomach knotted, but she still asked the question, "What happened? How did you come to the factories?"

He dropped his hand but remained close behind her. "A raid, standard at that time. In the middle of the night, surprising us all. They killed my parents. Took my sister. Left before dawn. No one expected the violence."

"You had nothing to defend yourself?" she asked.

The idea of living so easily, without thought to one's safety, was simply unrealistic. They must've gotten some kind of news of the world, from the markets.

"My parents fought with what they had on hand. Kitchen knives. A torch. But the factory men outmatched us in weapons and experience."

"Do you blame them? For not being able to save you?"

"I used to."

"What changed?"

He spun her around gently to face him, his hands gripping her upper arms. "I saw what they were up against. No one can face the factories alone."

A warmth spread through her, starting where his hands

touched the bare skin of her arms. She didn't move, wanting the moment to last. He stared at her for several moments, his eyes telling her that she wouldn't be alone any longer. That they had each other now.

Even if only until the wedding.

Chapter Twenty-Nine

Emil let Veronica return to the duke's townhouse on the sixth day after her kidnapping. He saw how often she reached for the tisane and how much her arm pained her. She would have a hard time hiding it from the duke, in spite of her previous acting experience. A glove could hide the hand, but not an involuntary reflex when someone brushed up against it. Emil hated sending her back. He could have taken her anywhere, away from it all. But then he'd be no better than Durad had been lately. Hiding. Watching out for only himself.

The entire time he spent with Veronica, Emil wondered how he could deceive himself. She was not *his* fiancée. Did he promise something without words but couldn't fulfill? He seized every opportunity to take her hand, her elbow, to show her he desired her. He let himself live a few days of a dream.

But she wasn't his. He shouldn't have stolen those days with his prince's fiancée.

If that weren't enough, how could he still plan to strike at the duke when he loved Veronica so completely? Perhaps he didn't understand love in the least. In the end, he'd kept a proper distance from Veronica. It wasn't so far-fetched, after all, that a love he'd always wanted would be out of his reach. In fact, it fit quite well with how his life had turned out thus far.

He stood now beside Durad, betraying him with every thought. He'd judged his friend when he needed to look into a mirror himself.

"Does she want to see me? Are you certain?" Durad adjusted his turban, the jewels catching a rare ray of sunshine just outside the Clarke townhouse.

It was mid-day, but clouds obstinately covered the city, obscuring all but the most persistent light. The line of carriages rattling through the square puffed steam, leaving behind misty clouds that left Emil feeling constantly wet and unclean.

He tried clapping a hand on his friend's shoulder, hoping the gesture felt real.

"Of course, Durad. Matilda told me she worried, like any female, how well she would look for you, but you were never far from her thoughts."

Durad's smile gleamed brighter than his turban.

The stiff, old butler answered the door and escorted them to the drawing room. Veronica sat on a small, wing-tipped couch across from a set of over-sized leather chairs. Her dress once again masked her, the marbled color of a rotten peach. She glanced up from what must've at one time been a needlepoint, but it now appeared more like the dark musings of a tortured seamstress. The duke sat at his desk, his back ramrod straight, studying a map. He rose when Durad entered the room and offered a small bow, a slight incline at the waist.

"Please," Durad waved away the formality, "there's no need, Your Grace. I appreciate the gesture but hope that the bonds of family will allow us some level of comfort with one another."

Durad turned to Veronica. "My dear. How are you feeling? I've been devastated by your illness." He lifted his foot to take one step forward but set it down and straightened up instead, folding his arms formally across his chest.

Aman Tanrım! The questions about Veronica outside the townhome, Durad's nervousness. The way he stood uncertainly. Durad was never uncertain.

How did Emil miss that his friend had developed real feelings for Veronica?

Veronica set aside her needlepoint and smiled at the prince. Emil had seen her smile many times over the last week. He knew when it tilted slightly from pain or widened too far to cover an emotion she didn't want to feel. When there was genuine pleasure, it was perfect. As it was now.

"How kind of you to visit. I'm quite well now, thank you." Veronica indicated the chair across from her.

The doors to the drawing room flew open, nearly clipping Emil on the shoulder. He stepped aside just in time.

"So, this is the groom! *Felicitationes, mon ami!*"

Alec entered the room, swinging a walking stick. He paused and bowed, a sweeping gesture that caused his stick to nearly clock Emil in the stomach. Once again, he stepped aside. He now stood flush with the heavy drapes, where obviously no one noticed him.

Veronica coughed. "Alec, you know quite well the prince's native language is neither Spanish nor French."

The duke's face flushed, and he escorted Durad to the set of chairs, asking him questions about Sombor's economy. Alec ignored them, whistling, and turned to his sister.

"I have, once again, proven there is nothing one cannot accomplish with the duke's resources. Your wedding will be the event of the Season. Not one person has sent their regrets."

She appeared to pale a little. "Thank you, Alec. That's simply marvelous."

Alec propped himself on the arm of the couch and leaned forward. Emil stepped out of the shadows in order to hear better. He'd had enough practice focusing—long nights casing factory districts—that he could shut out every other sound in the room except Alec's and Veronica's voices. Durad appeared not to be paying the lease bit of attention, back straight and tall as he answered the duke's continual volley of questions.

"Yet there's no excitement? Not even a little?" Alec gestured toward Durad. "When does such a fairy tale ending come to pass? The handsome prince? What's the matter with you, Peanut?"

Emil craned even closer for her answer. She glanced quickly at him and then back to Alec. She gave him the smile a hint too wide, and said, "I *am* happy. I could want nothing more." She patted Alec's knee.

Alec grimaced and then looked up. "Mr. Marcovic, come here, chap. No need to lurk about. Sit next to the bride-to-be. Plenty of room, now."

Emil hesitated and then complied. One didn't disobey a peer of the realm, though this one was the first to notice Emil. What was Alec about?

"My sister tells me you captain an airship named *Hırsız*. A rather peculiar title. Where did that come from?" Alec asked.

"It's a story I don't care to share." Emil tried to keep a modest amount of space between himself and Veronica, but the blasted couch was far too small. His leg kept brushing hers.

"No matter. I have many more questions. Is the scarf a symbol for a eunuch in your country? Or do you have a lady companion? What purpose do you serve to Durad? All muscle or do you consult with him on matters of state?" Alec prattled on, each question offensive and intrusive.

Emil had been warned about Alec during his time with Veronica. "His Highness does not, nor do any of the men in Sombor, have harems. There is no need for eunuchs. I serve Prince Durad in many ways, none of which I can share." Emil gave up trying to keep his distance from Veronica and she instantly sank into his side. In that moment, he reached out his hands to steady her and put her away from him. But when she glanced at him and didn't look away, he lingered a moment too long.

Alec's smile seemed to grow by the minute. "And my other question? Surely, you're married by now? A strapping fellow like you."

"My duty to my prince leaves me little time for such pursuits." Emil shifted and then rose abruptly. "If you will excuse me."

As he crossed the room to Durad, Emil heard Alec's whisper, "I see what you mean, Peanut. You weren't exaggerating."

Emil tensed as he took his position behind Durad. What in the skies did that mean?

Durad waved away the carriage and continued on foot toward the hotel. Sombor's royal colors disappeared in a cloud of steam. The prince appeared to notice nothing as he plowed down the street.

"Curse that ambitious father of hers. I got but a few moments to speak to her. She appeared well to me. How did she look to you?" Durad continued without waiting for an answer. "*Tomorrow*, Emil. I'll be married. I have to do this. There's no turning back. Sombor's future will be assured with England by our side. This is a good step for us. Very good."

Emil grabbed Durad's arm, forcing him to a halt. He pulled the prince aside into a nearby alleyway. He looked at his friend's face, tense and expectant, and the question he'd been rehearsing for the last hour came out.

"What I want to know is this; have you come to care for her?" The words came out even, impartial, just as he intended.

Durad's features relaxed and his smile blinded Emil. "You know, I believe I do. In all the time we've spent together, I see something in there she's unwilling to show most people. Kindness, compassion, intelligence. You wouldn't know it to look at her, of course. It's probably the duke that dresses her so poorly. He's a beast, one can tell. What kind of man would marry his daughter off to a foreigner he'd never met?"

Unwilling indeed. She was a downright master chameleon, but Durad had an uncanny ability with people, Emil knew that. His heart flopped in his chest, but he didn't look away from his friend.

"So, in spite of the circumstances, you may actually pull this off?"

Durad grinned. "I do believe this may work out, as the English say, to be a *smashing* success. Who would've thought?" He flung his arm around Emil's shoulders and strode with him toward the street. "If you hadn't dragged me here, I never would have met her. I owe you once again, my oldest friend."

While Durad prattled on about the coming day, Emil wrapped his memories of the past week in a box, shut it tight, and made a promise to himself not to speak of his feelings to anyone. In fact, he felt relief at not having told Veronica outright how he felt.

He would return the prince and his new princess to Sombor. He would help Veronica continue her work as the Eidolon. Neither of them were meant for anything more.

Chapter Thirty

"How on earth will you choose, dear Peanut?"

Alec twirled his stick. He sat on the settee in her bedroom, legs crossed, arms elegantly sprawled. He appeared far too delighted by the events of the afternoon.

"Choose?" Veronica asked.

She prodded the fire with a poker. She kept it going constantly since she'd returned home. Something about the metal in her skin seemed to give her a continual chill.

Alec snorted. "Don't play coy. Prince Durad is nuts about you. He practically tied his tongue in knots speaking to you."

She *had* noticed that. He hadn't seemed nervous around her before. Alec could be right, yet it seemed impossible. Surely, Durad couldn't have feelings for the vapid Veronica. If he did, she couldn't place much faith in his taste.

"And that muscular fellow. He was more discreet about it, but when you fell into him on the settee," Alec waggled his brows, "there was something there."

She adjusted her gloves, using the excuse to look away from Alec's teasing gaze. "Mr. Marcovic? I told you, I barely know the man."

In point of fact, Veronica knew Emil better than any man. This past week had been something of a marvel to her. Speaking honestly with a male who respected her opinions, treated her like something to be treasured and admired… it all had an ethereal quality.

How wonderful that might be, to share a future, spending days exactly like those. Emil could make her feel what she'd never believed to be real.

For a moment, her imagination chased away the chill and warmed her down to the tips of her fingers.

Alec coughed. "Peanut, dearest? Wherever did you go?"

She pulled her wrap tighter around her arms. "It's funny, you asking me that question."

He pointed his walking stick at her. "Don't deflect. I have to say, I find the mysterious Marcovic an interesting prospect. What happened between the two of you to make him stare at you so?"

Plenty. Not enough. "Why would any man stare at me, Alec? You know I'm nothing to look at."

"Peanut, you may not know much about men, *anything* about men. Well, how could you? It's not as if they've been lining up to call on you. Sorry, dearest, but it's true. You've a strength and beauty beneath those horrid silks you wear, but who would ever know? And now to have two strong, handsome suitors? It must be overwhelming." He delivered his opinions in a playful tone, but she sensed a serious question underneath.

Veronica picked up a pillow with her good hand and threw it at him. "Don't tease."

Alec caught it and tossed it into the air. After a moment, he stood and joined her at the fireplace. He lifted her chin, forcing her to look at him. "I'm right. And those two men know it. However, what they see or don't see scarcely matters at this point. Those children are obviously what matter to you."

She opened her mouth to protest, but he placed a finger on her lips.

"Now, I don't know why your love for those street rats has given Papá the leverage he needs to control you, but it seems that you've little choice here. In the end, it wasn't too bad of a bargain, was it? Prince Durad appears to be a genuinely good fellow, and he cares for you."

Veronica felt the truth of his words chase away her troubled thoughts of Emil and the discomforting possibility that men might not be such terrible creatures. She'd never had much control of her future, but now, with her orphans, she had none. Nor would she trade them, if she were being honest, for Emil. The happiness they eagerly handed her—a carefully drawn picture, a tight embrace, a kiss on the cheek, unrestrained laughter—no man, not even one as extraordinary as Emil, could match that.

"I told you I like the prince."

He lowered his hand, but his eyes wouldn't release hers. They were blue, murky like the ocean, and fierce as a storm. Veronica couldn't move. For a moment she felt a hint of fear.

"Peanut, you must get out of this house. Do you understand me? Papá has reached his limit with your behaviors, and were you to cry off, he would find a much worse fate for you. Something I would not be able to help you with." His eyes gentled. "I couldn't bear to see that happen to you."

Veronica didn't answer. It almost seemed like Alec genuinely cared. Not in a foppish, overly dramatic way but how he used to, when they were younger.

Alec placed both hands on her shoulders. "I know I've been a beast of a brother to you. I haven't protected you when I should have. I've been off dealing with my own inadequacies in nasty ways. But this wedding? It was my chance to make some of it right."

She couldn't believe he was admitting this to her. The words didn't sound insincere, but she still couldn't trust them. Veronica stepped back, breaking his hold. She was not, after all, the same weakling that used to seek comfort by his side.

"I'll see you in the morning, brother," she said softly. Veronica turned and rang the bell for Matilda.

Alec sighed and said, "Don't forget, you're doing the right thing." He left, tapping his walking stick along the floor with somewhat less exuberance than normal.

She belted her robe tighter and poked the fire again. The chambermaid should bring more wood. The weather had taken a turn and her room felt like ice.

Veronica flexed her new hand underneath her glove and then clenched it into a fist. The glove was a special material Dr. Hoch had delivered during her stay aboard the *Hırsız*, thick, durable, not easily torn. No one knew about her mechanical hand, not even Matilda. In fact, she'd told Matilda nothing, save that she'd needed a few days to tie up some loose ends before the marriage.

The image of Prince Durad's smiling brown eyes rose in her mind. What would he think of her, once he saw what she truly was? She thought of his enthusiasm for Dr. Hoch, for anything steam-tech. Perhaps he might find it fascinating. Perhaps it might even make her more interesting.

Or he might find it repulsive, monstrous. She wasn't sure she would blame him.

The door opened and Matilda entered the room. "My lady! It's a furnace in here, it is. Shall I open the windows?" She fanned herself.

"No! Keep it going all night. I'm exceedingly chilled." Veronica tugged her wrap more firmly about her body. Why could she not feel the heat?

Matilda smiled. "I saw that handsome Prince Durad today. You looked happy, m'lady. Does he mean that much to you, then? Do you care for him? Oh, he's a right handsome gentleman indeed."

"He's wonderful." *Just not the one who saved her and then made her feel strong again.* Her thoughts tangled again, this time adding Emil to the strong, heavy mess.

Veronica turned away, suddenly very tired. The tisane eased her suffering and gave her bursts of energy that left her drained afterwards. If she went too long in between doses, the pain returned so sharply she could hardly breathe.

"Never mind, Matilda. I'll take care of myself tonight. You may leave."

"Very well, my lady," Matilda said in a soft voice. "If you don't need my help." She waited for a moment. When Veronica didn't say anything, Matilda blew out a breath and words tumbled from her lips, fast and hard. "Land's sake, what happened during the past week? Why won't you tell me? I've waited and been patient, but you're being a stubborn ox!"

Veronica blinked once. Twice. Then found a grin curling the corners of her mouth. "An ox, am I?"

Matilda laughed and then placed her hands on her hips. "I'm quite serious. Tell me what happened this instant."

Veronica wanted to tell her. Watching Matilda's curls bounce as she tapped her foot, waiting for an answer, started that feeling of rare warmth inside Veronica. Matilda had sent Clank after her. Cared for her, even though Veronica lied to her and snuck out. Their friendship wasn't a fragile one. Matilda was strong and could be trusted.

Veronica carefully pulled off the glove on her left hand, one finger at a time, revealing the metal monstrosity beneath. Matilda gasped. Instant tears sprang to her eyes. She stepped forward, but Veronica drew her hand back.

"Don't come closer. I still don't quite know how to use it. I could hurt you," Veronica warned.

Matilda brushed away the wetness from her eyes, then rolled her shoulder back, all business. "Nonsense. You'd never hurt me. That bandage around your arm needs changing. Now, come here before I find your Tesla-ray and make you sit still."

Veronica sank down into a chair, and before she knew what was happening, Matilda took Veronica's metal hand gently in hers. Matilda turned Veronica's wrist to and fro, examining the contraption.

"Brilliant. Dr. Hoch's work, I assume?"

Veronica nodded. "It's dangerous though. Strong. I don't have control of it yet."

"You'll figure it out, my lady, you always do." She looked down at Veronica, eyes softening. "We'll figure it out together."

This wasn't the first time Veronica had underestimated Matilda. Hopefully, it would be the last. She used her good arm to pull Matilda in for an awkward hug. Matilda laughed and squeezed her tighter.

"We'll work on that."

Some impulse made Veronica cease her pacing and glance at her wardrobe. It'd been several days since she'd seen Clank. She'd been relieved he hadn't been captured. Such numbers, so many guards, would've overwhelmed even her most loyal companion. The thought of what Grillett might have done—attempted to re-program him maybe, make him his own—made her sick.

Veronica reached forward with her mechanical, left hand and slowly opened the armoire. The door moved silently, as it always did. She pushed aside the false panel. Light filtered in through the crack, revealing the unanimated face of a being more alive than most she'd met during her lifetime. Clank's eyes didn't begin their familiar whir. He didn't bow, nor step out of his hiding spot with his usual eagerness. She reached forward to see if he'd been charging.

Dr. Hoch never answered her question about the origin of her hand… and the reason he hadn't now stood before her. Of course, he would never have had such a thing lying about. She stared at the empty arm socket and then placed her mechanical palm on Clank's chest.

"I'm sorry, dear friend," she whispered. "Forgive me. And thank you. Thank you so very much."

Too cowardly to turn him on, she patted his metal head and replaced the false panel. She would have Matilda return him to Dr. Hoch when she left. She couldn't take him with her, after all. Silly tears threatened. Veronica would miss Clank. A being made of wires and cogs. One of her only friends. The fact that she took some small part of him with her comforted her in a way Alec couldn't.

Mercy. At some point during this past week, she'd accepted it. She was going to marry Prince Durad. It was her conversations with Emil, not only about the beauty of Sombor and its passionate people, but about the Eidolon's work. How she might continue it after her marriage. If that were truly a possibility, and she now believed it to be, with Emil's help, she might have even more freedom than she had now. With his help, and that of his ship and crew, she could do more. She could save more children.

The conversation of the women at the Steam-Tech Expo rose to the front of her mind. With her independent means as a princess, she could possibly recruit others to help as well. The defunct debutante they might not regard but royalty of Sombor?

As always, such a bright future came with a price. The heartache she'd feel working alongside the man she'd never thought existed.

Though how could she regret marrying Durad? She was certain his kindness would have a chance at thawing her already melting heart.

She had no other plan in place to thwart her father and save Bridges. With the duke moving up the wedding, and the week lost aboard the *Hırsız*, she'd had no time. Alec wasn't entirely wrong. She would marry Durad, and oddly enough, she would have a measure of happiness in being able to continue her work. She'd never thought it possible. Even if it wasn't what her soul hungered for.

Veronica glanced toward the trunk she'd instructed Matilda to pack. All of her ridiculous frocks, muslins, and wrappings. Nothing truly her. All that she owned that mattered were her memories of her rescued children, and they were safely stored in her heart.

Still, she wished for a set of the loose robes Emil provided her aboard the *Hırsız*. He must be escorting her and the prince to Sombor. Durad would hardly trust anyone else to do so.

She wrapped herself in a blanket and slid beneath her cool, silk sheets. In spite of Alec's words, in spite of her determination to marry Durad, Veronica felt her mind drift in directions she couldn't control. She remembered the feel of Emil's hand on her arm. She remembered the many times he'd adjusted her covers, fed her meals, and changed the bandages on her wounds.

Emil's firm touch, spiced scent, and smooth accent warmed her until she finally slept.

When the sun finally slid through her window in the morning, Veronica was already awake and ready for Matilda to help her into the wedding gown.

Chapter Thirty-One

Veronica turned sideways, examining her reflection in the full-length mirror. She'd never imagined her own wedding, though she suffered through many a conversation at Almack's on the topic. The endless debate over silk or chiffon never failed to send her daydreaming about her next fencing lesson. She would find herself thinking about Clank and Bridges and wondering whether the day would ever come that she would be free of the need for such tiresome society.

In fact, Veronica always thought Alec would be the one to carry on the Richmond line. With a title, money, his youth, and a face that made women flutter their fans and exclaim how warm it was, Alec's future was assured. He had his pick of partners, within the parameters the duke set, of course.

After Veronica's spectacular failure at her debutant ball—involving a dress she spilled on several times, many innocent yet inappropriate remarks, and many bruised toes—she'd been written off. "Hapless, hopeless and an utter disaster," was the phrase accepted by all. The duke had been livid. Dr. Hoch proclaimed her absolutely brilliant.

Standing here, now, in Westminster Abbey, preparing to be married, everything felt wrong. She wasn't supposed to be getting married. Ever. She was a fool. A bumbler. Nor was she supposed to have feelings for a man she wasn't marrying. A man that made her shiver with heat, with arms strong enough to carry her, and a heart big enough to care for the orphans like she did.

The one thing that was right was the dress. Alec was a genius. The only concession to the proper wedding gown was the color of the fabric. The white silk, overlaid with chiffon, appeared conservative enough, until one saw the white corset. The corset outlined her waist, defining her strong figure. Alec had provided a cropped lace sweater that matched the lace running vertically on the corset. He'd also laid out her butterfly necklace and a small, white top hat, meant to be pinned slightly askew on her head.

Without a need for concealment any longer, she could be herself. She hadn't even asked Alec what he'd planned for her, but as she stood there, she couldn't help but feel grateful.

"Lands, my lady," Matilda breathed out, her gray eyes alight and a little misty. "You look perfect." She fiddled with the laces on the corset, patting and smoothing the gown.

Veronica turned and stilled Matilda's hands with her good one. "Will you come with me? To Sombor? You don't have to answer right away. It's far from home, and who knows what circumstances we'll be forced into."

Matilda laughed, the sound bright. "My lady, we'll be living in a palace. I'm sure it will simply have to do."

"Are you quite certain?"

Her companion looked hurt for a moment. "You know I have no family left to speak of here in England. You're my family now."

The simple statement struck Veronica. She never truly believed in the idea of a family. Couldn't imagine the traditional concept of people who care for you above all else. The thought made her almost smile. Matilda. Suzie. Claire. Perhaps even Mistress Phillips. She might not have a family by birth, but she'd created one of her own.

She side-hugged Matilda while a few tears escaped her eyes.

When the doors to Westminster Abbey opened, a thousand people stood. Veronica clasped her bouquet of painted, steel roses, courtesy of her orphans, and stepped forward.

The organ sounded the wedding march, and her heart thumped right along with her steps. She could barely see Prince Durad at the end of the row of pews. Of course, the duke chose a place large and grand enough to make a statement about his loyalties to the queen. No one could be more loyal than a father that escorted his own daughter into the arms of a foreigner.

Veronica paused as the duke placed her hand on his stiff sleeve and marched in step with her. His touch was cold and hard, matching the disapproval she saw in his eyes at her dress and bouquet.

Whispers rose from each pew she passed. Some of the younger set matched the attire she'd seen last at Almack's; corsets showing like hers, dangling monocles, leather gloves. Veronica thanked the style for the cover it provided her, as she sported a set of white leather ones herself. Luckily, the duke hadn't appeared to notice that her hand no longer felt soft but was now firm and unforgiving.

As she approached the front, she glimpsed Lord Grillett. He stood to her left on the bride's side, his gold breastplate catching the occasional ray of sunshine through the windows and gleaming with a nearly blinding light. With his helmet removed and tucked under his arm, he saluted her. The thin smile he wore told her the action was a mockery.

Blackthorne could have revealed her identity before that night. Grillett might know who she was. Though there was little he could do now, in front of the people whose opinions and business he valued above all.

She forced her head back toward the front. Emil stood to the right side of his prince, wearing robes of white, a decorative turban on his head, and a white scarf over the lower half of his face. His eyes seemed to burn through her.

Veronica turned her focus to Durad. He smiled at her, white teeth gleaming, features brightening at her approach. He cared for her. Her life at his side would be considerably better than with the duke. How could it not? No longer would she have to worry about the many masks she wore. No longer would she have to endure nights of the endless, nonsensical prattle that enraged her. No longer would she be subject to the duke's threats. She would be safe.

Safe. The concept felt as unreal to her as Melilot's fairy tale ending, but here she stood, about to exchange her life of fear and secrets for one where she wouldn't have to worry about tests, punishments, or concealing the biggest part of her. The part she'd hidden since that day Dr. Hoch met her in the garden; her desire for change. To do something, mean something to others. Durad seemed to understand.

Veronica and Durad spoke their vows and exchanged rings. He leaned forward. She stood very still as he took her face in his hands and pressed his lips softly and sweetly against hers. She trembled at how the kiss made her feel, safe and loved. A little like Emil's touch, except she missed that hot current of energy, like the rush of jumping off a building or escaping guards. Emil enlivened her and forced her to feel. Durad's arms promised security and shelter.

She looked into Durad's warm, brown eyes. They were tender and soft. He smiled, his gaze widening in a way that he most likely meant to look innocent but failed. He leaned forward and kissed her again. This time, he dipped her back, holding onto her securely. She felt her world tip. His mouth slanted against hers. She wanted to laugh at his boldness, but all she could do was hold on.

Her life with Durad would not be the same as it would be with a self-absorbed earl, a stuffy general, or any other member of the *ton*. Her life with Durad might possibly be enjoyable, unexpected, and charming… exactly like the man himself. She was ridiculously fortunate in this match.

Amidst the cheers, Durad whispered, "I'm very lucky this day indeed."

Durad pulled her close for an embrace that was strong and gentle. He felt warm, solid, and smelled wonderful. Sandalwood, perhaps. Over his shoulder, she saw Emil, standing stiff, eyes scanning the crowd.

Maybe the warmth she felt in Durad's arms would replace the cold that gripped her heart every time she looked at Emil and wondered what could've been.

Lord Grillett bowed over her good hand. She wanted to yank it away, his touch sickened her so.

"Best wishes to you both, princess. Congratulations on such a successful match." The corners of his mouth pointed downward as he spoke, negating the sincerity of his words.

She didn't curtsey, clearly intending the insult to the society standing he held in such high esteem. "Lord Grillett. I hear you have quite a busy schedule these days."

Prince Durad stood by her side but attended to another guest. Emil never moved from his post behind the prince. Veronica couldn't tell if he noticed Lord Grillett, or if he persisted in ignoring her, as he had since the ceremony ended. In any case, she faced Grillett alone.

Grillett patted her hand and leaned forward as if to share a confidence. "My lady. Your Highness. I heard from a fellow by the name of Blackthorne that you have many names."

He did know. Blackthorne told him her secret. The one that could destroy her, the life she'd built and the orphans she cared for. She pulled her hand away.

"I'm sure I don't know what you mean. Though I've heard Blackthorne got into a spot of trouble from which he's unlikely to recover," she said in a light, pleasant voice.

Grillett smiled, an action as beautiful and fake as every word that came from his mouth. She couldn't imagine a more horrible sight. He lowered his voice even further.

"Following this reception, you will make your excuses and meet me at your workhouse, Bridges. Plead exhaustion, vapors, whatever you like, but you will be there by half past six or I will tell the duke exactly how his daughter rounds up the orphans she brings to Bridges. Do you understand, princess?"

Every muscle in her body seized and she found she couldn't say or do anything but nod. Of all the outcomes she imagined since she became the Eidolon, this was the very worst. The duke discovering her secret. Grillett stealing back her orphans and replacing their newfound hope and sense of safety with his cruelty and despair. They were hers now, fully and completely. She would do anything, absolutely anything to keep him from them.

Grillett left with a graceful turn, his gaudy, gold armor gleaming, sword swinging by his side. When the next person stepped forward to offer their congratulations, she responded automatically with a smile that felt as cold as steel.

An hour later, Veronica's face had grown numb with the tension born of false happiness. She pled the need to freshen up and kissed Durad on the cheek. Avoiding Emil's gaze, she tried not to run toward the bridal dressing rooms. Matilda followed close behind.

When they arrived at the suite of rooms, Veronica ushered Matilda in and then closed and bolted the door behind her. When Matilda noticed Veronica's expression, she froze. Veronica spun, presenting her back to her companion.

"Unlace me, Matilda. Hurry!"

She obeyed with quick, experienced fingers. "What's happened, Your Highness?"

"No formalities, please, Matilda. It's long past time you called me Veronica. I need out of this dress now. What clothes have you packed for me?" Veronica tried to be patient, but she longed to cut the laces of her dress with her sword.

Matilda didn't respond for a moment, her hands working quickly. When she finished, she tugged the dress off, but Veronica was careful to keep her gloves on.

Her companion said, "I brought *those* clothes."

She opened a trunk and tossed out fripperies until she reached a satchel at the bottom. With a sigh, she retrieved the cape, mask, trousers, shirt, and even the Tesla-ray, which Emil had presented to her on board the *Hırsız* the day after her capture. Clank had retrieved it from Blackthorne's body.

"Is it the children? Our children?" Matilda asked.

Veronica nodded and pulled on her clothes. "Grillett is waiting at Bridges. He's threatened to tell the duke about the Eidolon if I don't meet him there. You mustn't tell Prince Durad where I've gone."

Matilda huffed. "And what will I tell him when you turn up dead? You can't do this, my la— Veronica." With her eyes narrowed and her jaw tight, she appeared frantic. "You're so strong and you've proved the duke wrong and all of *them* wrong in every way. You've made a difference in hundreds of lives. There must be another way to do this. Even if you go in alone, what will happen after they kill you? They will only take the children back to the Grave. *Think*, Veronica!"

Veronica paused in the process of strapping a knife sheath to her leg. Bugger, but Matilda was right. She would willingly risk her life, but if she failed, she achieved nothing. Her children would still be in danger.

Veronica could think of only one person who would stand a chance against such odds. She closed her eyes, rubbed her temples. Even if she had no right, she would ask this of him, this one final thing. He wouldn't be able to refuse, not with so many children at risk.

She took a deep breath and opened her eyes. A few more hours with Emil before he vanished from her life forever. She'd made her choice. She didn't deserve to steal this time, but she couldn't help feeling like sunshine had just flooded the room.

"Fetch Mr. Marcovic," she ordered.

Chapter Thirty-Two

Emil couldn't bear to look at Veronica. She was so beautiful that something hurt inside him. He'd wanted to drag her away from the greedy eyes of the *ton* to somewhere private, where he could finally, *finally* gather her into his arms. As though nothing else in this blasted world mattered. Durad. Sombor. The steam-tech factories. Let it all melt away. But neither of them believed in the brand of selfishness that would betray Sombor and destroy Bridges and the Eidolon's work.

Emil had to stop thinking about her, cease getting distracted by his memories of the past week, by his feelings for her. He couldn't live like this, tormented by his obsession. Especially when he had more important matters to attend to. He'd delayed too long in the reason he came to London in the first place. He'd been greedy. He should have simply seen Durad married and been done with it all.

Instead, a woman with hard blue eyes appeared like a stroke of lightning and struck him hard, leaving him fascinated. Possessed by his feelings for her.

Now, she was gone. The idea threatened to make him into even more of the madman.

Durad appeared as happy as Emil had ever seen him, his eyes returning to Veronica over and over. When she excused herself, he looked worried until she smiled, with a bright enough light to prompt him to relax. He embraced her and told her to return soon.

But the way she left—footsteps clipped—something wasn't right. Emil wanted to follow after her and demand to know what was wrong, but he couldn't. He had to stop thinking about her like this, wondering and fretting like a mindless debutante.

After a few minutes passed, Matilda returned. She strode by, pressing a note in his hand. Startled, he nearly dropped it. He shouldn't look at it, but he did.

Grillett knows. Follow Matilda.

Everything paused. Durad's light laughter, the murmur of a hundred voices, even the smells of the roses seemed to hang in the air. Grillett. That's what upset her. He must've spoken to her during the reception. Emil had noticed him during the ceremony, sitting down the row from the duke.

Emil scanned the room. Matilda stood in the hallway to his right.

Veronica shouldn't face Grillett on her own, as she surely would without him. Look at what the woman had done before he rescued her, taking on a pack of Enforcers and Blackthorne. Not to mention the dozens of other times she'd done so.

He couldn't leave her alone. Not yet. Not now.

He turned to Rosseau, indicating the other guards. "Make sure Kasun and Sera stay at their posts. You are to guard the prince. I will return shortly." Emil nodded at Durad. "He will not even notice my absence."

The burly Frenchman lowered his voice in reply, "Of course, *capitan*. Go, look after your princess." He stepped forward to take Emil's post.

Emil didn't move for a moment, startled. Did Rosseau suspect Emil's feelings? He very well could, after the week they'd spent aboard ship.

Emil then tried to leave, but Durad's hand on his arm stopped him. He turned, stiff.

"First my bride, and now you. What about me offends this day? Are we not celebrating?" With his cheeks flushed and his tone bright, he smiled and the whole room turned sunny.

In a rare gesture, Emil reached out and embraced his prince. As he did so, Emil felt the ridges of the scars beneath Durad's thin garments. Durad hadn't escaped the factories or the wars without the marks that told his stories. The reminder of this, of their shared pasts, released some resentment he felt at Durad for marrying the woman he loved. None of this was Durad's fault, either the marriage or Emil's feelings for Veronica. That was all Emil's doing.

"Emil, has all this luxury made you soft?" Durad tilted his head as if examining him. "I cannot imagine such a thing. It must be the wine that is making you maudlin. Go, sleep it off."

Durad waved Emil away, his smile a little too wide to be real. As though he suspected why his bride and his bodyguard left so closely together. Suspected they could mean more to each other than they'd let on.

It wasn't entirely false, after all. It was, perhaps, a mercy to let him think that rather than to put him out in front of the danger, like Veronica and Emil were likely about to do.

Emil turned in the direction Matilda had gone. He scanned the room as he did so to see if anyone followed his movements, but he noticed nothing out of the ordinary. When he reached Matilda, she hurried forward without a word. They remained silent until they reached the suite of bridal rooms, former offices made over for the occasion. She made sure no one was watching, and then they both entered.

Veronica stood by the windows, hands clasped behind her back. In the armor of the Eidolon, she looked so much more like the woman he'd spent the last week with, confident and full of purpose. He waited for her to speak.

She did so without looking at him, sounding distant, formal. "He has the children, Emil. Dozens of Enforcers probably swarm Bridges by now. He's threatened all of them, and to reveal my secret to the duke, if I don't turn myself over to him." Her voice was resolute. "If I'm to succeed in saving them, I must defeat Grillett. I cannot do so alone."

The orphans she'd told him about. There were hundreds of them. If Grillett had them all in his grasp… his heart cried out and then hardened. He couldn't let Grillett take them back. No matter what. The idea of so many suffering again, after all they'd endured, sickened him until he trembled with the need to act.

"You need help. And a plan," he said in the same voice that commanded his crew.

Veronica turned to face him. He was surprised to see her face streaked with tears. "I need *you*, Emil. I'm so sorry to ask, I know—

"

He wanted to grab her. Hold her close until they shared the same energy, the same breath. Until she knew she would never be alone in facing Grillett, or any of her enemies.

Instead, he softened his voice and said, "Of course I will help, *kardeşim*. A plan. We need a plan. We cannot go in blind. The two of us together will still not be enough."

Veronica wavered, leaning toward him. She seemed to want to close the empty, energized space between them. Then she shook her head and stepped back several paces.

She stumbled, directly into a large mirror. She righted it, then paused. Reached her hand up to her face. Muttered, "That's it."

"Matilda, get Alec. Hurry, now. Tell him whatever you need to tell him to separate him from the champagne," Veronica ordered.

"But Your Highness! Look at what you're wearing. He'll know. He'll know all about—"

Veronica interrupted, "We have to tell him. Go!"

Matilda vanished through the door.

"What are you thinking?" Emil asked.

He kept his distance. Halfway across the room seemed proper enough when he really wanted to pull her into his arms, top hat and all.

She paced the length of the windows, black cape trailing behind her. "How loyal are your crew?"

He answered honestly. "It depends on the endeavor. Where profit is involved, I can count on them unquestionably."

"I can pay, whatever sum you think will secure their loyalty. They're good fighters, no?"

"The best I've found across Europe."

A strange look flitted across her face. "Though none can best you."

He lifted his shoulders in a shrug.

"Grillett's weakness is his vanity, his pride." She continued to pace, her steps slow, even, precise. "I mean to strike terror into him, threaten what he most values. I will expose what he conceals underneath that golden armor. By the saints, all of London will see that his greed runs as deep as any ocean and that his heart is not comprised of muscle but of gold-plated coal."

"Have you not tried to expose him before?" he asked.

Half of Veronica's mouth quirked up into a smile. Her hand went to the Tesla-ray at her side. "Young, naive Lady Veronica tried. Before she fooled the world into thinking she had little of anything—sense, brains, or beauty—in order to save those she loved most."

"What is the different this time?" he asked, trying to follow her thought process.

Why would she expose Alec to the Eidolon? How could that help? It seemed to Emil that even though Alec held title, his gurney racing and other vices prevented him from gaining society's respect. How could they leverage that against Grillett?

"My brother's image, in spite of everything, is useful currency. There are many privileged young men his age involved in the same vices." She looked around and found what looked like a cold teacup of the tisane. She used her good hand to lift the cup and drink it all.

Emil wanted to stop her from exposing herself as the Eidolon. *Keep yourself safe behind a mask*, he wanted to argue. Just as he had with *Kartal*. But he couldn't say a word. Not when he understood what the children meant to her.

Chapter Thirty-Three

Alec stepped through the door of the bridal rooms, bottle in one hand, walking stick in the other. He swung both in a gay manner, as though he had not a care.

"Sister, you looked marvelous out there! All of London…"

He stopped abruptly. His mouth fell open. He looked quite unlike his usual, dapper self.

"What's the meaning of this?" he demanded.

He straightened up in a surprisingly sober manner and jabbed his walking stick at the floor as he continued, "Is this some type of farce, Peanut? Is there a masque later on? Why are you dressed like that Eidolon fellow? And what's the burly fellow doing here?"

Veronica drew her Tesla-ray and flipped the switch to on. It hummed and she released the trigger. The beam shattered the full-length mirror. The crash made Alec jump.

"You knew I had secrets, Alec. You may not have asked me outright, but I know you're not the fool you play all of us for." She holstered the Tesla-ray and folded her arms across her chest.

It was time now to see whether or not he was capable of being truthful with her, or if her brother's time at Eton and Cambridge had forever changed him. If he couldn't, if he continued to hide his true self from her, her plan wouldn't work. And she could think of no other way to save her children.

If he wouldn't help her, she would never forgive him.

Alec sighed and sat in a nearby chair. He dusted imaginary lint off his sleeves, looking everywhere but at Veronica. "Of course I knew you were up to something, but I figured it to be slightly less suicidal. I thought you snuck out to care for those orphans. Or perhaps to meet up with someone." He glanced at Emil. "I never thought you were dressing like a man, killing people, and stealing children.”

Half-truths, most likely, but better than nothing. “You yourself were singing the Eidolon’s praises not a week ago at the supper table. Come now, no need to continue the games. You must know there is some truth to my work.”

“I’m not a complete ninny. I figured it out quite some time ago.”

“You did?” Veronica sank down into a chair. “Why didn’t you tell me?”

Alec rolled his eyes. “You seemed to value the whole secret identity bit, but why tell me now? I thought once you married that prince fellow, you would ride off into the sunset, as it were. No more sneaking out at night to do whatever it was you did. No more need to defy Papá, no more need to act out.”

“I’m not like you. I don’t abandon those I care about! And I don’t do this simply to irritate the duke or prove a point to him. I do this for Suzie, Claire, Agnes,” she choked. “All my orphans. There are hundreds of them! They all depend on me. Do you understand what kind of responsibility that is? Their lives are in my hands.”

Alec rose and glared to her. “I understand that you’ve been out there risking your life. Tell me, how many times have you been hurt? I’ve noticed you’ve been favoring your right hand lately. What happened to your left? What injuries do you hide?”

“That doesn’t matter now! Grillett has them! The orphans. He’s at Bridges and will tell the duke who I am if I’m not there in two hours. I have to make this right. Do you understand? They have only me!” Her body trembled with the restraint it took not to punch her brother until she knocked out all of his selfish words, all of his fake pretensions, all of his ridiculous lies.

He waved aside her words. “Send someone else! Tell Prince Durad to take care of it. But leave. You’ve done enough.”

She took a deep breath. Closed her eyes. Tried to picture her orphans. She gave her brother one final plea. “I need your help. You will do this for me. You will do this to make up for all the times you were not there for me, after you left for Eton. All the times the duke caned my hands for poor posture. Told me I was worthless, no good, and a disgrace, and I believed him because you weren't there to tell me otherwise. For all those years you left me alone with him."

Alec's left eye twitched and his mouth hardened. "That's why I'm trying to save you now. Talk you out of this madness." His voice lowered to a whisper. "Please, Peanut. Don't do this. You can't trust Grillett. Don't throw your life away."

"You've no right to ask anything of me. No right. Even so, just as my safety is seemingly important to you, I feel the same way about those children. They're my family. As much my flesh and blood as you are. I need you. Together, we can save them. We have," she glanced at the ancient clock on the dressing table, "an hour and a half. *Please.*"

Matilda stepped forward. Veronica had quite forgotten anyone else was in the room. Her companion chimed in. "She's brilliant, my lord. If she says it's possible, I would believe her." Alec stared and Matilda ducked her head, cheeks pink.

He didn't speak for several long moments. Veronica waited in agony. She would either love her brother forever or hate him.

"I'll need to hear your plan, but I do have one condition. You stay by Mr. Marcovic over there." Alec pointed his walking stick at Emil. "You will protect her?"

Emil bowed, the gesture formal and graceful. His turban dipped low, and when his eyes raised, they met hers once again, dark and strong.

"Dare I ask what you have in mind?" Alec sighed.

Veronica felt dizzy at her brother's changeability. She nodded. "We have to hurry."

Perhaps, just perhaps, her brother was not entirely lost.

Chapter Thirty-Four

Hale rolled the carriage to a smooth stop in front of Bridges, hopped down, and opened the door with a formal bow. Veronica exited, scanning the roof and nearby streets for Grillett's Enforcers. Four patrolled the second-floor balcony. An equal number were on the third. Five in the south alleyway. Six more there, across the way. Who knew how many were hidden in the shadows.

Emil took his place by her side. So strong, so steady. It felt entirely different from having Clank with her. Her heart refused to remain still within her chest, painfully wonderful, thrumming like the engine of their steam carriage that Hale could barely tame. Veronica waved Hale on.

He started up the carriage, and with a soft whir and pop, took off down the street. The other carriages—Alec's carriages—pulled up, turned off their engines and waited. They lined the streets, stacked one after another, like uneven books staggered on a shelf. The only sound was an occasional puff of steam from Bridges' ventilation system.

Veronica stepped forward. "Grillett! Will you not face me yourself? Or is that sword and shiny armor you wear only for show?" She stood her ground, back straight, hand on the hilt of her sword.

The door to Bridges swung open and a stream of red-caped Enforcers poured out. Without a word or barely a sound, they filed into a straight line. She counted at least twenty. In spite of her fear, she nearly smiled at the show of force. Exactly what kind of foe did he think the Eidolon?

The fading light caught the glimmer of gold as Grillett stepped outside. When he saw Veronica and Emil standing alone, he laughed.

"After all this time, this is how you face me? How have you survived this long, Angel?"

He drew his sword. With several quick, long strides he closed the distance between them and pointed his sword at her throat. He pressed the ultra-sharp tip into her skin, and blood, warm and wet, trickled down her neck. Emil's shadow flickered beside her, too tense to remain still.

Grillett continued, his tone dismissive. "This charade is over. The children will be returned to their rightful, productive place in the factories. And you." His voice trembled on the last word. He cleared his throat.

"And me?" she queried, keeping her voice flat, even.

Grillett cuffed her on the side of her head, sending her sprawling to the ground. She turned to look back up at him, tasting blood in the corner of her mouth. Her arm ached, and she wished she'd had a second cup of Dr. Hoch's tisane earlier. The cobblestones' chill might have made her shiver, but the fire of anger heated every part of her.

"Too cowed to fight a real opponent?" Grillett removed his helmet and tucked it under his arm. "Come, I will allow a fair fight. Show me the woman that can best my Enforcers."

Veronica used her left hand to propel herself onto her feet, the movement swift and uncanny. "I will gladly accept your challenge, *Lord* Grillett. In very point of fact, I anticipated such an opportunity and have invited a few friends to witness the occasion."

She nodded at Emil. He made a gesture with his hand and light flooded the street. The doors to the waiting carriages opened. One by one, elegant gentleman stepped out and approached Veronica and Lord Grillett. Men of all ages, from several boys just out of Oxford to a man with graying temples. They all wore leather, buckles, goggles, top hats, dusters… the wardrobe of the New Era. It looked like a night at Almack's, without the crinoline, chiffon, or silk. Several of Emil's crew, hidden among true nobility, appeared distinctly uncomfortable, tugging at their trousers and squirming in their fitted vests.

Veronica spoke, her trembling voice carrying through the crowd. "They know everything, my lord. I've shown them just now. Taken them on a tour of the Grave, since you left it so thinly guarded. My, my, what a filthy place. Not at all like the papers show! No fat, healthy children there. Only skinny little things, hardly strong enough to stand."

Lord Grillett's eyes flicked from one dandy to the next. He swallowed, any honeyed words he might have planned to say vanishing down his throat. His weight shifted, and he rocked back on his heels. Then he straightened his posture immediately and lifted his chin in a perfect disdainful tilt.

Grillett started to talk, but Veronica cut him off. "They feel very sheepish to have been so deceived by you. In fact, you've made them quite angry. They plan to do what they do best, spread the word about who you truly are very quickly. By tomorrow, all that matters to you will be lost forever."

Alec stepped forward, tipped his hat and said, "Grillett, old chap. You remember my friend, Lord Walter, Baron of Ghent? And His Grace, the Duke of Grafton? Or perhaps Sir Howard, heir to the Earl of Essex?"

Grillett opened his mouth, and then shut it again. He glanced down the row of nobles and closed his eyes briefly.

Veronica waited, her sword still drawn. It was working better than she'd hoped. Now, all he had left to do was prove the coward and run. Leaving the children to her.

Grillett's eyes flew open, squinted in calculation, his lips curved into a sneer.

"My apologies, my lords and Your Grace, for what you've heard. Unfortunately, I cannot have such lies spread among my peers." He gestured toward Alec and the others, turning to speak calmly to his Enforcers. "Leave no one alive."

Chapter Thirty-Five

Emil drew both swords and took his stance by Veronica. *Hayır, olamaz.* Grillett had just ordered a mass murder of members of the peerage. The golden man himself vanished behind his sea of red.

"Run!" he ordered Alec and his friends.

A few ducked back into carriages and took off, but Alec and several others remained. They drew rapiers and stood ready.

Out from behind Alec's group, the shadows moved, and a hundred men charged the Enforcers. Brandishing knives, clubs, and steel bars, they whooped as they crashed into the red capes.

"Who are they?" Veronica asked, her voice raised above the din.

Emil grinned. "The secret society that supports the Eidolon." Giles and all his friends. He'd sent word as soon as he realized Veronica's plan. "They, like us, are very, very angry."

She smiled that perfect smile, a bright, forceful thing. Her body loosed and she raised her sword and whooped just as they had. She charged into the fray, knocking aside one Enforcer and then another.

She was magnificent. Tall. Strong. Fierce as she whirled to face each new foe. Her cape swirled behind her with each fluid thrust and parry of her blade.

Emil's men followed her, with Alec's friends close behind. They met the Enforcers, steel on steel. A deafening clang shattered the air. Emil cleared a path to Veronica. He guarded her left, wishing she would use that blasted powerful hand hanging by her side.

Veronica turned, saw Alec nearby, and yelled, "What are you

doing?" She parried a blow and shoved a man aside. "Go! Please, Alec, go!"

Alec thrust his sword at an oncoming Enforcer. With a few surprisingly deft moves, he struck the blade out of the other man's hands and cuffed him on the head, knocking him out.

"Really, Peanut. Do you think I learned nothing at Eton?" And with that, he vanished into a sea of red.

Aman Tanrım. Alec would make a mess of it, but Emil didn't have time to follow him. He met several Enforcers at once while Veronica watched her brother vanish into the crowd. It took her a few moments to snap back into focus. When she did, she drew her Tesla-ray and sprayed a beam in a circular motion around her. Six men dropped to the ground, stunned.

She holstered it and said, "We have to get inside."

Emil nodded and led the way. He swung his blades, cutting a path through a river of red Enforcers. They were very good, really. Just no match for him.

Veronica fought at his back, favoring her right hand, which brandished her sword. In spite of their trainings together, she didn't use her left. It hung by her side, an awkward prop.

"Do not push it too far," Emil warned as they reached the entrance to Bridges.

He pulled her inside the doors, searching for a place to rest. Several more red capes descended upon them. He shielded her from the worst of it, but he couldn't take them all on at once. The beam of her Tesla-ray broke through, sending the last few to the floor. One of his crew followed them inside the building, fending off Enforcers that broke through the crowd toward Emil and Veronica, but he couldn't tell who it was.

Veronica holstered her gun and lifted her goggles onto her hat. "Charge is almost gone." Wiping her damp forehead with the corner of her cape, she continued, "We've got to find Grillett. Quickly, now."

Hayır, olamaz. It was too soon for her to be fighting like this. Still, she'd never been more stunning, with her mouth twisted in pain, the sweat of battle on her brow, and a fierce, desperate fire burning in her eyes.

They stood in what appeared to be a receiving lobby. A

chalkboard with a scribbled price list stood off to the right. An aged but clean desk off to the left. Several large bins were grouped in a corner, with etched metal signs hanging from the brims.

"Where do we look?" he asked. "Should we split up?"

She didn't answer, simply took off down a hallway to the right. A single Enforcer rushed his left side. He dispatched the man with one uppercut to the chin, sending him sprawling to the floor. The crewmember that had followed them inside—Emil still couldn't see who it was—continued to cut through the streaming red capes as more and more Enforcers entered the building.

Emil took off at a run in the direction Veronica had gone. Cursed, wonderful woman. Now that they were within reach of her children, she must be half mad to find them.

He found her jogging down the hall, looking in each room she passed. She muttered to herself, "They must've gotten warning and reached the hiding place."

"Hiding place?" he asked.

"Cellar. Below the kitchen. I had it dug out when I bought the building. The children hopefully took refuge there before Grillett got to them."

"You have a warning system in place, *camm*?" He couldn't help grinning. The woman was always ahead of Grillett. Always looking at the situation differently from anyone else.

She nodded, unaware of his endearment. "We run drills every day. Saints above, I hope it worked."

"Of course it did."

If not, if Grillett held even some of the children captive with him… there couldn't be casualties. He wouldn't allow it. Thank the stars Veronica was as brilliant as she was caring.

They neared the end of the hallway. She pointed to a door a few feet away.

"There's the common room. It's our gathering place. I think—" she paused. Crept up to the closed door. Listened. Nodded. Continued in a low voice, "Grillett's in there."

The cries of the battle grew suddenly louder as part of the fray entered the hallway. More of Emil's crewmembers joined the first, their fancy leathers at odds with the swift and brutal way they fought. A thrust of the sword followed by a fist. A spin and a low, sweeping kick. It was a beautiful sight.

Veronica reached forward and eased the door open a crack. A gun popped, the sharp report loud in Emil's ears. He dropped to the floor. At the same time, a figure hurtled out of nowhere, knocking Veronica out of the way.

Emil looked around, unsure of where the bullet had come from… The fight behind them in the hallway or the room in front of them? He reached forward and slammed the door just in case. To his side, Veronica sprang to her feet.

"Emil?" she asked sharply. She looked shaken as she took a hesitant step toward him.

He smiled beneath his scarf at her concern and placed a hand on her shoulder. She felt strong beneath his touch, yet her skin was pale as the moon.

"I'm fine, *canım.*"

He allowed himself a moment to look at her. The soft shimmer of her eyes. The hard line of her mouth. She swayed under his scrutiny, her expression flickering.

He dropped his hand at once. His thoughts had turned far too dangerous for both of them. She stepped back and they glanced down to see who'd saved her, which of his crew Emil planned on awarding a generous token of his gratitude. The man lay groaning on the ground.

Emil cautiously turned him over, hoping he was okay. Veronica let out a startled cry, and it was then Emil noticed the man's face.

"Durad? Durad!"

His prince's eyes were closed, his breathing labored. Emil tossed aside all of Durad's goggles and gadgets and checked his wound. A hole. On the left side of his chest. Emil heart grew heavy, until he thought he might be sick.

"What are you doing here? How did you get here? Rosseau—"

It was impossible. An illusion. A dream. His prince. His oldest friend. Hit by a bullet. Lying here in his arms.

Emil had seen such a wound in battle. Durad might not survive. He would grow pale, pass out from the blood loss, and then his spirit would leave him empty and cold. Emil would know the moment it happened. The body would grow still and silent with nothing left to animate it.

"Skies, Durad. What on earth were you thinking?" he groaned, felt his vision blur and his scarf become wet.

Veronica stripped off her cape and pressed it to Durad's wounds. She leaned forward, great tears falling from her eyes.

"Where did he come from? How did he know, Emil? Will he be all right?"

He glanced away, unable to tell her the truth of the matter. The clamor of battle grew louder as Giles and his men reached the hallway. With a loud yelp, they crashed into the Enforcers from behind.

Emil clasped Durad tightly. He had to get his friend somewhere safe, but he was trapped. Grillett in the room just ahead and Enforcers behind.

Veronica wiped her eyes and stood. "I'll take care of Grillett. Wait here. Make sure no more harm comes to the prince." She checked the charge on her Tesla-ray and lowered her goggles.

"No!" he said. Durad's eyes fluttered at the loud noise. "Absolutely not. You have no idea what is in there. And he has a pistol, which he has probably already re-loaded. There could be a dozen more Enforcers. You cannot do this alone," Emil babbled, unable to form any coherent strategy to keep her from taking such a risk while unable to help her.

She glanced at the fray behind them and then back at Emil. "Take your prince and leave. Emil, you and Prince Durad have done enough. I never intended to involve you in all this, but I had no choice. Claire and the others," her voice choked. "I did what I had to do. You've gotten me this far. You'll never know how much it means to me, how different you are. Now, go!"

Emil took note of her rigid, unyielding stance. She would enter that room. Face the gilded shadows that chased her night after night. Fight bravely, with all her heart, for the children that had long ago claimed her love. Most likely, she would lose against such odds.

Emil whistled and Kasun came running to his side. He handed Durad gently over to his crewmember and said, "Nothing happens to him."

The ever-smirking Kasun took the prince's body and for the first time appeared solemn. He nodded and took shelter by the wall, shielding Durad with his body.

Veronica already had her hand on the doorknob. Emil snatched her shirt and whirled her around. He tilted her chin and stared into her eyes.

"Me first."

She looked startled for a moment, then she took up a post to the right of the doorframe. He spent one last moment memorizing her before he turned, kicked open the door, and spun to the side. He ducked and rolled as he entered the room. Another bullet whizzed by, just above his shoulder. When he stood, Veronica was there, unharmed, staring behind him.

Emil followed her gaze. Grillett no longer pointed the Smith & Wesson pistol at the doorway, but at the head of a petite, big-eyed, brown-haired girl of about seven or eight. Dressed not in factory rags but a bright blue dress, she must be one of Veronica's charges. The rest of the room, however, was filled with older boys of sixteen or seventeen wearing filthy, gray shirts and trousers. Grease streaked their faces and their hair stood up in uneven spikes, as if cut by a mischievous child. They carried broken rods, knives, and whatever one might find on a factory floor. Each wore looks varying from fury to fear as they looked at Veronica.

Emil's heart ached. It felt as though Grillett held up a mirror. Emil would look into it and see a tall, stick-thin boy wearing nothing but angles and deeply hidden fury. He would see a boy dangerously deep in his own mind, with little left to lose but a flickering flame of hope that would soon be extinguished by the next crack of a whip. He lowered his weapons. Their weight felt too much to bear.

Grillett spoke in a pleasant, crisp tone. "These boys, they've heard stories about you, Lady Eidolon."

Veronica didn't move, didn't speak. She simply stared at one boy after another, her hands tense by her sides, as though to keep them from reaching out. Emil felt the same impulse.

A smirk crept across Lord Grillett's face. "They know how you steal away others like them, give them hope of a different life. Why, look at this fat, healthy child I found picking weeds in the back alley. So bright. So innocent. You provide all this," he paused and lifted a brow, "and then give them to your father. The front lines need fresh blood… isn't that right?"

Veronica started and sputtered, "What? Of course I don't! I love them!"

The girl beside Grillett looked like she wanted to reach for Veronica but could only stare at her with pleading eyes.

Ridiculous, but brilliant. He'd turned the tables neatly. Emil wanted to smash his hand into Grillett's confident face.

Grillett interrupted. "Tsk, tsk. This little brat is part of your plan. Make them think they're safe and secure. Then send them to be slaughtered. The duke, why, he has the golden touch! No one can defeat him. He's never lost, they say. Well, of course he hasn't. He has an endless source of fuel for his battles."

"That's ridiculous! Why would I bother to feed them and make them feel secure before giving them to die? Why would I go to the time and expense to do all this?" Veronica's arm swept out, gesturing around the room. "Not one child has left this workhouse. I haven't found a safe place to put them and I would never—"

Grillett laughed. "These boys have seen bodies return from the front. So young. So mangled. They know there's no better existence beyond the factory doors than the productive and safe one I offer them. I feed them, clothe them, and give them purpose."

Veronica moved to step forward, but Grillett pressed the pistol tighter into the girl's temple. She froze. Emil inched up behind her slowly, when all he wanted was to cut Grillett down with a few swift strokes and end the boys' thrall.

"What bodies? You must be referring to those who die in your care. Those who become an unfortunate statistic in your profitable enterprise." She laughed, a bitter and hard sound. "Now you've managed to turn the tragic deaths of your orphan slaves into a twisted motivational tool for your remaining workers?"

A few of the boys shifted, exchanging glances with one another. The current of energy in the room wavered. They no longer clutched their weapons as tightly. The redness of anger in their cheeks paled.

Listen to her. Emil wanted to shut Grillett's lying mouth and tell the boys his own story. *There's hope. She can give it to you.*

Emil stepped closer to Veronica's side. Some of the younger boys appeared unconvinced of either tale, Veronica's or Grillett's, but the older ones were too far gone. Lost, hope's light brutally stamped out. They believed Grillett, because he'd delivered on every promise he'd made. These boys would attack Veronica, because they knew with ruthless certainty that if they didn't, they'd suffer. None of them had remained alive this long by being noble, by protecting others. They did what they had to in order to survive.

They were Emil, before he met Durad.

And now, surviving meant killing Veronica. Nothing would stop them.

Chapter Thirty-Six

Veronica had seen many terrible sights in the factory district. Children lashed by a cattail, cuffed and beaten for not meeting quota, denied food for bad behavior. The smell of the streets alone was nearly unbearable, filled with filth of every kind.

Nothing could compare to this. Here were the children that haunted her, the ones she hadn't saved. Ragged and thin to the bone, they were naught but lean muscle and anger. They provided the greatest contrast imaginable to Claire. Round-cheeked and healthy, she rarely smiled, but the darkness had at least been chased from her eyes.

Now, pale and frightened, she still looked at Veronica with complete trust, as though she'd always known Lady Flowers was also the Eidolon. Had they all known?

"What is it you want?" she asked Grillett.

He laughed, a bitter and hard sound. "You've taken from me the only thing I ever truly wanted. Now, like a promiscuous debutant, I am ruined." He shrugged. "It's only fair I seize everything from you. My boys here have their orders."

A shout rose from the boys and they lifted their weapons and advanced on her. She stumbled back. She would not fight them, though they were nearly grown. She looked into one pair of eyes after another. The despair she saw buried deep matched what she had coaxed away with dozens of others. They could yet be saved.

She dropped to her knees with her hands raised in surrender.

"Boys, I will not fight you."

Emil rushed to her side and drew his swords, pointing them at the closest ones.

"Do not take another step," he said.

The boys came to an abrupt stop, arms raised to ward off a blow. Veronica wanted to do what she did with all her orphans; wrap them in soft clothes, feed them until they felt sleepy, and then tell them the lovely story of Melilot. She wanted to gently reveal a candle of hope, give it to them and encourage them to feed the light until it revealed all the dark corners.

"You can't stop us," one boy said.

He was taller than the rest, his expression chiseled in hard, defensive lines. He moved forward with a deliberate step, his wiry strength clear in the way he spun a crowbar in his hand.

"I won't hurt you. I won't make you do anything. You don't have to listen to me, but you certainly don't have to listen to Lord Grillett, either," Veronica said.

Without hesitating, she tossed aside her hat and goggles. Her long hair tumbled down on her shoulders, thick and unruly. She paid no heed, slowly sweeping her gaze from one side of the room to the other. As she met one pair of eyes after another, most flinched and dropped their gazes to the floor. As though no one had really looked at them in a long time.

One boy with white-blond hair whispered, "She *is* a' angel."

"You dolt. It's not real." A taller boy clapped the speaker on the side of the head. "Don't look at 'er. She'll draw ya into her lyin' eyes." His voice wavered as he spoke, possibly uncertain in the face of such an unfamiliar sight, a person who might care.

Grillett sighed. He pointed his pistol at her. "I don't blame you, lads, for not seeing what she truly is. That pretty face has fooled the entire *ton*, why would you be able to discern what they have not? Now, go on." His voice hardened into steel. "Make her pay for her lies. Show her what you think of adults who ship children off to war."

The tall boy who'd challenged Veronica growled, the sound deep and feral. The noise echoed through the crowd, growing in strength, until it became a wave of pain and hatred.

Veronica remained kneeling. She would block their blows, but she wouldn't hurt them. Beside her, Emil sheathed his swords and stepped forward to shield her. He was fierce and elegant as he disarmed them with quick, efficient moves, trying not to harm them. Emil couldn't save them all from harm—several fell to the floor, groaning—but at least they lived. The boys tried to surround Veronica, but Emil fought as he did that day on his airship. Defending the center point presented little challenge to him. Veronica stood behind him, knowing she couldn't match his skill at keeping the boys at bay without casualties.

A moment later, Grillett stepped forward, his gun still drawn. Emil cried out a warning. Grillett pulled the trigger. Veronica threw up her arms to protect her face right before the bullet slammed into her, knocking her backwards.

Chapter Thirty-Seven

Veronica waited for the wave of pain to wrap her in its familiar embrace, sharp and hot, but she felt nothing, save the tightness in her chest from the anticipation.

Emil's hands cupped her face, damp and warm. "Veronica!" His breath warmed her brow. "Where did it hit you?" Blood streaked his forehead and his turban was gone. Black hair wound around a top knot on his head, frayed and wild.

She pushed herself to a sitting position. Emil dropped his hands but hovered inches away, his eyes frantically searching her person. Her clothing was smattered with a bit of blood here and there, most likely from Enforcers she'd fought. She put her weight on her right hand and lifted her left.

There was a hole in her glove, directly in the center of her palm. She clasped and unclasped her hand. Still strong. Still metal. She looked through the hole to see a completely intact hand. Not even a dent. *Bugger,* the metal was strong.

A great breath escaped her lungs, the air burning as it left her lips. She was alive. Unharmed.

Alive.

Suddenly, the odd quiet of the room penetrated the fog in Veronica's mind. The boys surrounded her, weapons dangling by their sides. Even the fiercest of them looked unsure. Several scurried over toward Claire. The usually calm and quiet girl appeared even more so in this moment. Her gaze was on the floor. Fixed on the body on the floor. Lord Grillett's.

"You are all right, *canım*?" Emil asked in a low voice.

She nodded. "The bullet bounced off of my hand." She held it up for inspection. "Must have saved my life."

His scarf rose at the corners, indicating a smile. "You, my princess, are very hard to kill. A good quality in a ruler, I'd say."

Veronica answered with her own smile. She got lost in the brightness of relief in his eyes for a moment.

Then, she remembered. "Grillett? What happened to him?"

Emil inclined his head toward Claire. "He lies there."

"Did you… is he dead?"

He stood and then pulled her gently to her feet. They approached Grillett with cautious steps. The golden giant looked small and rather pathetic lying on the floor, his icy eyes closed, his army scattered and unsure.

In the very center of his forehead, just below the rim of his helmet, a large hole fed a river of red spreading down his face. The blood coated his once unnaturally pale white face, ugly now, with the bits of skin and clumps of blood clinging to his cheeks. Veronica reached for Claire's hand with her good one and squeezed it in reassurance. Claire relaxed, leaning into Veronica's side, her eyes closing at the sight.

Emil prodded Grillett with the toe of his boot. He didn't move. Emil sank to the floor and placed his fingers on the pulse at Grillett's neck. Then waited. Shook his head.

Yes, Grillett was most certainly dead.

It didn't seem possible that such a goliath could fall. His golden armor caught the shifting light and nearly blinded her. Veronica stepped back. Had he moved? She shook her head. Of course not, what a ninny she was. Afraid of the man, even in death.

"He is dead. With a wound like that, he went pretty quickly." Emil said quietly. He didn't look at her, his gaze remaining on the boys still surrounding them, weapons in hand.

"Whose bullet did this?" Veronica asked. "Was it…?" She held up her left arm.

Emil nodded. "I only heard the one shot. After that, I noticed nothing else." He kept his eyes on Grillett, as though his confession made him uncomfortable.

Veronica turned Claire away from the body, knelt, then reached forward a trembling hand and checked Grillett's pulse again. She had to be sure. It seemed impossible that he lay here at her feet.

Nothing. Not even a flutter. The leathery skin felt cold and dry beneath her fingers. Chilled perhaps by the metal entombing his upper body. Or by the ice that had long ago splintered and frozen his heart.

The tallest boy, the one with the feral smile, stepped forward. He opened his mouth to speak, but at that moment, the door slammed against the wall and the room flooded with soldiers in the uniform of Her Majesty's army. Veronica rose and stepped in front of Claire, blocking her from view of the door, and gripped the Tesla-ray at her side.

Mercy, it couldn't be. Her mask, where had she dropped it? She searched the floor, unable to find anything among the heavy pairs of black boots now concealing the carpet. After all she'd done to conceal her true self, she felt exposed and raw. The remembered chill of those snowy days she'd spent hiding in the garden offered to numb her heart, but she resisted. The children had changed her, strengthened her heart.

The group of soldiers parted, and the Duke of Richmond, Her Majesty's favored general, the Hero of the Skies, stepped through the doorway. He was still in the full officer's uniform he wore at the wedding. Unmistakable blood-red coat, startlingly white gloves.

"Take these delinquents into custody," he ordered with a nod at a soldier wearing an officer's braid. The officer signaled his men.

Grillett's boys, only half of them still armed, looked to their feral leader. The boy glanced at Veronica, his expression impossibly dark for such a youth. She silently pleaded with him. *Surrender. Don't try anything.*

He lifted his chin. For a moment, it looked as though he would order a fight. His shoulders rolled back. Fingers tightened on his weapon.

Don't. Please. She didn't flinch at his continued stare.

All the boys here would perish at the hands of these experienced soldiers. There could be no other outcome.

The feral boy bared his teeth but raised both his hands in surrender. He never took his eyes off Veronica. Not when the soldiers cuffed his hands. Not when one burly sergeant raised his arm and struck him across the side of the head and shoved him forward. Not until he was herded out the door, followed closely by his crew of misfit boys. Their feet dragged the floor, backs hunched, in a pose so familiar to Veronica that her anxiety for their safety flashed into an anger that flamed hotter as each boy left.

Veronica watched Claire slide behind Emil into a wall panel behind the curtain; one of the many passageways to the safe room she prayed contained the rest of the children. She knew the protocols for emergencies and had been caught off guard outside, the poor dear. Mistress Phillips would do her best to keep her safe now.

The duke took several slow, even steps forward, hands clasped behind his back in a pose so straight, Veronica knew it to be painful. He glanced down at her black boots, then at her men's trousers, her shirt, at the Tesla-ray at her side and the sword strapped at her hip, and finally up to her face.

He stared, relentless in his perusal. Though she wanted to flee, escape his awful eyes, she did not. She let the duke, her papá, see her for the first time. She looked at him straight on, gilded with armor she'd never had before, armor stronger than Grillett's... the knowledge that she'd done something right and good.

When the duke spoke, he aimed his words like a sword, quick and sharp. "You're a *traitor*. After dedicating my life, my whole life to the crown, I discover this. That my own blood has turned into something twisted, wrong, and evil. I find that not only have you been dressing as a man, but you have blood on your hands! You've murdered men. Took it upon yourself to administer justice, rather than trusting in a system I've supported and built up for decades."

She opened her mouth to respond, but he backhanded her with a force that sent her flying several feet. The slap echoed like a gunshot. The light dimmed as her vision blurred and sound muffled. Her cheek burned. Pain resounded in the rest of her body, reminding her she wasn't fully healed. She tried to rise, but the floor didn't remain steady.

Emil reached down to pull her up, his gentle touch converse to the wrath in his eyes. As he put her on her feet, he whispered, "Let me do it."

It took her a moment to realize what he offered. Her head ached and her body burned with pain. Before she could consider his words, the duke continued his rant.

"Your husband lies nearly dead in the hallway, and I find another corpse at your feet. A peer of the realm! There's something evil in you, child, that I could never fix. No matter how hard I tried. The shame you bring upon me and upon the Richmond name is worse than any punishment you could have ever devised for me."

Veronica had long anticipated such a final judgment from the duke. His words flew at her, but she stared them down until they vanished, utterly powerless. If she cared in the least about his opinion, Veronica would've never become the Eidolon in the first place.

The duke seemed to realize exactly how far she'd grown apart from him during her silence. He gestured around the room. "This—Bridges—will be sold. Your orphans turned over to the factory district for a chance at a useful life. And you." His voice lost all hint of emotion, turning bland and even. He might've been ordering Critchton to fetch him his nightly port. He turned his eyes on her, vacant and dead. "You, Veronica, will be executed for your crimes."

The duke nodded at a soldier standing near her. Veronica heard the rush of air and then her legs were swept out from under her.

Chapter Thirty-Eight

Emil reached out and snatched Veronica before the soldier could land his blow. He hoisted her up into his arms, cradling her close. She bled from the cut to her cheek, her face sallow and pale.

"Enough. She's a Princess of Sombor," Emil growled.

The duke made a slashing gesture with his hand yet spoke in a mild voice. "Veronica committed crimes against the Crown. Her newfound royal title will not protect her against that. You will hand her over to me, or I will bring all of England's might against your ridiculous country." He stepped toward Emil but had to look up to meet his gaze. Emil raised a brow.

"Boy, I don't know what *relationship* you had with Veronica," the duke said with a twist of his mouth, "but you must now choose. Your country or the girl?"

Emil wanted to plunge his sword into this man's belly and watch as the light left his eyes, but if he did, the duke's soldiers would attack without hesitation. He counted at least a dozen in the room, but he'd no idea how many more waited outside. Veronica couldn't help, and he couldn't protect her while taking on so many at a time.

He couldn't let the duke take Veronica, could he? After a few moments, a plan grew in his mind. Though his entire being trembled with hearty vehemence, Emil inclined his head stiffly.

A soldier stepped forward to take Veronica. She turned away from Emil, while squeezing his hand. She understood and was giving her permission. His heart twisted.

He whispered, "I'm sorry," and set her on her feet.

He wanted to reach forward, pull her back, cut down any that would challenge him. He wanted her to know he had the beginnings of a plan, that he would still come for her and save her, that he could never leave her. He settled for a light touch of her back as she stepped away from him. He felt the space between them chill, and his heart turned cold as iron.

After one more quick glance at Emil, Veronica held her hands out to be cuffed.

Trust me to save you, he wanted to say.

The duke used the toe of his highly polished boot to nudge Lord Grillett's prone body. "This workhouse is a futile symbol of those who refuse to face the world as it is. It, too, will burn, leaving behind only cold, useless ashes."

The duke turned to leave. He threw a final command over his shoulder to the remaining handful of soldiers. "Kill him."

Emil whirled and sliced his sword across the arm of the last soldier. The soldier dropped his blade and collapsed on the floor. Emil kicked him, rendering him senseless. A quick search told him all the others remained down and out. He sheathed his sword and wiped the sweat from his forehead with his sleeve. The duke's men hadn't presented as much of a challenge as he'd anticipated. These soldiers fought cleanly and efficiently, but Emil did not fight cleanly. A swift kick to knock a man's feet out from under him or a simple punch and they were defeated.

Emil rushed into the hallway, searching for Durad. He found Kasun in his same post, blood staining his fancy togs. Durad's body lay behind him, appearing untouched. Several other bodies lay before him. When Kasun heard Emil's footsteps, he swung wildly toward him.

Emil held up his hands. "Kasun. Well done." He let gratitude soften his voice. "Very well done."

Kasun sheathed his sword with an unsteady hand. The scars on his face appeared in sharper relief as he spoke in an unsuccessfully casual tone. "Captain. The prince is alive and safe."

"Thank you. Now go. Find Rosseau and bring him to me." Emil paused, watching Kasun use the sleeve of his jacket to wipe the sweat from his eyes. It surprised Emil that the fierce Serbian had defended the prince so intensely. "You've done me a great service."

Kasun straightened and nodded. He saluted Emil once, crisply, and loped off down the now empty hallway.

Emil knelt by his prince. Durad's chest lifted and fell slowly, his eyes remaining shut. Where had he come from? He must've suspected something when both Emil *and* Veronica left the reception. Durad was nearly as good as Emil at slipping in and out of places unseen. What a horrible skill to teach him. Emil certainly hadn't thought that through.

As Durad's blood soaked through Emil's robes, he wished that life would not, for once, find the worst way to cause him pain. He wondered, in fact, if his pain or Durad's were worse. Emil wasn't sure he could survive this. It had never been his plan to outlive Durad. Emil was to give his life for the prince, not watch him bleed until he could no longer keep a mortal body.

Emil half-whispered, half-groaned, "Wake up, *hayır, olamaz,* wake up!"

Durad's eyes twitched open and he coughed.

"What did I do now, Emil?" he whispered. "I'm constantly disappointing you, am I? And now I got myself shot."

Emil raised his friend's head and torso with gentle hands and clasped him to his chest. "Getting shot is a beginner move, Durad. Do not let it happen again." His words faded at the end. He couldn't quite bring himself to a show of optimism, even for his oldest friend.

Durad smiled, a desperate, twisted one. "I won't." He coughed. "Who knew my lovely wife was such a hero? She's that Eidolon, the one Grillett's after, isn't she?"

"I am afraid so," Emil answered.

"She's good for us. For Sombor. She'll save us all. Keep her safe, Emil."

Durad clasped Emil's hand and gave him a look filled with a meaning Emil didn't understand. His prince's chest rose and fell one more time, and then lay still.

Emil leaned down and pressed his forehead to Durad's. His soul had indeed risen and vanished to whatever world awaited them after this life. For a moment, Emil wished he could follow. What was this life without the charming, maddening, always grinning Durad? A deep wrenching in his gut strengthened that desire. He felt his strength leave him, and he sagged against the wall.

"What happened, *capitan*?" Rosseau's voice interrupted his thoughts as he rushed down the hallway and then sank heavily to the floor beside Emil. "The prince! I've been looking everywhere. What happened?"

Emil's head snapped up and looked into the shocked eyes of his first mate. It took him several moments to re-surface from the tide of his grief. He shook his head, trying to disperse the fog.

"*Capitan*?" Rosseau asked again, this time softly.

Emil forced himself to stand, carrying Durad's limp body with him. "Not now, Rosseau." He headed down the hallway. Rosseau followed, shuffling dejectedly after his *capitan*.

"Is the prince dead?" he asked.

Emil nodded. "We have to find the children. They were not with Grillett."

"My deepest apologies—" Rosseau began, his voice strained.

"Not. Now," Emil interrupted.

He couldn't deal with his first mate's regrets right now. Not when he carried his friend's body in his arms. Later. When he wasn't soaked in blood. When the edges of his sorrow weren't so razor-sharp, shredding his heart and mind.

When they rounded the corner, a small face peered out of a nearby room, only to vanish once again. Emil motioned for Rosseau to be silent. Rosseau held out his arms and Emil carefully handed over Durad's body.

Emil then padded softly into the room, calling out in a quiet voice, "The danger is gone, little one. The Eidolon has saved you once again. There is nothing more to fear."

He glimpsed a shadow flicker off to his right. Emil dropped to his knees and placed his hands behind his head.

"Will it help if I surrender to you?"

He waited, trying to keep his breath even, but his pulse raced. There was so little time. Of course the child would be frightened, but how long could he afford to wait? Several seconds passed.

"Emil? *Ağabey*?" the child asked. She stepped forward into the light, her eyes wide. "Is that you?"

A thrill rushed through him, so strong that the shock of it brought instant tears to his eyes. "Suzanna. *Camm*," he whispered, barely able to form the words.

His sister rushed toward him and threw her arms around his neck. He buried his face in her shoulder and wept. Emil's heart lifted from the pit where it had fallen, brightening his whole being until he laughed as he never had before. The sound was so light, it floated away, trailing hope.

"Ya foun' me, Emil! How'd ya fin' me? Where'd ya come from? Do ya know the Eidolon? Why'd it take ya so long! It's bin eight years! Why you wearin' that scarf?" Suzanna pulled away from Emil with a grin that spread from one side of her flushed face to the other. She was ten now, and though small for her age, her face was rounded with health and free of the pain that never left the factory kids.

Emil placed his hands on Suzanna's cheeks, her skin smooth and warm. "I never stopped looking for you. *Never.*"

She shrugged. "I know. I never stopped waitin'."

He smiled. She hadn't known English before the duke took her. She must have picked it up from the street rats at the factories. Every word she spoke sounded beautiful to him.

As he gazed into his sister's face, he realized that Veronica did this. She had saved Suzanna. Another dark, twisted part of his soul broke free; his life, once more, brightened by Veronica.

Emil stood and took Suzanna's hand. "Come, show me where the other children are and then I'll take you to my ship. I am a captain, you know."

She smiled again and led him out of the room. When they saw Rosseau, still holding Durad's body, Emil's sorrow returned, sharp and hard. Suzanna squeezed his hand and helped him take a step forward.

Chapter Thirty-Nine

Emil reached Buckingham Palace well past midnight. Suzanna was safely in his room at the hotel, guarded by Rosseau. Rosseau wouldn't let her out of his sight.

With Suzanna's help, Emil had found the rest of the orphans, hidden in the cellar with tear-stained faces. Thank the skies they were safe. Since Suzie had been the longest at Bridges, she knew every hidden corridor, and swore no one would have been able to find her if she hadn't wanted to be found. Emil guessed they would have a lot in common, even after so many heart-breaking years apart.

Alec had suddenly re-appeared with a casual, "The rest of Grillett's men disappeared. Where's Veronica?"

"Gone. Your father took her," Emil said.

Alec's usual grin wavered. "Do you have an idea, then? I assume you're going to get her."

"I might. I don't suppose you know anything about Buckingham Palace security?"

The fop broke into a laugh and told Emil enough to shock him speechless. Emil then put Alec in charge of the children and left. Surprisingly reliable, that brother of Veronica's. Wouldn't have guessed. Emil needed to stop underestimating that family.

He had to save her. The one. *His.* Emil felt his heart pound harder every moment that she remained under the duke's power.

From what Emil could see through his scope, several dirigibles lazed above Buckingham Palace, armed with heavy artillery. Guards patrolled the roof and the grounds. The building was enormous, with rooms stretching out endlessly in both directions.

Luckily, he didn't have to guess which one housed the queen.

How Alec knew, Emil didn't care to guess.

Emil motioned toward Kasun, and their airship went black. All lights extinguished at once. After a few minutes, Emil slowed the *Hırsız* and handed the wheel to Kasun. They'd reached the west wing. He swung over the side and onto the window casement. He landed a little harder than he intended, making a scraping sound on the stone.

He reached down to open the window but found it tightly wedged shut. After a few noiseless pushes, Emil realized he would have to break the glass. He hadn't planned on announcing himself in such a fashion, but he hadn't the time to find another entrance. With a hard push, he flipped off the casement and through the window.

Emil crashed onto the floor of the bedroom, bits of glass nicking him everywhere. A long blade pressed against his throat. The scent of jasmine filled the air.

"I'm in a playful mood this evening, or I might have killed you. I still could. Say the wrong words, and I will succeed where my guards have not," Queen Victoria said.

Her silver hair ran unchecked down her fine, white lawn nightgown. She held the blade—a long, wickedly sharp thing— right up to his artery. Her eyes met his, full of power and authority. Everything that Emil thought Durad might have desired.

Sombor's future, Veronica's life, his life, all depended on him. Emil had no doubt she would kill him should he fail. Yet he'd watched her at Almack's, the night Veronica had been presented to Durad. Emil *had* to be right about her.

"You may notice, Your Majesty, I am not armed." Emil held up his hands. "It might make you curious to know why *Kartal* came thus to your private chambers."

The queen's brows lifted, and with a flick of her wrist, she cut his scarf away. When she saw his scars, she laughed, sounding delighted.

"This is better than anything I could dream of. Come, sit. Tell me your tale." She motioned with her rapier toward a settee.

He obeyed.

Chapter Forty

When Veronica woke, pain knifed through her arms and she nearly cried out. She lifted her head to find both her wrists clasped in irons, which were in turn bolted to the wall. She hung, her feet brushing the floor. Her mouth was so dry, she could barely swallow. There was a pool of blood on the floor beneath her right wrist where the shackles had sliced through her skin.

The glove on her left hand remained, covering her macabre fingers, while the one on her right was missing. After all the duke had uncovered about her, and after leaving her here raw and aching and alone, at least he hadn't discovered that one secret. She glanced around. She was in a cell somewhere, with nothing but a pile of straw, a bowl, and several insects and scurrying creatures.

Where was she? The duke had found her, accused her of treason, and then… Emil. He'd been forced to choose between her and Sombor. He'd done the right thing, of course, but leaving his side, returning once more to the duke's steely embrace, had wrenched her heart in half. Her metal hand had clenched into a fist, and she'd wanted to swing it at every smirking face in the room. She'd wanted to show the duke she had power to match his, with Emil at her side. The duke wouldn't threaten the Somborian soldier so lightly after seeing him fight.

She hadn't risked the odds. Along with the dozen or so soldiers in the room, there could've been ten times more lining the hallways and guarding the doors. If she and Emil lost, the duke wouldn't hesitate to attack Sombor, simply for the insult of not taking his threat seriously.

She'd gotten one last glimpse of Emil—rigid, eyes blazing at the duke—and then she'd been dragged out of Bridges and into a waiting carriage. She'd instantly missed his solid shadow. Without Emil, she felt as alone as she always had. The awful, familiar emptiness swallowed her, and this time, she wasn't sure she could keep that small, flickering flame of courage alive. Several blocks later, when the tisane wore off, she'd passed out from the pain.

What had happened to Claire? To the rest of her children? She hadn't seen them on her forced march to the duke's military carriage. She hoped they'd taken refuge in the cellar. They'd practiced the drills enough times, but they were only children. Emil would find them, if they hadn't been captured. He wouldn't forget. Of course he wouldn't. Even if they had been taken, he'd find them.

But he couldn't find Veronica. No one could. Not here. She glanced around again. She must be entombed beneath the military headquarters, swarmed by EurAsia's finest. The duke's office took up most of the main floor of this building. He wouldn't let her go far.

Even if Emil knew her location, he couldn't save her, not with the duke's threats. She wouldn't see Emil again. Wouldn't watch him dance among his enemy, savage and strong. Wouldn't stare at his scarf and wonder what secrets a man so fierce would need to hide.

Pain. It kept her conscious now. She glanced up at the thin stream of moonlight through the tiny window. Nearly dawn. The duke's favorite time of day. She had maybe an hour left.

Not only had she left Emil behind, she'd left all her children. Claire's thin, strong arms thrown around Veronica's neck. Suzie's nonstop chatter. Faces, one after another, smiling and hesitant, flooded her mind. Memories, telling Melilot's story, watching the children paint away their grief in those heartbreaking self-portraits, Agnes' hand taking hers, Landon's eyes, focused unwaveringly, as he built a winding, intricate train track.

All of it, all she'd done, every child's life she'd changed... she would never do it again. Never watch the emptiness fill with love, laughter, and healing. Hundreds saved, but there were thousands more. In the end, had she done enough? Why hadn't she tried to train another in her place? Why hadn't she thought to leave behind someone who could carry on her work? Even Matilda, or perhaps

Clank.

Alec. She might've confided in him. He could obviously swing a blade, maybe even well enough to become the Eidolon. He'd given her clues here and there. Glimpses of who he could really be. Brave. Resourceful. Capable. Would the duke announce her death at the breakfast table this morning, as though he'd always known Veronica would end up this way? A disappointment beyond imagining?

The duke might even wonder if Alec hid confidences like hers and order a full investigation into his activities. What would he find? She hoped Alec hid something worthy. She believed it possible. Even after all those years she cried out for him in their winter garden, waiting for him, hoping to hear the crunch of his footsteps as he arrived to put his arm around her and lend her some bit of bravery.

Hope for Alec, like her flame, could apparently not be extinguished.

Hope and pain. Co-existing opposites. Her body shouted at her, but she paid it no heed. She had to get free. She mustered her strength and pulled at the chains. Her left arm, still not quite healed, burned and tore. The chains held comically fast, seeming to laugh at her attempts to escape. If only they had bound her hands instead. Then her unnatural fingers could serve a practical function. Her metal fingers couldn't reach far enough to tear at the chains.

Veronica took a deep breath and tried again to pull her chains off the wall. This time, when the chains held, her body jerked. Pain exploded through her arms and she blacked out.

Cold water drenched Veronica, a sharp sensation that took her breath away and woke all her senses at once. A soldier stood beside her, a key in hand. He inserted it into the manacles about her wrists. When the second one clicked and the chain released, Veronica dropped to the floor.

The soldier instantly cuffed her and hefted her over his shoulder. She grunted. The stench coming off this man was horrible, like rotten eggs wrapped in old fish. She blinked, trying to formulate a plan as he carried her up the stairs, but her mind remained fogged with pain.

Veronica flexed her metal fingers, trying to reach down to her cuffs. She had managed to get one finger underneath the opposite cuff when the soldier grunted and shifted, breaking her grip. She continued to try, but the man strode down the hallway at a near jog, jostling her about.

Needles of pain shot through her arms as she tried to twist her hands without getting caught. The great oaf turned right down a hallway. The light streaming through the windows caught her full in the face and she winced.

Dawn. It was time.

She slipped her index finger once more under the cuff and pulled. The metal tore but didn't break. They must've been made like the Enforcers' blades, nearly impossible to even scratch. She stared at them, wondering at how useless they made her feel, how helpless.

There had to be another way. She could whip her heel back and catch the man in the face…

Now they were outside. Fifty or more soldiers stood in formation around a raised platform. The duke was certainly taking no chances on her escape. Much like Lord Grillett, this show of strength forced a corner of her mouth to lift in a half smile.

The soldier shifted and she was flung onto her back, her breath knocked out of her lungs. Sunlight flashed before the duke's face darkened her vision.

"Lady Veronica Clarke. For your crimes against Her Royal Majesty, Queen Victoria, you've been sentenced to hang by the neck until you are dead."

The duke's familiar face stared down at her, impassive as always. Veronica tried to speak, but her voice was hoarse from the ordeal of the last few hours. If she were to face death at his hands, she wanted to tell him everything she never had. She wanted to tear off the mask she'd worn since childhood and rail at his cruelty, at every lash and cane and every moment of pain and misery she'd endured at his hands.

The duke's eyes burned into her. Those eyes, so much like hers in color and shape, but with none of the same feeling.

He leaned in closer and said, "You've failed, Lady Eidolon, and shamed us all. You're worthless, no better than those gutter rats." The words were crisp and polished, smooth as a sharp knife through skin.

Veronica pushed herself to a standing position with her metal hand, chains dragging the ground. She steeled herself against the hot rush of pain, quivering with fury. She faced him, shoulders square, back straight, and cleared her throat. He'd said those words to her hundreds of times, but this was the last. Words tumbled from her mouth, strong and clear.

"I'm *not* ashamed of what I did as the Eidolon. Even if I may have, in the end, failed those I tried to save."

She shuffled forward, lifting her shaking, joined hands to point at him. He returned her stare, unblinking, hard as stone. "No matter how hard *you* tried, Papá, you did not extinguish the flame burning inside that is uniquely me. I believe that children are good and innocent. I believe they're lovely and useful and worthy of being saved. And most of all, I believe that you are everything you despise. Useless. A drain on society."

She reached out and poked the duke in the chest with her metal index finger. He stumbled backwards, his face flickering in confusion.

"You're weak. Vulnerable. Blind. Useless. A waste of society's resources."

The duke straightened up and grabbed her wrist. "You're stalling. Don't think I'll delay."

Stall death? That's the only thing she'd done since her birth. The duke had broken her time after time, waiting for her to give up, waiting for his punishments to become too overwhelming to handle. Now, he would have to hang her to achieve the result he'd worked so hard for.

He released her and clasped his hands in his familiar, painful position behind his back. "Since the opportunity for truth presents itself, I will reveal to you what all your cleverness could not uncover."

He smiled for the first time Veronica could remember. It was cold, sinister, and black as sin. It made her want to crawl for cover, to do anything to escape the focus of such an expression. Even the soldiers around her shifted. She tried to fold her arms across her chest but found her hands still cuffed. She focused on a spot over the duke's left shoulder, unable to keep her eyes on such a horrible, hateful expression. Her empty stomach twisted with dread.

The duke spoke softly, his words rich with a sly enthusiasm. "I gave Grillett the funding he needed to start the factories. I told him where to find the orphans. I hired the convicts that work as guards and Enforcers for him. All of it is my doing, you little fool. You think you made a difference? I will undo all of it. I will return your precious children to the Grave. I will burn down Bridges, and I will make sure this never happens again."

She stumbled. Fell to her knees. It made morbid sense. All of it. His rants about the orphans. The military getting the first pick on all of Grillett's dirigibles. Her arranged marriage to the ruler of a country that controlled a large amount of fuel. Even the cover Bridges provided, so that, should the whole thing be blown wide open, Queen Victoria would never suspect the duke.

The duke stepped back and spoke loudly. "Make her ready!" he ordered.

A soldier pushed her roughly up the stairs and onto the platform. Another stepped from the thick shadows behind the platform and lifted her hair, fitting the scratchy noose around her neck. The fibers rubbed against her skin, burning and biting, as the soldier tightened the noose.

She closed her eyes. Emil's black eyes filled her mind, dark and gentle. Claire's brown ones followed, soft and trusting.

"Now!" the duke ordered.

Swish.

Chapter Forty-One

Veronica fell. Waited for the snap of the rope. Instead, landed in something hard.

"Mmph," the thing said. Followed by a few curses. "Didn't think you'd weigh this much, Peanut."

Alec set her on the ground inelegantly, and she stumbled backward, nearly falling.

Her brother. Here. Wearing a mask? Bending over with his hands on his knees, seeming winded. She looked up at the hole in the platform and then brought her hands up to her neck, searching for the rope. It was still looped around her, the clean-cut end dangling halfway down her torso. Once slice from her metal finger and it fell to the ground.

Alec had come for her. The little girl, alone in the garden, waiting for him year after year. Now realizing she hadn't stopped looking and hoping. First, at Bridges with Grillett, and then here.

Veronica used her non-metal hand to swipe at the wetness in her eyes as she stared at him.

"We're not through this yet, Peanut. Musn't start that. Here."

He winked and tossed her a rapier. She caught it out of reflex. Before he turned to face the guards, she thought she heard him mutter their old phrase. *Together, forever.*

Veronica stepped forward to join Alec as he rushed back out to join the battle, but the duke blocked her way, his own rapier drawn. Without a word, the duke's face red with contained rage, he advanced, his strokes quicker than the eye could see. Veronica parried with her metal wrist and with her rapier, almost too slow. She fell to her knees under the force of the blows. Sweat blinded her vision. Her arms, her wrists, on fire. Here she was again, on the ground. Where she always ended up in front of the duke.

After all this. The kidnapping. Blackthorne. Grillett. Her hand. Losing the children. The Eidolon. No. She wasn't the same girl with open palms waiting for the cane.

As the duke's sword descended, Veronica's metal hand reached up and grabbed the blade. She concentrated. Squeezed. The metal snapped in half.

Emil stepped forward from the shadows. With Alec's help, he'd joined the group of guards for Veronica's execution. It hadn't been hard to take out the platform guard and slice the rope. Thank the gods they'd been on time.

Emil heard the movement before he saw it. A sword appeared in his vision, and he blocked the blow without a thought. Another soldier stepped forward, and another, until they ringed Emil.

The soldiers surrounding Emil advanced, but Emil's crew, disguised in the group, pounced. With sweeping legs and quick, brutal punches, they confounded the duke's soldiers' orderly fighting style. Emil stepped through the chaos and toward Veronica, but it felt too slow. *He* felt too slow. No matter how quickly he told his brain to move, his body couldn't keep up. He distantly heard the crowd shouting for Veronica's head.

Veronica fell to her knees under the force of the duke's blows. Emil shoved aside one man, and then another, but he still wasn't close enough.

Suddenly, the duke stumbled backward. Right into Emil.

Emil yanked the man's arms behind him with one hand and held a blade to his throat with the other. Veronica collapsed, but Rosseau was there. He caught her with a fierce look of concern.

"I gave you a fair chance," the duke said to him. "Sombor could have existed peacefully as an ally of England. Now, I'll absorb it, take your resources. Your children."

Emil nicked him with a quick, measured stroke, satisfied to see the line of red on the duke's neck. "I do not see how. I have explained to Her Royal Majesty, Queen Victoria, the full conditions of the factories and what the Eidolon has been fighting for."

"Impossible." The duke said in a conversational voice more fit for a drawing room. "Who are you? A simple bodyguard."

A brother. "I believe your queen awaits your presence."

"You know who I am. Let me go. I will not ask again."

Emil turned the duke back toward the platform. A uniformed official, one of Victoria's trusted inner circle, stepped forward, along with a dozen of his men.

"Tell this man to release me at once," the duke said.

The official raised a pistol and pointed it at the duke.

Emil sheathed his sword and shoved the duke away from him. He had what he wanted. Veronica. Suzanna. He would leave the duke in Victoria's capable hands.

The duke smiled, a twisted, horrible sight, and said, "Her Majesty will not stand for this."

The official gestured for the duke to follow. The duke obeyed, striding toward the palace, the specter of Emil's words on his heels.

"Where is she?" Emil asked as he leapt over the side of the *Hırsız.*

Rosseau was to bring Veronica back and prepare the ship for launch. The burly Frenchman emerged from Emil's cabin.

"I had to give her a sleeping draught. She would not let me attend her injuries. She kept going on about Claire and Suzie and her children and refused to sit. I told her they were fine, that they were safe at Bridges, but she insisted on seeing them with her own eyes. I believe she was in too much pain to think.

"Once she fell asleep, I set her arms and bound her cuts. She had pulled one shoulder out of its sockets and cut her wrist so deeply it is a miracle she could stand upright. As it is, she will need substantial time and nourishment to recover. I gave her some of the tisane."

A shoulder dislocated? In addition to her barely healed hand? Yet she survived. Just as he had, long ago in the factory escape, she had survived. *Aman Tanrım.*

Emil clapped his friend on the shoulder. "Thank you, Rosseau. It was well done."

The Frenchman would not meet his eyes, keeping them cast on the ground. "*Capitan*, I will be leaving after we reach Sombor." He bowed and turned to leave, but Emil caught his arm.

He didn't speak for a moment. Rosseau's shoulders, always so proud, now hunched, burdened. Like Emil, he carried a nearly untenable guilt over Durad's death. How did one get past such a thing? Was it possible?

Emil swallowed, thinking of all the times he'd failed Durad. The years he'd been gone. Falling in love with his fiancée. No one person would carry the guilt for Durad's death.

"My friend," Emil said to Rosseau, "the loss of the prince will not be laid at your feet. Not now, not ever. The prince chose to put himself in harm's path, just as he chose to deceive you by leaving without informing you. Had he done so, you might have been able to save him. I hope you will not leave me. I have lost enough this day already."

Rosseau's head lifted, eyes drooping with sadness. He nodded. "I will think on your words, *capitan*."

Emil watched him go, hoping it wouldn't take long for his first mate to obey this particular order. Then, he strode toward his cabin and entered quietly.

Veronica lay on the bed, her eyes closed in heavy slumber. Her mouth remained tight, as though her dreams haunted rather than comforted her.

He sank down into the chair and took her hand.

Chapter Forty-Two

This time when Veronica awoke, she didn't feel the cold embrace of steel at her wrists, but a soft pillow at her cheek and a warm brick at her feet. She sat up quickly and swore, her head swimming. Bugger, Rosseau. He must have given her another sleeping draft. He'd been doing so for a week, slipping it in her food and drink. After she'd learned the children were safe and out of the duke's reach, she had let him. The pain from her wrists and arm had been overwhelming.

Where was she? Veronica swung her legs over the side of the bed. She didn't seem to be on an airship any longer but in a decadent room. Light, red silk drapes hung about several large windows. An oddly shaped writing desk, formed like a crescent moon, sat in the corner. A small fire burned in a fireplace, with two chairs flanking either side. A set of columns divided her room from a sitting area, which contained an oriental-looking couch and another set of chairs. Was this Durad's room?

Blessed saints, here she lived while he did not. Veronica never thought she would mourn the loss of any man. Yet Durad had surely changed her, as much as the new hand she now wore. Charming as spring and good to his soul, she'd liked him.

The people of Sombor might blame her for his death. She would either be a princess in their eyes or a murderer. Veronica would not fault them for their choice, but she wanted to make things right. She wanted to help Sombor. Even if only for Durad. Would they allow her? They might think a princess who is also a masked crusader a ridiculous figure. London certainly had, but as always, she couldn't quite fight the spark that told her she could make a difference, that she was different from the duke.

The duke. He'd turned out to be the biggest liar and murderer of them all. How could she not have known? She should have at least suspected the duke had something to do with it. It seemed incomprehensible that he would dirty his hands or lie to the queen he loved and admired.

She stood, noticing that she wore a soft chemise. Her shoulder no longer ached, and the pain in her wrists beat like a dull, worn-out drum. Her left hand where Dr. Hoch had attached the new one still chilled her arm, but the giant, burning ache had vanished. She lifted it, gloveless now, and examined it in the soft light. She flexed her fingers carefully. This contraption had saved her life. Saved her from the duke. And from Grillett. Maybe, like Clank, like Lady Flowers, it could do something good for the world.

The door to her room opened, admitting a girl of about nine years of age with beautiful, brown skin the color of Veronica's favorite tea. She padded forward and bowed, presenting Veronica with a platter. A note lay on top. Veronica took it, unsure how to thank the girl. She must be in Sombor, surely, where else would they have gone aboard the *Hırsız*? Veronica smiled and the girl returned it, her face glowing. She perused Veronica's attire and then her hand. Giggling, she turned and left.

Veronica slit open the note with the finger of her left hand. A black half-mask fell out. She automatically picked it up as she read.

Princess, your presence is requested on the balcony.

She stared at the note for a moment longer, then looked around her room. What balcony? Why the mask? She rubbed her eyes.

The drapes to a window in her room fluttered. She looked around for a robe and found one laying across a chair. She slipped it on, crossed the room, and moved aside the curtains. A black-cloaked figure stood on the balcony, staring out into the city below. Veronica joined him, recognizing his large shoulders and the wary way he stood.

A sprawling, humming city lay below them. People dressed in all colors, forming an odd rainbow that flowed through the streets, calling out in words that carried the same cadence and form as

Emil's frequent Turkish phrases. The air drenched her, hot and humid, forming an instant film on her skin. The familiar spiced scent Emil carried on him drifted pleasantly into her senses.

"How are you?" he asked, his familiar, deep voice winding into the empty places of her heart.

"You've seen me through worse," she said as she stepped closer.

He nodded, still not looking at her.

Veronica had so many questions for him, so much she thirsted to know.

"How are the children?" she asked first.

"They are all at the workhouse Bridges and accounted for. The queen released Claire. They know now, of course, that the Eidolon and Lady Flowers are the same person. I think the little scoundrels knew all along. When Claire told some little brown-haired, freckled thing, she did not seem surprised. Nor did many others." His voice lightened as he spoke of the orphans.

She grasped the railing. She felt as light as the warm breeze. "Thank you. Oh, thank you."

"I found them after you were captured. I left Rosseau in charge while I came for you."

While I came for you. The words were so sweet, she dared to let them make her feel valued. Cherished.

"Alec is all right? Was he injured? What about the duke—"

"Your brother is fully capable of taking care of himself. I do not think the duke ever saw him during either fight. Alec returned home, and the last message I got from him was something along the lines of, 'Tell Peanut to hurry up and get well, because I want to show off the Eidolon to all my society friends. It's terribly dull here without you.' "

Combined with the growing warmth inside her, the knowledge that Alec had actually helped her and was unharmed made her tremble. He'd caught her. Hadn't let her fall.

"What about the duke? Won't he come after us? Won't he come after the children?"

"The queen was not pleased when she learned how Lord Grillett truly ran his *orphanages.* She's ordered an official investigation. Your father is still imprisoned for the moment."

She glanced sharply at him. "You know, then? About his involvement with Grillett?"

He nodded. "Yes. I knew he ran the factories alongside Grillett."

"And you didn't tell me?" She turned away. How could he have kept that from her?

A hand landed on her shoulder softly. "Veronica, I knew the duke by his face only, not his name. He kidnapped my sister many years ago. I thought her dead. I have been searching for him ever since. I did not figure out who he was until the night before the engagement ball."

"I'm sorry. How awful, Emil."

He gently turned her. She was surprised to see light in his eyes. It seemed a direct contrast to his sorrowful tale.

"I found her, Veronica. At Bridges. She had been going by the shortened name of Suzie."

She gasped. "My little, bright-eyed, matter-of-fact Suzie? Is your sister?" She smiled, wide enough that it felt unnatural. Surreal. Nothing about her current situation seemed possible.

"She is safe now, in a chamber down the hall. She is ecstatic to be living in the same wing as Lady Flowers. And she has been pestering me to see you."

"I can hardly believe it. I have to admit, she's one of my favorites. She never fibs, over anything. Always tells it like it is. Mistress Phillips adores her, too. She can always trust Suzie to help her get to the bottom of things. She was one of the first the Eidolon rescued." Veronica knew she was babbling, but she couldn't help the happiness bubbling out of her.

"Thank you, *canm*," he said softly.

She stilled. She was unable to move, weighed down by his emotion, and by a longing to reach out and feel if his skin was as warm as his gaze.

"I did not tell you about my involvement with the duke, or the duke's with Grillett, because I planned to kill him," he said suddenly.

She felt little at his declaration except sorrow for Emil. He thought the duke had killed Suzie. Veronica most likely wouldn't blame him if he had killed the duke. Particularly since she knew and loved Suzie so much and cared nothing for the duke.

"Why didn't you?" she asked.

He lowered his voice. The words floated toward her, wrapping themselves around her. "Because after I met you, I... you changed things. I put off getting my revenge until I knew how it would make you feel."

Veronica scrambled to try and organize her thoughts into words. "I tried for so many years to see the queen, but I was never granted an audience. How did you get through to her? Get her to consider that the duke might not be who he seems?"

Emil's eyes lifted at the corners, a sign that underneath his scarf, he hid a smile. "I slipped into her chambers and offered her a cup of tea."

She laughed. The sound nearly startled her. When had she last done so out of true amusement?

"You did not!"

He nodded. "Oh, but I did. Once I told her who I was, she was intrigued. The woman likes a man who has seen battle and lived to tell the tale."

"Who you are? What do you mean? The life of a bodyguard is that fascinating to the queen?" Veronica asked.

Emil lifted his right hand and slowly removed the scarf he always wore on his face. She kept her expression even while her heart pounded. After all this time imagining how he looked, wondering if she'd be repulsed or attracted, she saw the scars that crisscrossed the lower part of his cheeks. One tugged at his lower lip, making his mouth look as though it gaped constantly.

Veronica's breath faltered as she lifted her hand to trace it. It felt warm and alive underneath her hand. Emil remained still, his eyes not leaving her for a moment.

"The scars of *Kartal*," Veronica said. "I thought it a story to breed fear into the hearts of your enemies. I told those tales to my orphans as a bedtime story."

He closed his eyes but remained perfectly still under her touch. "Durad exaggerated, but the basic tales are true. I let him tell the story to gather strength for our cause."

"Astonishing," she whispered.

She rather liked his scars. Particularly how he seemed to enjoy her exploration of them. He'd have the *ton* swooning in fear should he remove that scarf in public. Next to the polished perfection of the gentleman, he would appear savage and beautiful.

A breeze lifted and the forgotten mask she still held fluttered to the ground.

Veronica leaned down and picked it up. "Why did you give me this?"

Emil's eyes flew open, bright and full of a kind of playfulness she'd never seen in them. He fingered the mask.

"This is yours. From the masque. When I nearly kissed you."

He smiled, the motion stretching his scars. Veronica found it to be the very opposite of the smiles she saw every day, so cultured, perfect, and empty. Emil's was dark, mischief curling the corners.

He said, "I fell a bit in love with you that night. I have thought about kissing you ever since, especially when I discovered who you really were. And every moment we spent during our week together about the *Hırsız*. When you married Durad, I thought I had missed my chance at happiness."

"Happiness doesn't exist," she said.

Emil tilted his head to the side, considering. He still hadn't moved. She could feel the rise and fall of his chest as he breathed.

He leaned closer and whispered, "What about Melilot? You would not dare deceive those sweet little children?"

She looked into his familiar eyes, and a dozen memories flooded her—Emil tucking an extra blanket about her when he noticed her shudder, Emil constantly keeping a warm cup of the tisane on hand in case she felt any pain, Emil kissing her on the forehead after revealing how much he understood about her, Emil rescuing her from the duke, when no one had ever been able to do so. Warmth, fiery and pleasant, rushed through her.

Emil seized her face in his strong, warm hands and kissed her. A current ran the length of her body, reminding her of the beam from her Tesla-ray, bright and powerful, but instead of numbing her, it did the exact opposite. She felt everything. From the way his nose brushed hers, to the way his hands felt as he threaded his fingers through her hair and pulled her even closer to him.

The feelings rushing through her felt painful. Not in the same way as her hand or any of her wounds in the past. She didn't dare believe in this kind of happiness. She simply held on to him as tightly as she could. After a few moments, she felt nothing but his hands as they held her firmly in place, and his mouth on hers.

Yes, a kiss like this would have changed everything.

A door slammed somewhere in the distance. Emil set her down suddenly and stepped back.

"I—" He shrugged, as though sheepish.

Veronica grabbed him and pulled him into her room. She shut the window and pinned him against the wall, her non-metal hand on his throat. His eyes widened, and he looked strong and unbelievably handsome there under her command. She liked his face without the scarf. She could see how it might have been handsome and symmetrical at some point, but now, with the story of his survival written on it, it was truly pleasing to her.

She raised a brow. "You may think you have the upper hand, *Kartal*, but simply remember that it is only because I allow it. I liked that kiss and I don't believe I told you to stop."

Chapter Forty-Three

Veronica prepared to address her people for the first time. Emil watched as she strapped on her weapons, lifting her skirts to buckle one on each lovely ankle. He'd done his best to prepare her for what he knew of the politics of Sombor, but he hadn't been here in a while, and there were many holes yet to fill.

Upon learning of the nocturnal activities of their new princess, Sombor's initial hesitation turned quickly to acceptance. Very few of their citizens hadn't lost a relative to the factories before Durad's rule. She bolstered their strength. A strength that had already faded to memory, though it had only been a few years since the wars. They were falling in love with her. She represented all that the Somborians were: proud, forward-thinking, and rebellious.

Veronica seemed to feel something she couldn't quite embrace yet. Emil noticed a shadow still veiled her eyes, but here and there, it lifted for a few moments. When he delivered a gift from yet another Somborian admirer, thanking her for what she'd done for all of them. When one of the many younger maids swept her a curtsey with tears in her eyes.

And, of course, whenever Emil kissed her. Or she kissed him, more often than he expected. Much to his delight. Not in public, of course. They were discreet. Sombor still mourned Durad. In spite of his fall in popularity toward the end of his reign, he was more beloved now than he'd ever been. He had died saving their new princess. Not one of them could conceive of a more heroic death.

Once she arrived, Matilda hadn't made any bones about urging Veronica to accept her people. Telling her endlessly that not everyone was the duke. Emil had sent Rosseau right back for her after successfully installing Veronica in the palace. The small, capable companion became Emil's unexpected ally and proved to be Veronica's biggest supporter.

Emil snatched one of Veronica's knives and reached forward. Taking her ankle in his hand, he slid the knife into the sheath.

When he straightened up, she grabbed his collar and pulled him toward her. With the other hand, she reached up and gently pulled his scarf from his face.

"I don't want you to hide who you are. A princess needs a man by her side that others fear."

"Once they know who I am, people will want to test the famous *Kartal.*"

Veronica smiled, a glint in her eye. She took his face in her hands, her metal fingers cool but gentle, and pressed her lips on his.

"Are you questioning your princess, Emil?"

This confident Veronica made him lose his words, so he just stared. Neither of them deserved such happiness, yet somehow, they'd found it, even in the embers of such destruction and loss. No one could take this moment from them. Not even justice or fate or whomever dictated the role of a man's life.

She said softly, "And so you see, my dears, that when night is darkest, when you have gone without even the barest of necessities, you can yet be brave. If you do, you may not have a dress covered with glittering stones, but you can still shine just as brightly…"

"Melilot," he said.

"One story in exchange for another." She looked up at him and smiled. The perfectly happy smile. She lifted a hand and traced the scars on his face, as she often did.

Her touch burned him, as it always did, but instead of leaving behind scars, it propelled him forward, away from his fears and uncertainties, like the *Hırsız* from an oncoming storm.

Epilogue

Alec tossed his sword onto his bed and growled at Critchton. "Be gone, old man. I've no need of your help this night."

"You've no valet, my lord," Critchton said with one slow blink.

He didn't move otherwise, his stiff posture suggesting he wouldn't be dissuaded. The wrinkles on his face sagged in an even, orderly fashion, as though he'd arranged them just so.

Alec hated the old man. He had ever since he'd obeyed his master's orders to lock Veronica in a closet for an entire day as a punishment for sub-standard academic work. He'd refused Alec's pleas with a heart of stone. He was carved from the same cold, inflexible granite as the duke, with the same slippery mind.

Alec ripped off his cravat, the delicate, expensive silk tearing as he did so. Critchton flinched at the sound. Alec stalked back toward his bed and picked up his blade. With a few swift movements, he cut off his waistcoat and fine lawn shirt.

Now down to his undershirts, he spread out his arms and said, "There. Why should I need a valet when this can get the job done in half the time?" He flourished his sword and then pointed it at the old butler.

Critchton bowed and then left, unnaturally fast for his age.

Finally. Alec splashed his face with water and began the routine of washing up. Curse his stubborn sister. She'd escaped with that hulking bodyguard, Marcovic. Off to Sombor, leaving behind a royal mess.

One he'd have to deal with, yet again.

Queen Victoria was not happy, and she'd let Alec know it. After her midnight visit from *Kartal*, she'd appointed one of her newest chief advisors to "investigate" Bridges and the Grave. Alec would likely have to help. In secret, of course.

By the by, who knew the silent, socially awkward Marcovic hid a secret as big as that? Hero, indeed. More likely a collection of tall tales spun to gather in the masses like the finest threads, until they were so tightly woven into a blanket of adoration they couldn't escape. Still, Alec had to admire the man. Valid reputation or no, he had saved Veronica's orphans and Veronica herself.

Alec dried his face with a soft towel and flung himself into a chair beside the fire. He could barely feel the heat, even though his skin was now ice cold. In spite of his sister's safe ending, he hated that everything had been blown wide open.

He hated having to expose the Dragonfly Order to Grillett and Veronica. He didn't think Veronica suspected anything more than they appeared to be—a group of titled men who happened to have a fencing hobby—but he couldn't be sure. She had become adept at hiding her thoughts and feelings, even from him.

Without bothering to don a shirt or jacket, he strode out of his room and straight outside the townhouse. The chill, damp night air was frosty on his skin, but he felt little. His feet led him to the barn. He went straight to the family carriage Veronica had monopolized often enough. Where he intended to go in this state, he couldn't say.

To his surprise, the carriage door opened, and Marcovic emerged and then helped Veronica down. *Kartal's* robes swirled about him, the darkness seeking him out and embracing him. Veronica wore the same monstrous ensemble she had as the Eidolon, those hideous pants, billowy shirt, and top hat. No self-respecting member of the Order would wear such a thing. He might have to have a word with her about that. In any case, she should be dressed in full mourning, no matter that Sombor didn't have such customs. Marcovic remained in the shadows, though his body angled toward Veronica's protectively.

Alec rolled his eyes. Heavens, that didn't take long. Durad's funeral had only been, what, three weeks ago?

"Why are you here?" he asked, using the droll tone he always reserved for his sister. He knew it irritated her beyond measure. There had to be some fun in this part he played.

Veronica took a hesitant step toward him, then closed the remaining distance and pulled him in for a firm hug. He stiffened. The few times they'd embraced could all be accounted for within the past month. Alec was still unused to such affection between them.

After a moment, he lifted his arms and patted her back awkwardly.

She laughed and swatted him. "You can't possibly be angry with me, brother. If anyone has cause to be so, it's me! How long have you played the fool, the drunkard, the gamer to me? Your own sister?" The joy in Veronica's eyes dimmed and she punched him in the shoulder with her non-metal hand.

Alec knew about the transplant, of course. Dr. Hoch couldn't keep it a secret long. Poor sod loved to brag, but only to Alec, thank heavens.

"I can't believe you had me so fooled. A gambler indeed. Think on this year we missed out on! Why couldn't you speak plainly with me, Alec?"

Veronica tilted her head, blinking up at him with that naive, endearing kind of hope he loved. After all this time, how could she still do so? That she hadn't given up on him was some kind of absurd miracle.

He'd never given in to her before, and he didn't plan on doing so now. She couldn't know, mustn't suspect how deep his involvement ran. While she dammed a current in the stream, he had to stop a waterfall. He braced himself, yet again, to lie to her. Yet another reason he hated this day.

"Peanut, darling, what would we have to discuss? You worked with Dr. Hoch on your little operation, whilst I trained at fencing with some of my associates." Alec sauntered over and plucked Marcovic's sword from his scabbard. Marcovic didn't look pleased. "We had a bit of a lark, pitting ourselves against each other. It became a type of obsession, until we became the very best at White's. Not many knew. It was our own private matter. Except for the wagers placed on the side. You know, who would win, etcetera. That racket funded the whole thing." He flourished the blade, then tossed it up and caught it again. "I won, of course."

Alec hoped just enough of his story rang with truth. He

couldn't have her suspecting any more. His heart ached to tell her. How many years had he kept his plans a secret, kept her at a safe distance? But still, she'd nearly died. Twice! Quite the protector he'd turned out to be.

Veronica remained silent for a while. Oddly, he enjoyed the play of emotion across her features. She'd spent so long concealing it with a vacant mask. While he didn't relish the pain he caused, at least he could see her as she really was.

With a sigh, Veronica said, "If that's the story you wish to tell me, I will tell you in return that I believe you." She stepped forward and placed both strong hands, one hot and one cool, on his arms. "When you're ready, brother, there's a place with us in Sombor. By my side, where you can fight freely and openly."

He didn't answer. What could he say? The further away from him, the safer she was? If she knew, if he admitted they both were in danger, Veronica would talk him into leaving with her… and Alec would let her do so.

Veronica kissed him on the cheek. "You needn't be alone anymore, but I won't force you, even though I quite likely could." She flexed her metal hand and flashed him a wicked grin. "If not with this, my Tesla-ray is fully charged."

He sniffed. "I quite like your new hand. Pretty soon, the papers will get hold of the Eidolon story and you will no longer be featured in *Defunct Debutantes*. Lady Ambrose will be de-throned, and all the young ladies will be wanting an appendage removed."

Veronica and Marcovic laughed. *Kartal* stepped into the light, as though his distance from his princess made him nervous. It was the first time Alec had seen him without his scarf, and the shock of it nearly made him flinch. *Kartal's* strong, brown face told a story of survival and courage, with dozens of small scars crisscrossing the lower half. If it had been handsome once, Alec couldn't tell. Now, it was simply fierce, and because of that, it held a kind of beauty even he could admire.

As a match for Veronica, a legendary hero might do. He liked the idea that *Kartal* would be protecting her. Even if she might possess a little skill on her own and a metal hand.

Alec replaced the sword in Marcovic's scabbard. "Marcovic, my good fellow, show that face in public and the men will follow suit and cut themselves shaving. Now those are movements I can get behind. Iron-fisted women. Deformed men. London will be so smashing!"

His sister smiled that half-smile he'd seen before. She recognized what he was doing. This time, though, that glimmer of hope in her eyes didn't fade.

"Like I said, brother, when you're ready. *Always.*" She blew him a kiss with her mechanical hand and re-entered the steam carriage. Hale appeared out of nowhere and started the thing up.

As they disappeared into the night, Alec shivered.

Coming Soon

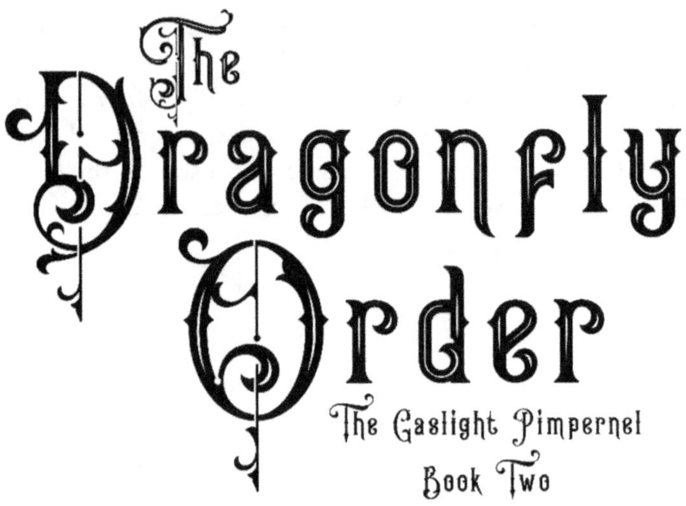

"Rebellion runs in the family."

by

Tiffany Dominguez

Fall 2020

About the Author

Tiffany Dominguez has a degree in Entrepreneurial Business from Brigham Young University and runs a Real Estate business. She has loved to read ever since she was old enough to drag a red wagon to the library.

Tiffany has been writing for fifteen years and won an award for her short story, "The Healer", from Writer's Digest. Her favorite hobbies are talking endlessly about kpop, baking and eating chocolate breakfast cake, and teasing her children.